The Sparks

BOOK ONE OF THE FEUD TRILOGY

KYLE PRUE

Barringer Publishing, Naples, Florida
www.barringerpublishing.com
Cover, graphics, layout design by Lisa Camp
Editing by Jessica L. Delashmit

ISBN: 978-0-9903935-8-0

Library of Congress Control Number: 2014951949
The Sparks / Kyle Prue

Printed in U.S.A.

Dedication

To Seacrest Country Day School.
It truly was a magical journey.

In memory of Drew Harrison.
I never would have had the courage to
express my creativity if I hadn't met you.

Characters

The Vapros Family

~ Neil Vapros

~ Rhys Vapros

~ Jennifer Vapros

~ Victoria Vapros

~ Sir Vapros

The Taurlum Family

~ Darius Taurlum

~ Michael Taurlum

The Celerius Family

~ Lilly Celerius

~ Anthony Celerius

~ Lady Celerius

~ Sir Celerius

~ Thomas Celerius

~ Jonathan

The Empire

- ~ The Emperor
- ~ Saewulf
- ~ Carlin Filus
- ~ The Empress
- ~ Virgil Servatus
- ~ Quintus
- ~ Captain of the Guard

Citizens of Altryon

- ~ Bianca Blackmore
- ~ Robert Tanner
- ~ Anastasia
- ~ Alfred the Bartender
- ~ The Pig

Altryon

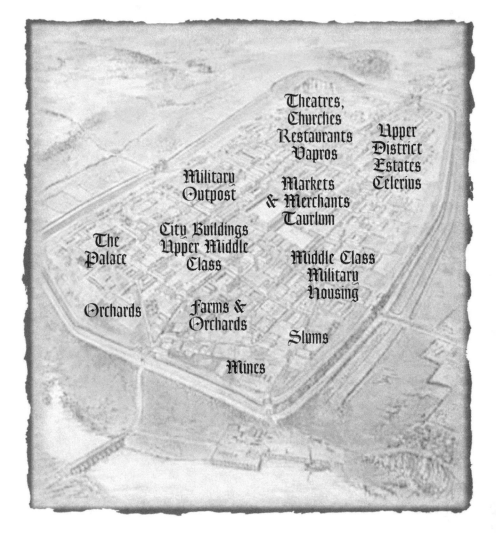

Theatres,
Churches
Restaurants
Vapros

Upper
District
Estates
Celerius

Military
Outpost

Markets
& Merchants
Taurlum

City Buildings
Upper Middle
Class

The
Palace

Middle Class
Military
Housing

Orchards

Farms &
Orchards

Slums

Mines

Part One
The Families

Vox Populi Vox Dei
The Voice of the People is the Voice of God

Chapter One
Taurlum Mansion
Neil

Slide the knife between the third and fourth rib.

Neil's father's words rang in his ears as he pulled his dark, ornate hood over his head and raised his cloth mask to cover his mouth and nose. He knew all Taurlum had several weak spots on their bodies, but only one was vulnerable enough to cause an instant kill. All he needed to do was thrust his knife directly between the ribs *(the third and fourth ribs,* he reminded himself*)* and straight through the heart. Neil's father had taught him this trick on his tenth birthday. It had been one of the more pleasant ones.

He spent a moment adjusting his mask, making sure his face would remain concealed. Not that it really mattered; during the middle of the day, the mask would do little to camouflage him. Any Taurlum would spot a Vapros like him from a mile away. The disguise had been given to him mostly for the sake of preserving his identity. Nobody needed to know *which* Vapros boy had made the kill.

Neil ran his finger over the hilt of the knife. His father had presented it to him upon completion of his assassin's training. Engraved in the handle was the Vapros family crest. The background of the crest was purple and black, with a raven embedded in the center. The Raven was the family nickname, as the black-haired, green-eyed descendants seemed to favor their swift, calculating animal mascot. The raven was known as the bringer of death: an appropriate symbol for the trained assassin. The family motto was inscribed along the bottom: Victory Lies Within the Ashes. Neil loved his knife; it made him feel like a real assassin.

Neil craved the assassin's glory but knew in his gut that he desperately needed another assassin to assist in this mission. Two stealthy ravens against a Taurlum bull was still a risk, but they would have the element of surprise on their side. Alone it was a certain death mission, but his father's orders were clear. Neil was desperately alone.

Making it into the giant Taurlum mansion had been easy. Navigating its giant corridors would be harder. Neil glanced carefully around the marble corner. A single guard stood watch. The man wore simple plated armor with red and gold war paint but had removed his helmet to reveal his entire head. *Not a Taurlum,* Neil thought. The guard lacked the golden blonde hair shared by every direct descendant of the Taurlum line; therefore, this man was not worth his time or effort. Neil squinted in concentration, and then threw all his energy into dematerializing. He reformed a split second later on the other side of the corridor. The guard continued watching the hallway and never noticed Neil materialize just behind him. As silently as he could, the Vapros boy made his way down the hallway toward the communal baths where his target would be waiting.

A Taurlum family crest hung above the door to the bathhouse. Its colors were the same gold and scarlet that covered the uniforms of the Taurlum guards who roughed up villagers in the market. A proud-looking bull stood in the center of the crest, eyes narrowed, as if challenging all who dared to oppose the name of the "great Taurlum." At the thought of eliminating his first Taurlum man, Neil's heart began to quicken, jump-started by adrenaline. He reached for his crossbow and fired a bolt directly into the bull's pretentious forehead. Then he opened the door and dematerialized as quickly as he could.

He reappeared behind a marble pillar a few feet away from the entrance. The inside of the Taurlum mansion was lavishly decorated with red and gold, from long velvet banners to giant tapestries depicting the family's crest. The manor itself stood in the center of the marketplace so that all the merchants affiliated with the Taurlum could get home quickly if the mighty Vapros warriors showed up. Even though Neil was disgusted at the opulence of the mansion, he couldn't help but admire how impressive it was. The entirety of the Taurlum mansion was made of polished marble to accommodate the great weight of its residents. A marvel like this had never been built before and was quite a change from the wooden and brick buildings that filled the city.

A door on the opposite wall opened. Neil risked a glance around his pillar. Two towheaded men wearing red and gold swimwear came into the bathhouse. Neil resisted the urge to snort. They never missed a chance to bear their family colors and boast of their "superior lineage." The two Taurlum were young, one looked to be Neil's age, the other a few years older, and they were unarmed. But their skin, Neil knew, was hard to pierce. The boys might as well have been made of iron.

Neil glanced around the corner to look at their swimwear. He had never seen anything like it. Most people in Altryon didn't have the money or opportunity to swim for fun, but when they did, their swimwear covered their chests along with their legs. These boys wore nothing except what appeared to be swim shorts. This was most likely because they wanted to show off as many muscles as possible. The taller one chatted loudly and easily to his companion. Neil dared to relax. They didn't suspect he was here. The shorter Taurlum was quieter, but the proud, almost cocky way he held himself when he walked made Neil roll his eyes.

"So," the taller boy was saying as he walked into Neil's line of vision. The Vapros boy held his breath. "Did you hear about the Pig?" Neil recognized this boy now: Michael Taurlum, known as "the Nose" among the villagers because of his prominent snout. He wore a gold ring on every finger, and the multitudes of bracelets adorning his arms clinked loudly. Any normal man would struggle to carry all that jewelry, but Michael's skin bore the weight easily. His droopy, yet unsettlingly alert eyes were fixed on his Taurlum companion and he had a thin, blonde beard growing on his iron jaw. He didn't see the Vapros enemy behind the pillar, which was incredibly fortunate for Neil. Michael wasn't well known for his mercy.

The younger, clean-shaven boy sank into the warm bath water. "The Pig?" he asked, raising an eyebrow.

Michael climbed into the bath beside him, not bothering to remove his jewelry. "Come on, Darius, learn the damn city." His voice was louder and bolder than his brother's. It was almost as if he wanted the entire city to hear him, and to hear him clearly. It made Neil want to shoot him on the spot. Patience, he reminded himself. He couldn't make his move yet. If these two realized he was here, he would not only fail his mission, he would probably also be killed, or worse, held for ransom. Even if his family paid the ransom to get him back, Neil's cover would be blown and he would be forced to spend the rest of his days working as a socialite. That was not the life he'd been working toward for all these years. He was trained to be an assassin. He could not mess this up. Failure would not be tolerated.

"The Pig is the guy who owns the mask shop in the market," the Nose was explaining to the one called Darius. Neil focused his energy and rematerialized behind another pillar a little farther away from the boys.

Darius cocked his head. "And why is he called the Pig?"

Michael waded into deeper water and smiled. "Because he's a pig," he chuckled. "And because he's famous for forcing himself on women."

Darius's mouth stretched into a grin. "You shouldn't be talking. You're kind of famous for that, too."

Michael's smile quickly turned to a frown. Behind the pillar, Neil nearly laughed out loud. This Darius wasn't afraid to speak his mind. From across the room, he heard the men continuing with their conversation, but he couldn't stay to listen. There was a mission at hand.

He rematerialized behind a new pillar, edging his way closer to the other side of the room where the door to the next room was waiting. Coming to the baths had been a waste of time; neither Darius nor the Nose was his target. Neil could still hardly believe his father had chosen him for this critical mission. His target was the Taurlum grandfather, the titular head of the Taurlum family. The Vapros controlled the nightlife district and the production and distribution of ale. The Taurlum controlled the markets. But in an unexpected power play, the Taurlum were attempting to corner the market on barley, wheat, and hops, buying up the ingredients needed to produce the Vapros ale. This assassination was in direct retaliation for this ill-advised maneuver.

Neil dematerialized again, and then again, and then stopped short; he was out of pillars. Nothing but empty space stood between him and the door, but it was too far. He wasn't strong enough to rematerialize that far away. Neil felt his heart begin to pound and he ran his hand through his raven hair angrily. He was stuck.

He considered his options. He could try to make a run for it. Darius was sitting with his back to the exit, but the Nose wouldn't sit still. If he turned at just the wrong time, he would spot the Vapros boy. Neil pulled his knife from its sheath. It had been specially curved so that it could slip in between a man's ribs. However, that tactic would prove ineffective against a Taurlum, unless Neil was perfectly precise. The only way to kill a Taurlum was to press the knife into a pressure point. Once the knife pierced the skin there, and the Taurlum started to bleed, he was as easy to kill as any other mortal. It wouldn't be so hard to sneak up behind Darius and stab him, and then it was just a matter of Michael. The Vapros loved to tell stories about how much of a brutish monster he was in combat. Michael also had the added advantage of his massive size. Neil estimated that he stood at nearly six-and-a-half feet tall, and every inch of his body was composed of hard muscle. Darius was smaller and leaner, but Neil didn't let that fool him. Darius was lean, but he had an athlete's hard body and definitely wouldn't go down without a fight. If Neil could only strike down Michael first somehow ….

Suddenly, the door Neil had come through burst open, and a guard came running into the bathhouse. "Sirs!" he cried. "We have reason to believe there is an assassin in the house!"

Neil almost dropped his knife. Michael leaped out of the pool, bracelets clanging obnoxiously against each other. The other boy didn't move. "What makes you think there's someone in the house?" asked Darius with a raised eyebrow.

"There was a crossbow bolt fired into the Taurlum seal over the door to this very room," the guard said nervously. "A Vapros weapon, from the looks of it. We are on high alert. Either one of you could be the target."

Neil shoved a hand through his hair and cursed his own arrogance. He slid the curved knife back into its sheath and planned his next move. Fighting had seemed like a good idea when it was only two boys in a bath, but now he had lost the element of surprise.

On the other side of the room, Michael scoffed, "I fear no assassin. I am going to go get my hammer and then I am going to find him and use his insides to decorate the floor."

Darius stepped out of the bath and put a restraining hand on the Nose's shoulder. "Settle down, Michael. The guards will take care of this. Any assassin stupid enough to fire a bolt into our crest is not stealthy enough to stay hidden for long."

Darius and Michael left the bathhouse together, leaving puddles in their wakes. Now, only the lone guard remained. Neil waited as patiently as he could but the man didn't seem to have any intention of leaving. Neil took a breath and tried to still his hammering heart. He had never actually killed a man before. Carefully, Neil raised his crossbow and fired a bolt into the back of the guard's head. The guard let out a surprised gasp as he began to fall. Neil materialized behind him and grabbed the back of his neck before he hit the ground. As he held onto the lifeless body, he began to gather all his energy and then, with a strong exhale, he released it. The guard's body instantly dissolved into ash—clothes, weapons, and all. Every fiber of his being was cremated in less than a second. The ability to dissolve his enemies into ash was a useful one, but for Neil, it only worked on bodies that were already dead, and it would be ineffective as a tool in the coming assassination.

Neil doubted anyone would notice the ash on the ground until he had already completed his mission, but he kicked through what was left of the guard for good measure. A pang of guilt began to arise in his chest and he clutched his stomach. He felt his face grow warm and for a moment, he was sure he would faint. He very quickly found himself vomiting onto the marble floor. He sighed and approached the pool. With cupped hands, he brought some water to his mouth. He swirled it around and then spat it out. *Don't feel guilty,* he told himself. *Any guard who decided to work for a prominent family like the Taurlum understood the risks.* He started toward the door, but fatigue and shortness of breath made him pause and double over. Materializing took an inordinate amount of energy. He had been stupid to use his powers so often in such a short amount of time. He stumbled to one of the pillars and leaned against it as he tried to stay conscious. A full minute passed before he felt well enough to stand, and as he made his way to the exit, he promised himself not to materialize again unless it was absolutely necessary.

The exit took him to the bottom of a giant spiral staircase. He climbed the steps with as much vigor as he could muster in his weakened state, panting a little from the effort. By the time he reached the top stair, he was gasping for breath. Before him stood a giant door which stretched up to over three times his height. Why was everything in this house so tall? It was as if the Taurlum mansion was built for a community of elephants, instead of men who just happened to have tough skin.

The door didn't have a handle. Neil threw himself against the wood with all his force, but it held fast, and with a sinking heart, he realized someone with the strength of a Taurlum warrior designed the door. No one without such strength would be able to push it open. Not for the first time in his life, he wished it were possible to materialize through walls.

As Neil backtracked a few steps to try throwing himself against the door again, it was pulled open with a staggering amount of force from the opposite side. The Vapros assassin found himself face to face with a familiar pair of Taurlum brothers, now armor-clad and holding weapons. "Got him," the Nose said to Darius, brandishing a hammer high above his head. Neil forgot every bit of his training and made a run for it.

In spite of promising himself not to, Neil materialized behind the two brothers and bolted into a circular room filled with armor and weapons. He gasped as he entered and realized this was a dead end. He didn't have the energy to materialize again. The two Taurlum turned to face him, amusement spreading across their faces. Michael stood back and watched as Darius began to walk forward to confront Neil. "Remove your hood, Vapros," he commanded.

Neil pulled away his hood and mask to reveal his face for the two young men. Michael seemed slightly surprised by his age, but Darius held his icy composure. Neil was finally able to see Darius up close. He had wavy golden hair and something in his blue eyes that was almost intelligent. Neil quickly decided that Darius's eyes didn't show wisdom but more of an ironclad determination. Unlike Michael, he didn't wear any jewelry. It was as if his entire outfit had been designed to be practical and battle efficient. This didn't stop Neil from noticing the blood smeared on his armored chest. Neil was ready to bet that it wasn't his. "Who are you here to kill?" Darius asked, advancing slowly. Neil backed away until he was pressed up against a giant floor-to-ceiling stained glass window. He glanced over his shoulder. The window would be easy to shatter, but a fall from this height was risky.

"The oldest Taurlum," Neil answered finally. "Your grandfather probably. I haven't exactly looked at your family tree recently."

Darius narrowed his eyes. Neil braced himself for a deathblow. "You're kind of an idiot, aren't you?" the Taurlum boy said, a hint of laughter in his eyes.

This question caught Neil off guard. "Not exactly. I'm just unlucky. Why?"

"Look at you!" he laughed. "You've run right into a dead end. You aren't even remotely in the right part of the house, if you're looking for my grandfather. Was that your intention?"

Neil tried to stand up straight as he responded sarcastically, "Well, if you could point me to the right part of the house I'd be on my way."

Michael sighed heavily through his oversized nose and rubbed his bearded face leisurely. "On with it, Darius. I want to continue my swim."

As Darius took a step closer to his target, Neil realized he might have stalled long enough to gain back sufficient energy for one last escape. He concentrated his energy and prepared to materialize somewhere near the door. Darius realized what Neil was doing too soon, and before Neil could disappear, the Taurlum had planted his right foot against Neil's chest and kicked him straight through the window.

As Neil fell, he used the last of his energy to rematerialize slightly closer to the ground. He hit it chest first with a thud. Neil groaned as he tried to get up. His breastplate was horribly dented and his mouth tasted of blood. He slowly made it to his hands and knees and realized he was facing the markets. The city walls loomed in the distance, shrouded by a thin fog.

He rolled around and tilted his head back to glare up at the window. He made eye contact with Darius, who now held a mammoth war hammer. A small smile played around the Taurlum's lips as he raised the weapon above his head. Neil realized what was going to happen just in time. The hammer hit the ground with such force that it tore apart the bricks where Neil had been lying a moment before.

"Is that the best you can do?" Neil shouted. Darius scowled and stepped straight out of the broken window. He plummeted to the ground (as did Neil's jaw) and landed so hard that the cobblestone street beneath him shattered and sent up a cloud of dust. He rose from the rubble, dusted himself off, and swaggered over to Neil. "If you value your life," he said, pulling the massive hammer from the ground, "you should run."

A group of villagers had come running when they saw the boy thrown from the third story window of the Taurlum mansion, but as Darius advanced on Neil they turned to flee. The citizens of Altryon knew what happened when members of opposing houses came across one another. Better to get as far away from the coming brawl as possible.

Neil met Darius's icy gaze and tore away his dented breastplate. For an instant, he considered fighting. Darius raised a challenging eyebrow and stretched out his arms threateningly. Neil took a step forward, threw his breastplate to the ground, and turned tail to run for his life. Darius smiled and waited a few seconds to give Neil a decent head start. Then, hoisting the hammer above his head, he let out a roar and chased after the terrified Vapros would-be assassin.

Chapter Two
Celerius Estate
Lilly

illy Celerius frowned at herself in the mirror and decided that being seventeen years old looked exactly the same as being sixteen. She lifted a comb and pushed it through her lengthy auburn hair, then gently guided the stray strands into place with her fingertips. She passed her palm down the front of her military coat, checking to make sure each button was still fastened, and then reached up to dab away a bit of smudged lipstick from the corner of her thin lips. She had wide mahogany eyes and well-defined cheekbones. These were common Celerius traits that she wore with pride. She nearly always looked presentable, but this was a special occasion. Nothing could be out of place—not today.

The door to her bedroom opened quietly, and Jonathan came inside. Lilly didn't bother to turn around. She looked his reflection up and down in the mirror. "Yes?"

The servant bowed, then stood at attention like a loyal guard dog. "Are you ready, Miss?"

More ready than you are, she thought, sighing. Jonathan's black hair hung down over his forehead, unkempt and far longer than a servant's hair was supposed to be. His royal blue coat, which had clearly been made for a much taller man, dangled past his ankles. The coat, Lilly knew, had been a gift to Jonathan from her father, and the former wore it proudly almost every day, in spite of the fact that he appeared to be drowning in it. "Let's go," she said, giving her hair a final pat. She hesitated for a quick second to readjust Jonathan's collar for him.

Jonathan bowed again, gestured to the door and answered, "After you."

She exited briskly and he trotted after her, stumbling slightly as he hurried to keep up. The poor man had never made it past five feet tall and he had to maintain a steady jog to stay next to his mistress. "When was the last time you saw General Anthony?" he asked, trying to sound serious in spite of his hurried pace.

Lilly took pity and slowed her steps. "It's been weeks, understandably. He's the busiest man in the entire realm." Anthony was the General of the Imperial Army.

"But it's nice of him to make time to see you on your birthday," Jonathon replied.

"Yes." From the corner of her eye, she saw Jonathan give a little sigh of contentment, which stung her heart, until she realized his relief was probably in response to her slowing down rather than her brother's absence.

The Celerius estate was vast and their manor lavishly decorated. Each wall was adorned with their blue and gold colors, and decades worth of medals and weapons hung side by side. These were their trophies. Lilly paused for a moment to admire the crest positioned on the wall at the top of the staircase on the second floor. A downward facing sword above golden stitched writing was all the Celerius family needed to prove their worth to passers-by. The gold writing read, "Highest Honor." Lilly nodded at it and straightened her coat with a quick pull. Jonathan fixed his posture and tried to do the same.

They proceeded toward the grand staircase that led to the front entryway of the Celerius estate. As they descended the long flight of steps, Jonathan comically reached around to hold the back of his jacket to keep it from dragging on the ground like a wedding train. Lilly would have laughed if things weren't so important today.

"Have you heard the rumors?" Jonathan asked.

Lilly stopped walking. She turned her head slowly and looked down at him, "About Anthony?" Jonathan gulped and nodded as he tried desperately not to meet her icy stare. "Yes, Jonathan," she said, "I've heard the rumors. They are nothing more than Vapros lies and deceit."

Jonathan nodded, but Lilly didn't lift her glare. Although one would normally associate such large brown eyes with warmth and kindness, Lilly's eyes could practically freeze time with their intensity. He tried not to squirm in discomfort. Finally, she started walking again, and he closed his eyes and let out a breath he didn't remember holding before tripping after her.

As they exited the house and stepped onto the gravel road, Lilly gazed across the distant fields that comprised her family's estate. Jonathan offered a hand to help her into the carriage, but she ignored it and climbed aboard herself. "Miss," the driver said, turning in his seat to face her, "we can't get to the military outpost without crossing through the marketplace or the nightlife district."

Lilly sighed. Jonathan grunted a little as he struggled to climb into the carriage. "So it's either Taurlum territory or Vapros territory."

Jonathan opened his mouth. "I think we should—"

"Marketplace," Lilly decided firmly. "It's closer, and if we are attacked, we will have an easier time fighting off one bull rather than ten ravens."

The Vapros usually travelled in teams and the Taurlum tended to operate alone.

"That's what I was going to say," Jonathan muttered, settling himself into the seat opposite his mistress. The driver clucked to the prized Celerius horses and they sprang forward, seamlessly pulling the carriage down the road with a smooth, steady haste. In no time, they had entered the city district. Lilly stared absently out the window at the glorious stone walls of the bank where her family stored their endless funds. Selling weapons had proven to be a lucrative business.

"I think we're almost to the markets," said Jonathan quietly. "Hopefully everything goes all right."

Lilly didn't appear to hear him. The carriage began to bounce up and down furiously. Jonathan was nearly thrown from his seat. Lilly closed her hands into fists at her sides. "Why are there so many potholes?" she asked through gritted teeth.

Jonathan chuckled a little, but stopped when Lilly turned her glare toward him. "This is Taurlum territory," he said. "There are bound to be a few holes in the road." Suddenly the carriage came to a halt. Lilly's annoyed expression turned to one of fear. She shared a knowing look with Jonathan and they both reached for the door simultaneously.

As Lilly stepped out onto the street, she realized how very out of place she looked here. Her military coat and dress were both a bright royal blue, a color nobody else seemed to be wearing. The crowds of villagers were clad in darker colors, the fabrics stained with sweat and hard work.

It was never difficult to determine someone's social class; all that was needed was a quick look at their clothes. A large mob had gathered in the streets, blocking the carriage. Lilly looked at Jonathan expectantly, waiting for her servant to order the crowd to move, but he seemed too terrified to speak. She sighed and approached the nearest merchant, checking first to make sure he wasn't blonde. "You," she said flatly.

The villager jumped and stared up at her as he wiped his hands on his stained apron. "Me?"

"Why is the road blocked?" She phrased her sentence the way her father always did; it was an order, not a question. That was the best way to command respect.

The commoner looked at her coat instead of her face as he answered. "Darius Taurlum caught some Vapros kid in his house. He's about to kill him."

Lilly suppressed a smile; it was always satisfying to see her two worst enemies fighting it out. "An execution?" she inquired.

"Not yet. Darius is still chasing him, but he doesn't play around. The kid will be dead before lunch."

Lilly smiled and then nodded appreciatively. "Thank you, sir."

She glanced back at the carriage and realized that it would take some time to turn around. This made her nervous; the Celerius weren't exactly beloved in the working parts of Altryon. The Celerius estate was on the eastern edge of the city, past the Imperial Palace and the nightlife district. Most people from the working class wouldn't have any reason to venture so far east. Lilly hardly ever journeyed out past the protective gates of the family estate, unless she was accompanying her father on business or to visit other nobles in the area. However, her desperate need to see Anthony had led her to pass through the working class area and the markets on her way to the military base on the northwest edge of the city.

She stood, her face hard, as her driver and Jonathan struggled to redirect the carriage. She could hear a few men in the crowd whispering as they noticed her, but she forced herself not to betray any emotion. "Hello, lovely," called a large, sweaty man, as he broke away from the crowd. "I like that coat of yours."

"Then you should understand what it represents," she said calmly, wrapping her fingers around the handle of her sheathed sword.

The man growled and wiped his forehead with a massive hand, leaving a trail of soot behind. He looked strong. Lilly guessed he was a blacksmith. "You've got quite a mouth," he said, advancing toward her, "and I'm not sure I like your tone."

Lilly took a quick glance at the carriage. Jonathan and the driver were arguing about something and didn't seem to notice her new friend. "Leave me alone," she snarled, as he took another step. "That's your one and only warning."

The man noticed how tightly she was gripping her sword. He snickered. "I've heard a lot about your family, girlie," he taunted. "You're supposed to be quick. But I'm the strongest and quickest in the market. What do you say to that?"

"I'm a lot more than just quick," she fired back. "Do you require a demonstration?"

Jonathan had finally noticed Lilly was in danger. "Miss?" he asked as he trotted over to her. "We should be going."

The blacksmith glared at him. "Take a walk, slave," he growled. "Me and your master are just getting acquainted."

As inconspicuously as she could, Lilly began to remove her sword from its sheath. Her adversary saw the blade catch the sun and quickly pulled a knife out from a holster on his hip.

Lilly didn't appear to be fazed. "Last chance," she said calmly.

They had attracted the attention of a few villagers who gathered around to gawk at the confrontation, but Lilly only had eyes for the blacksmith. "You sure you want to do this, woman?" he asked. "If you engage me in a duel, I'm sure it's completely legal for me to cut you up. Even if you are a lady."

"Ah." She cocked her head and a reminiscent smile crept across her face. "So you underestimate me because I'm a woman." She let the blade slowly slice through the air. "That's a mistake."

He took a moment to size her up. He was around six feet tall and had a large weight advantage over her. With a glint in his eye, he lunged forward with his knife.

She evaded him easily, leaving him to slice nothing but air. He recovered somewhat gracefully, pivoting on his heel to face her. He lunged again, faster this time, but still managed to hit nothing. He swung wildly at her outstretched arm and, to his relief, made contact. His knife nicked her hand and a stream of blood fell to the street. He grinned and took a step backwards. "What now, love?" he asked, arms spread wide.

She held up her hand so that the blacksmith could see it. Before his very eyes, her skin reformed around the wound and left her with nothing but a quickly fading scar. "Now," she said, slashing across his neck with her sword, "you yield."

His hand flew to his throat. Blood dripped between his fingers and puddled onto his toes. It was nothing but a small cut along his throat; Lilly knew it was not enough to truly hurt him, but enough to make him scared. It would have been easy for her to extend a bit more and decapitate him, and he knew it. He dropped his knife, cursing, and retreated into the crowd.

Jonathan was trying not to beam. "Back to the carriage, Miss?" he asked.

She nodded silently and sheathed her sword, eyes still on the place where the blacksmith had disappeared, and led the way back to her awaiting carriage. "Apparently the road is blocked because of a fight. Taurlum against Vapros," she explained upon re-entering the carriage.

Jonathan grinned. "So I guess we don't have to worry about being ambushed," he concluded. "Our enemies are busy killing each other."

Lilly gave Jonathan a rare smile as the driver directed the horses down an alternate route. Every street in the marketplace was Taurlum territory, but the back alleys were frequented by villagers and merchants, neutral commoners who held no grudge against the Celerius house. Nobody tried to stop the carriage again.

When they reached the military establishment, the soldiers on patrol waved them through the giant gates and directed the carriage to the stables where the horses could rest. Jonathan insisted on leading Lilly inside, and even though she knew the military base backwards and forwards, she humored her diminutive servant and allowed him to accompany her to her brother's quarters. Lilly had grown up playing in these hallways while her father and brothers worked in their offices.

The small office was empty. "Where do you think he is?" Jonathan asked with concern.

"He's just late," Lilly reassured him, sinking carefully in a high-backed chair. "He's busy. He'll be here. He's expecting me."

It wasn't long before the door opened to reveal Anthony Celerius. Lilly rose automatically as he entered the room, her eyes sparkling but her face arranged in a respectful countenance. Her brother was a large man, and when they were younger he used to hoist her up on his shoulders and gallop around the estate like a pony. Those days were long gone. His broad body was clad in shining armor, probably polished just this morning, and a royal blue cape that was draped over one shoulder and connected with a gold brooch that bore their family crest.

Lilly's eyes widened as she took a closer look at his face. Anthony once had an iron jaw and long auburn hair, but now his once-youthful face was marred with premature wrinkles and his hair was covered in streaks of grey. Being the youngest general in the history of Altryon was clearly taking its toll. "Anthony," she whispered, dropping a curtsy.

He smiled. Lilly was relieved to see it made him look younger. "Lilly, happy birthday, darling girl." He came forward, armor clanking, and wrapped her in a bear hug. She allowed herself to grin. "We will speak in the war room," he said, releasing her and nodding to Jonathan, who had bowed so low that he was having trouble standing up again.

They followed him down a hallway into the renowned war room. Anthony pushed through the door, chatting easily, as if he did not realize how old and exhausted he looked now. "You remember Carlin Filus," he said, gesturing to the corner where Anthony's second in command stood at attention.

Carlin offered the trio a smile, bearing crooked teeth so different from Anthony's perfect, pearly whites. Lilly suppressed a shudder. Carlin and his smug smile had always unsettled her; he looked like he knew something she didn't. He slid his palm over his brown military-length hair and came forward. "Lilly Celerius," he grinned, reaching for her hand. She held her breath and offered it to him. "It has been too long. How are you on this fine day?"

She was close enough to see the stubble lining his cheeks. He had gained a fair amount of battle scars during his time as a warrior; most noticeable was a deep cut on the upper right side of his lip that made him look like he was permanently scowling. "I am well, thank you," she replied carefully. He pulled her hand to his lips and kissed it formally, his dark brown eyes not leaving hers. It was almost as if he were telling her something silently with his eyes, that he had a terrible secret that he wasn't willing to disclose. Lilly felt the hairs rise on the back of her neck. Then, with a bow to Anthony, he brushed past Jonathan and hurried from the war room, red cloak billowing behind him.

Lilly shivered once he was out of sight. "He's terrible," she said to Anthony, wiping the back of her hand on her dress.

Anthony moved to close the door. "You don't know the half of it," he muttered as he sank into one of the large chairs. Lilly took the chair opposite his, leaving Jonathan to stand awkwardly by the door. "I assume you've heard the rumors?"

Lilly nodded. Anthony flicked his eyes to his sister's servant. "Jonathan," he said, not unkindly, "leave us."

Jonathan looked mildly offended. "Miss?" he asked, looking at his mistress with wide eyes.

Lilly nodded. "It's all right, Jonathan," she said, and he went, head hanging down like a kicked puppy. As the door closed behind him, Lilly abandoned her perfect posture and leaned toward Anthony intently. "Are they true?" she asked urgently. "The rumors? Jonathan can be trusted, you know."

Anthony shook his head and replied, "Not with this." He rose and retrieved a bottle of gin from the other side of the room. With a heavy sigh he sat back down and poured himself a glass. "There's something very important we need to discuss." She saw him slide a hand over one of his eyes and she realized he had brushed away a tear. "But before we begin, understand that I love you very much, Lilly."

She blinked and shook her head. "Begin what?"

"Our last conversation," he whispered as he took a sip of his drink.

Chapter Three
The Markets
Neil

Neil didn't know Altryon's markets as well as he knew other parts of the city, but he knew a few key things. For instance, half the market was divided into stalls for farmers and other small businesses, and the other half was dedicated to large stone stores that sold luxury goods. Most of the buildings in Altryon were several stories high. This was due to the fact that the city was walled and needed to accommodate its rising population. This information, however, did not help him make a decision about which way to run for his life.

Just as Neil began to gain a lead on his pursuer, the hammer soared within an inch of his head and embedded itself in the wall of a clothing shop. He ducked into an alley, clutching at his chest as he ran. He couldn't take much more of this. The physical exertion was wreaking havoc on his body. Every muscle screamed at him to stop running, to take a break, but Neil couldn't risk stopping.

As he hurtled down the alley, lungs burning, he remembered something his father had told him the very first time he'd collapsed after overusing his powers: "You'll get older and stronger, and so will your powers. Someday, materializing will feel like nothing."

Easy for him to say, Neil thought, pushing his raven hair back off his forehead. Neil's father was the strongest Vapros man alive. He had pushed his abilities past every limit imaginable. He could turn his entire body into smoke, envelop live men, and turn their bodies to ash. Moreover, he could accomplish it without even breaking a sweat.

As Neil neared the end of the alley, he allowed himself a quick glance over his shoulder. The alley was empty. Darius wasn't following him; Neil either lost him, or the brute had given up altogether. Nearly crying from relief, Neil let himself stop running. He was safe. It was over.

For a few blissful moments, the alley was silent other than Neil's heavy breathing. Then the sound of heavy footfalls came within earshot, and Neil cursed and raised his crossbow. As Darius rounded the corner, Neil fired a bolt; the weapon hit Darius's forehead and broke, not even putting a dent in the Taurlum's skin. Darius didn't even seem to notice. Neil sprinted down the alley. "You can't run forever!" Darius shouted after him.

Neil was about to collapse. "If you would hold still and let me shoot you, I wouldn't have to!" he shouted back over his shoulder.

Darius roared as he charged after him. Neil loaded another bolt and fired. It sailed harmlessly over Darius's head. Cursing, Neil rounded a corner and tore down a new street, heading for the square. Darius was gaining, but if he could make it to the busiest part of the marketplace, maybe he could blend in with the throngs of villagers.

Neil had almost reached the square when he was yanked off his feet and into the air. Darius let out a scream of triumph and threw him to the side, sending him flying into the wall of a nearby store. Darius held his hammer high, posing dramatically for the crowd that had gathered to

29

witness the brawl.

A broad-shouldered man in Imperial armor stepped between the boys. Neil recognized him as the Captain of the Guard. "Taurlum," he ordered, drawing a long sword, "by order of the Emperor, I command you to...."

Without taking his eyes off his prey, Darius swung his arm and knocked the Captain of the Guard into a wall, where he left a sizable dent. Darius blinked and glanced at his victim, acknowledging the fact that he might have gone too far.

Neil lay on the ground, groaning in pain. Darius sneered down at his victim. "Here's to my family," he said, grinning. "And here's to the end of yours."

Just as he began to swing his hammer down, a silver blur shot through the air and imbedded itself in his neck. A small trickle of blood dripped down onto his shoulder. The impact made Darius jerk his arm to the right, and the hammer hit the ground just shy of Neil's head. Darius's expression changed from savage triumph to one of confusion, and then fear. His precious iron skin had been pierced at a pressure point. He was now just as mortal as everyone else around him.

Neil staggered to his feet, smiling in relief. "Today is not your day, is it, Taurlum?"

Darius ignored him. His hand was against his neck, pulling the silver weapon (a throwing knife, Neil now realized) from his skin. "It was a second ago ..." his adversary replied.

"Go home, Darius," Neil said loudly. Darius growled and held the knife tightly in his fist. A few villagers began to whisper nervously.

"I'm still strong," he snarled.

Neil shrugged. "Yeah," he agreed, "but I have backup." He gestured to the knife in Darius's hand.

Darius narrowed his eyes. "Who threw this knife?" he roared, spinning to glare at the crowd. The villagers looked terrified.

Neil was regaining energy fast. "You won't find her over there," he said quietly.

"What?"

"I said, you won't find her there," Neil repeated with more volume.

"I heard you," Darius said angrily.

"You just didn't understand." Neil nodded. "It doesn't make much sense, does it? Who would have thought, a great Taurlum man like you, bested by a girl?"

Darius blinked. "Bested by a—"

Before he could finish the sentence, an iron bar had collided with his skull. He stumbled two paces closer to Neil with his arms outstretched and then collapsed. As he hit the ground, a girl with shimmering ivory hair stepped out from the shadows, an iron staff held loosely in one hand.

She smiled. "You fight like a girl, Neil," she said calmly, dropping her iron weapon.

The crowd of bystanders, realizing there would be no execution today, began to disperse.

Neil looked the girl up and down. "You dress like a man, Bianca," he countered playfully.

She looked down at herself briefly before meeting his eyes again and asked, "What's wrong with armor?"

Neil grinned. "Most girls who look like you tend to prefer dresses. Besides, isn't leather armor a Celerius thing?"

Bianca shrugged. "I could wear a dress, I suppose, but I wouldn't want to drive you crazy. You might get distracted and lose another fight."

"I had it covered."

She snorted. "Of course you did."

Bianca was several inches shorter than Neil and had a shapely figure. The noticeable curves were a recent development that Neil expertly pretended not to notice. Her grey eyes always seemed to retain a smile.

She had a small smudge of ash on her cheek. Neil could only guess where that had come from. He glanced around at their surroundings. "You should get out of here before more Taurlum show up," he warned. "You know how word spreads around here. They'll be after us both as soon as they hear Darius Taurlum got his ass kicked by a girl from the markets."

Bianca sighed and tried to pry her knife from Darius's iron hand but she realized that it wouldn't budge. "Yeah," she muttered, "I probably made some enemies today."

Neil stared down at Darius's body. "Are you gonna kill him?" Bianca asked.

Neil drew his knife. "Yeah," he said quietly.

He approached Darius and pulled his head up by the hair. He felt a familiar dizziness beginning to arise but suppressed it. Bianca watched him with quiet curiosity. Neil sighed and dropped Darius. "No, not with all these witnesses …. He's learned a lesson, I think."

Bianca raised an eyebrow in disbelief. "Whatever you need to tell yourself," she sighed. "I'm sure we're both going be on the Taurlum's most wanted list after today, anyway."

"True," Neil said and started down an alley. Bianca followed, matching his pace easily. "But things aren't all bad."

"Why not?"

Neil grinned and slung his arm casually over her shoulder. "At least you get to walk down the street on the arm of a handsome Vapros warrior."

Bianca laughed and ducked out of his embrace. "Yes, it's an absolute privilege," she said with a mock curtsy, and then she tossed her hair over her shoulder and skipped down the street ahead of him.

Bianca knew the streets better than anyone else and she led Neil through a twisted back-alley route until they reached the safety of the nightlife district. Neil had dozens of memories just like this one. Since they were children, Bianca always knew how to get where she wanted quickly and she loved to drag Neil along.

Neil slowed as they approached the Vapros house. It wasn't a grand, pretentious building like the Taurlum mansion; in fact, most of the building was underground. The only part visible from the street was a small shack with the Vapros crest etched into the side. The family motto was inscribed on the door: "Victory Lies in the Ashes." Neil put his hand on the iron door as if he meant to open it, then sighed and let it close.

Bianca offered him a sympathetic smile. "He sent you alone. It was practically a suicide mission. He should be happy that you made it home alive."

Neil stared at the ground. "I don't …" his voice faltered, "I don't think he's going to give a damn."

Bianca squeezed his hand. "Good luck."

He smiled at her weakly. "Please. I don't need luck. No one can resist my apologetic smile."

Bianca turned to leave. "I've seen your apologetic smile," she called over her shoulder. "It needs work."

Neil managed a little smirk in her direction before he sighed and knocked on the heavy iron door. A hatch about the size of Neil's torso was opened from the inside. Neil materialized through the hatch and found himself face to face with his younger brother.

Rhys was Neil's opposite in nearly every way. While both shared the Vapros dark hair and green eyes, Rhy's eyes were jade whereas Neil's were emerald like those of his sisters. While Neil was tall and more athletic, Rhys was smaller and more slender than the other siblings. He was a quiet, intelligent type, with hair he kept short and eyes that were constantly darting around. With his innate curiosity, his eyes were constantly wide with fascination.

"How'd you do?" Rhys asked, cocking his head to the side curiously.

"The twins and I have been waiting to hear, and—"

Neil brushed past him and started down the narrow staircase. Rhys followed and called after him. "Calm down. I don't think he expected you to be able to do it anyway." Rhys's voice was always soft, but at the same time filled with energy and intelligence.

"Comforting," Neil mocked, stopping to glare back at him and then continuing through the entry hall to one of the corridors that stretched even farther underground.

Rhys kept up, but just barely. "He shouldn't have sent you. Your advanced abilities haven't even developed yet."

"Easy for you to say, Rhys. Maybe Father thinks he can't wait … I may never develop advanced abilities."

Rhys tried to grab Neil's arm, "You can't compare yourself to me. You know it's different. I suffered a major trauma. You said yourself that maybe I got them so early because of that traumatic event."

Neil didn't even stop to look at his brother. "This conversation is a traumatic event," he said. "And putting people to sleep is not what I'd call 'advanced powers.'"

Rhys caught Neil's shoulder. "Think logically."

"Do you think I can manage it?" Neil asked sarcastically without turning around.

"I've seen how you are with people, Neil. You're charismatic. You're good at talking. You're perfectly cut out to be a socialite. Why are you so desperate to be an assassin?"

Neil finally stopped walking. He ran his fingers through his hair and then met Rhys's eyes and said, "Because socialites aren't impressive. How hard is it to go out and sweet talk people into funding our projects? Not hard at all. Even Jennifer can manage it when she tries, and Jennifer has terrible people skills. Assassins, though—they're rare and powerful— "

"Like Dad?" Rhys interrupted.

"This isn't about Dad."

"Okay." But Rhys didn't look like he believed that.

Neil sighed. "It doesn't even matter. Dad's going to hate me no matter what I choose to be."

"He doesn't hate you."

"He does. And he has every right. In his mind, I tore our family apart."

Rhys shook his head. "Don't say that. That wasn't something you could help."

"I have to make it up to him," Neil said. "I want to make him proud of me, even if it's just for *one second*. And that's never going to happen if I'm a socialite. So there you go."

"I support you," Rhys said, "but he might not." He gestured to the door at the end of the hall. "I'm sure he won't, actually."

Neil sighed and closed his eyes. "Thank you," he said slowly as he tapped his brother between the eyes, "for that vote of confidence."

Rhys smiled slightly. "Good luck."

Neil pushed through the door at the end of the hallway and walked into his father's study, shoulders back, head high, just the way he'd been taught. He offered Sir Vapros a little bow.

Sir Vapros sat behind a massive desk that dwarfed nearly everything in the room. After becoming patriarch of the family, he had asked for it to be specially crafted. He shared the common Vapros traits: he was classically handsome, tall with dark hair and vibrant forest green eyes. But he wore an expression so stern that he could silence nearly anyone with a simple look. He was elegantly dressed in evening attire, and his hair was neatly styled. Neil knew the polished exterior was a façade; Sir Vapros was a warrior. Underneath his sleeves, Sir Vapros's body was decorated with tattoos.

This was a Vapros tradition: every assassination earned you a ceremony where the patriarch would award you a tattoo representing your most recent kill. The only tattoo visible at the moment was a bloody coin on the back of his right hand. It was new. Neil's sister, Victoria, had told him that it was from killing the head of the Imperial Bank of Altryon. For some unknown reason, the banker suddenly refused to do business with the Vapros establishments stationed around the city. Sir Vapros suspected that the Celerius, with their strong ties to the banking industry, were trying to cripple his businesses in an attempt to expand into the Vapros territory. Sir Vapros had personally gone to "renegotiate" the deal.

Sir Vapros slowly put down the paper he was examining and looked at his son with a deathly calm expression. "I heard what happened in the markets." His voice was cold. Neil hated that his father could make him feel this way, as if he were five years old again and being punished for staying up past his bedtime. "Is it too optimistic of me to ask if you reached your target at all?"

"There were complications," Neil said through a clenched jaw. "I couldn't—"

Sir Vapros raised a hand to silence his son. "You were ejected from the house by Darius Taurlum. You fled instead of fighting."

"He would have killed me," Neil started, but his father interrupted.

"At least you would have died a man!"

Neil felt as if he'd been dunked in icy water. "I'm sorry," he said quietly.

His father didn't appear to hear him and continued. "And after all that, Jennifer tells me you needed help from a commoner. And not just any commoner—that commoner." He put his face in his hands. "I've asked you repeatedly to stay away from Bianca Blackmore. We don't accept help from commoners, Neil." He ran his hand through his straight black hair the same way his son always did. "On top of it all, you had that Taurlum completely at your mercy and you failed to end his life."

Neil felt his heart twist with shame.

Sir Vapros spoke as his eyes drilled into Neil. "Any blood he sheds from this day forward is on your hands."

There were a million things Neil wanted to say, but he settled on, "You had Jennifer spy on me?"

"I didn't. Your sister did it all on her own."

And she didn't even step in to make sure I wasn't killed? Neil wanted to say, but he held his tongue. "Give me one more chance."

Sir Vapros raised an eyebrow and noted, "Not everyone is cut out to be an assassin, son."

"I am," Neil insisted.

Sir Vapros countered, "You're pretty. Become a socialite."

"One more chance," he repeated stubbornly.

Sir Vapros sighed. "I can't afford to give you one more chance. This is too important. Do you understand what happened nearly three hundred years ago?"

"Of course," Neil said, trying as hard as he could not to sound disrespectful, but he knew that if Sir Vapros got started on the family history, his great passion, there was no stopping him from launching into one of his infamous sermons. It was too late.

"Our ancestors, four brothers, who were the leaders of Altryon, stood in the giant palace as it fell under siege," he said. "The savages broke through the door and prepared to end their lives, but something happened to change the course of history. Do you know what happened, Neil?"

"The glowing man appeared," Neil said unenthusiastically.

"Use his full name. I won't tolerate blasphemy in my house."

"The Man with the Golden Light," Neil amended. "Sorry."

Sir Vapros continued, "Our powers were given to us by a deity, Neil. That's what you don't seem to realize. Protecting Altryon is our divine purpose and only one family can truly protect Altryon. It's not the Taurlum, it's not the Celerius and it's not the family that's already perished. It's us, Neil. It's the Vapros. The people seem to have forgotten all we've done for them. Many are hesitant to let us rule or trust us, but there are certain gifts we have bestowed that even they cannot forget. For instance, our ancestors built the wall. No matter where we go in this city, the wall is always visible, reminding us that we are safe. Do you know what's outside the wall, Neil?"

He didn't wait for an answer. "It's a wasteland. It's a desert. It's dead earth, crawling with savages who want to come within our paradise and steal it for themselves." Sir Vapros had a faraway look on his face. "But the greatest threat to Altryon was still inside the wall."

Neil tried not to sigh.

"The brothers all married and bore sons and daughters, and each child inherited powers of their own. They competed with each other, testing ability against ability. Grudges were born. Tension grew between the relatives. Their competitions became increasingly violent. The Taurlum drew first blood. I'll be dammed if I let them draw last."

Sir Vapros drew a long breath. "This feud started before you were born, before any of us were born. It's not ideal. But we still have to protect Altryon. There's no choice. We have to carry out the destiny laid before us by the Man with the Golden Light. It has to be the Vapros, Neil. The other families are inferior to us. They just aren't capable."

Neil felt like screaming but knew better. "But we aren't carrying out the destiny. We aren't in charge anymore. None of us are."

Sir Vapros drummed his fingers along the table. "It's true. An emperor took control, and now his descendant rules the city. But we're still here. We rule Altryon through other means. We use our wealth, our businesses. We provide the people with jobs."

"I just don't see what our family history has to do with me wanting to be an assassin," Neil said, trying to keep the stubbornness out of his voice.

"If you look back through history, you will see that we only accept the best." Sir Vapros slammed his hand against his desk to emphasize each word. "The Taurlum children, they're all trained as warriors. Even though half of them are hopelessly unskilled with a hammer, they all become warriors. And then they all retire and become merchants, and the other half is hopelessly unskilled at mercantilism. Half of their house is forced into jobs that do not make the best of their skills. The Celerius are similar in that they all go into the military and then into business. We Vapros, we are more . . . efficient. The ones who are good at being assassins will be assassins for life. The charismatic ones will be socialites for life. We play to our strengths. And that is why we are better." He looked down at Neil. "You've just turned sixteen and it's time you choose a permanent career. With that charming personality of yours, son, you would make a first rate socialite. Play to your strengths. Do it for Altryon."

"Father," Neil said carefully. "Please, I just need one more chance, a new mission. Give me anyone, I don't care who it is, I'll kill him."

"I cannot be embarrassed again, Neil."

"If I fail," Neil said, "I'll give up the dream and become a socialite."

Sir Vapros stood from his chair and approached Neil. "Don't talk back to me. Do as you're told."

"One last chance," Neil said again, with more force this time.

Suddenly Neil felt a blow to the head. With his cheeks burning and ears ringing, he realized that his father had struck him. This was not exactly uncommon in the Vapros house, but still Neil was somehow surprised. Rage filled him but he did not flinch. He blinked back tears and fixed his posture. He glared at his father who almost looked like he regretted striking his son. "One last chance," Neil begged quietly.

Neil's father looked thoughtful for a moment. Neil thought he caught a glimpse of admiration in his eyes. After what felt like an endless pause, Sir Vapros sighed. "Okay, one last chance," he decided, putting his hands on his son's shoulders. Neil tried not to flinch. "Now put on a smile, boy.

We're going out tonight—all of us, as a family."

Neil could feel the pain fading and his excitement building. *One last chance.* "Where are we going?" he asked.

Sir Vapros sported a smile of his own. "Tonight, we're going socializing."

Chapter Four
Vapros Bunker
Neil

After taking a few moments to shed his assassin cloak and don his evening clothes, Neil approached the mirror in his bedroom. It was connected to a small dresser nudged into the corner of the minuscule room. The dresser and bunk bed were the only furniture that could fit into a room so small. Neil examined his reflection and hoped the red mark in the shape of his father's hand would soon fade. Neil had an angular face with a strong jawline. His eyes were a distinct emerald green and peeked out from behind his long messy hair. He examined the black locks for a moment and decided to brush them back out of his face. He hoped it would make him look slightly more presentable.

Rhys entered the room briskly and grabbed his own coat. He appeared to be deep in thought, but stopped upon seeing Neil. "You didn't have that mark when you came back today …"

"You know where it came from," sighed Neil.

Rhys looked at the floor for a moment and nodded.

They ascended the spiral staircase that led to the undersized entryway where his family waited. Everything about the Vapros bunker was specifically designed to be small, and with good reason: no Taurlum invader could charge through these narrow hallways. No Celerius sword could swing down to deliver a deathblow with these low, sloping ceilings. Cramped spaces did nothing to hinder materialization, and so the family had built their dwelling accordingly. Even generations ago, their house had played to their strengths. *Father would have been proud,* Neil thought as he jumped the last few steps and joined the throng of siblings and cousins packed into the foyer.

"Neil!" The cry came from a black-haired beauty. "Neil! Over here!"

Neil threaded his way through the crowd to meet her. "Jennifer," he said to his sister. *Thanks for spying on me,* he added internally. *Thanks for standing by while I almost died.*

Jennifer grinned enthusiastically. It made Neil nervous. "Victoria and I were just talking about you!" Victoria, Neil's sister and Jennifer's twin, reached out to straighten Neil's collar.

"We've been waiting for news about your mission," Jennifer said.

Victoria gave Neil a smile that was much gentler than her twin's maniacal grin. "We already heard some news, actually."

Neil glared at Jennifer. "News travels fast around here, doesn't it?"

Jennifer laughed loudly. "It was too entertaining to keep to myself."

"You didn't have to tell Dad about Bianca," Neil grumbled to Jennifer as she turned to face the entrance to the bunker.

"Yes, I did," she said, and just for an instant Neil thought he saw her eyes soften. "Don't socialize with people you're not supposed to, Neil. It never ends well."

"Is everyone ready?" thundered the voice of Sir Vapros before Neil could respond. Sir Vapros opened the hatch at the front of the door and materialized through it. The group followed suit one at a time. They gathered in a circle around Neil's father. He waited until everyone was there and a small grin began to split his face. "Is everyone familiar with Quintus, the emperor's advisor?"

A murmur of consensus went up among the group.

"Tonight, we spread the rumor that Quintus has been visiting the brothels due to his failing marriage."

Neil saw Jennifer smirk. The plan was becoming clearer. Until about two hundred years ago, the families were the collective leaders of Altryon but were overthrown by the people due to the fact that their constant infighting made it impossible for them to pass badly needed laws to benefit the people. Fed up, the citizens had gone on a citywide strike that crippled the economy. The families reluctantly relinquished power to a newly anointed emperor and were forced to rule through other means. They had divided the city into three parts: the Vapros controlled the nightlife district, the Taurlum the markets, and the Celerius the banking system. They paid taxes to the new empire, and an uneasy truce had been established.

With each new emperor, the families maneuvered politically in order to maintain favor with the emperor and the citizens of Altryon. Whenever the emperor had an advisor that displeased Sir Vapros, they usually didn't last long. Quintus, for example, was famously anti-Vapros. This was a mission of defamation.

"We also," Sir Vapros continued, "will drop hints that he is battling alcoholism." A grin nearly broke his icy expression. "If any of you finish early, you are encouraged to head down to the Opera House. Tonight's performance is going to be a very special one."

Neil knew all about the new opera because his father had been going on about it for weeks. Apparently, it was finally going to be an "accurate depiction" of the history of the families.

Sir Vapros pointed to the twins. "Jennifer, Victoria, you take the Opera

House. Entertain the nobles. Gather information and keep them drinking."

Jennifer pulled her hair back into a tight ponytail and gave her father a nod of affirmation. Neil felt a tiny twinge of jealousy. She looked exactly the way an assassin should look. Despite her delicate facial features, she always had an expression of readiness and intensity. Unlike her socialite twin, she only had the appearance of being slender. Neil knew that the coat hid her well-toned muscle and a multitude of tattoos.

The first tattoo was always given in private and represented the first kill, but the rest were accompanied by a family celebration. Jennifer had been the guest of honor at countless "family dinners." Neil, on the other hand, had never known the honor of such a celebration. She probably had more tattoos than anyone else in the family, aside from Sir Vapros, of course. As the twins began to stroll down the street toward the Opera House, Sir Vapros called after them. "Victoria!" She turned.

"I don't want to hear about your little boyfriend ending up at the Opera House."

She blushed. Jennifer smirked.

"He's not the one I'm asking you to entertain. Do you understand?"

Victoria nodded, lowering her head so her hair fell in a curtain around her face. Jennifer let out a laugh as she grabbed her sister's hand and pulled her down the street.

Sir Vapros turned his attention to Rhys. "There is a masquerade ball near the palace. Go. Meet people. Engage in conversation. Make friends." Rhys smiled as he realized he'd be able to spend the entire night conversing with intellectuals. He trotted down the road toward the mask shops.

One by one, Sir Vapros assigned his family members to different areas of the nightlife district until only Neil was left. He looked down at his son thoughtfully. "Go to the pub near the Opera House," he decided.

"Buy a couple of rounds—flirt, boost morale, all that. If you have time, go meet up with Rhys near the end of the night." Neil gave a bow so subtle it could have been a nod and walked away. "And Neil," Sir Vapros called after his son, "do not disappoint me. Once was quite enough for today."

Neil clenched his teeth and materialized onto a roof where he could see the city better. Down below, the older members of his family were heading into restaurants. In the distance, he could barely make out the twins skipping hand in hand toward the Opera House. He began to walk along the rooftops, materializing between buildings when he had to, heading in the general direction of his favorite bar, The Laughing Mask Tavern. His father's voice rang in his ears. *Do not disappoint me. Do not disappoint me. You have one last chance.*

Sighing, Neil materialized down to the street in front of the bar. He inspected his evening cloak quickly to make sure it was in presentable shape. It was a long, black cloak that lapped near his knees and hugged his sides nicely. It also had a subtle, purple trim to let everyone know who he was. He put on a fake smile and pushed through the double doors with a cry of jubilation. Everyone in the bar turned as he came in, and then echoed his cheer. The girls all sat up a little straighter, and even some of the men improved their postures. They all knew what it meant when a Vapros showed up in a bar—free drinks.

Neil swaggered through the masses of people up to the bartender. "A round for everyone!" he shouted, throwing his hand in the air. The bar erupted into applause. For them, this was a kind gesture, but it was nothing for the Vapros. They owned the bar and they even manufactured the beer. Grinning, Neil scanned the crowd for possible sources of information. If he returned tonight with intriguing gossip, maybe his father would finally realize his worth.

Through the hordes of men chanting tuneless drinking songs, Neil spotted a table of girls giggling and chatting. Women were always good for gossip. In the center table, a group of Imperial soldiers were sitting, laughing, chugging and waving their tankards in Neil's direction. Perfect. Neil leaned over the counter and grabbed the bartender by his lapels. "Keep their glasses full," he whispered, gesturing over his shoulder at the soldiers.

The bartender smirked, nodded knowingly, and remarked, "Soldiers— a wealth of information there. Excellent choice, sir. But are you sure it's not that table you want drinking?" He jerked his head toward the girls in the corner.

Neil grinned, "I don't need booze for that." The bartender nodded in approval. This bartender knew the drill and loved the Vapros like most did. The Vapros kept him employed and provided protection. After Neil returned the nod, he waded through the crowd to the table of women. "Hello, ladies," he said, sweeping a bow. "How are you this fine evening?"

A few of them giggled. One finally spoke up. "We're all doing well. And yourself, Mr. Vapros?"

Neil pulled up a chair. "Can't complain." That was a lie. He, of all people, had every right to spend a great deal of time complaining. His father didn't approve of his dreams. His sister had willingly sold him out, most likely because she saw Neil as a threat to her position as top Vapros assassin. His younger brother's powers had advanced farther than his own, and he'd ruined his family's reputation by running for his life through the markets, until a girl from the streets saved his life. It had not been a good day.

"So," Neil remarked, "how's the city treating you all tonight?"

The girls exchanged a glance and burst out laughing. "We heard it hasn't been very kind to you," one of them said finally.

Neil repressed a groan and tried to fake a smile. "Hey," he said, "I've been through worse."

"Worse than almost dying?" the girl sitting across the table asked.

Neil shrugged. "I could have killed him if I wanted to," he said slowly, making it up as he went along. "But the first thing they teach you in assassin school is that you are only allowed to kill your target. That Taurlum boy wasn't my target. I had to let him chase me." He shrugged. "Call me a pacifist."

The girls, amazingly, bought into his lie. Neil signaled to the bartender to bring more drinks. "So, ladies," he said leaning in, "just out of curiosity, have you all heard about Quintus, the emperor's advisor?"

Chapter Five
Celerius Estate
Lilly

Across town, the carriage ride back to the Celerius estate was a silent one. Lilly stared blankly ahead, ignoring Jonathan in spite of his best attempts to talk to her. When they pulled up to the main house, she jumped to the ground without waiting for assistance and walked quickly to lock herself in her room. She exhaled slowly and let herself fall onto her neatly made bed, smoothing down minuscule wrinkles in the comforter with her hands. Lilly liked everything to be tidy; cleaning and straightening up provided her with a good distraction from the chaos that followed her everywhere she went.

A knock at the door made Lilly jump. Glancing in the mirror briefly, she smoothed down her hair and rose to admit the visitor. Lady Celerius stood outside the door, cupping her hand around her tight blonde bun to make sure it was still perfectly in place.

"Mother," Lilly said, automatically dropping a curtsy.

Lady Celerius nodded in acknowledgment and came into the room.

"Close the door, Lilly," she said. Lilly obeyed. Lady Celerius looked as if she hadn't slept in weeks. The bags under her eyes were too heavy to be concealed by makeup. "What did Anthony tell you?" she asked, skipping over the formalities of small talk.

Lilly stared at the wood of her door, willing herself not to cry. "He says the rumors may be true," she whispered. "His life is in danger. There are changes happening in the Imperial Army—big changes." She took a deep breath. "They're going to execute him."

"No." Lady Celerius sank down on the bed. She did not abandon her perfect posture, but her face grew white. "I was afraid of that."

Lilly didn't reply.

"Why not ask him to step down?" Lady Celerius asked. "Why not just dismiss him?"

Lilly clenched her fists at her sides. "Because they're trying to send a message. They want everyone to see that the families aren't all-powerful. That's what Anthony said."

"I believe in Anthony," Lady Celerius said. "We are very hard to kill. He may have a chance."

Lilly turned to face her mother. "That's not all of it," she said.

Lady Celerius pursed her lips. "What do you mean?"

She took a deep breath. "If Anthony resists—if he fights back at all— the emperor will send his Imperial soldiers here ... to kill us. So Anthony ... he says he isn't going to resist."

Lady Celerius clutched her daughter's bedpost. "But that means ..."

Lilly closed her eyes. "He won't risk our lives. He isn't going to fight back. He's going to let them kill him."

Lady Celerius rose and took her daughter's hand. "There is still a chance the rumors aren't true. This could just be more Vapros lies to force us to move against the emperor," she said.

Lilly shook her head. "I think they might be true. So does Anthony," she said, voice cracking. She leaned her head against her mother's shoulder and cried harder than she had in years. "I hope he fights anyway," she choked out between sobs.

Lady Celerius hugged Lilly tightly. "I hope he doesn't have to. We'll discuss this with your father when he returns from his trip tonight. He will never let this happen. If the emperor really wants to send us a signal, we'll send one right back. We'll see him bleeding on his own palace floor."

Chapter Six
The Laughing Mask Tavern
Neil

Neil was getting frustrated. He had easily convinced the girls at the bar that Quintus was a womanizing alcoholic, demanded all their gossip in return, and bought them so many drinks that most were past offering any more reliable information. Now there was nothing to do but wait for the Imperial soldiers to become intoxicated enough to spill their secrets. He sighed and set his chin in his palm, gazing absently at his targets.

"… Captain of the Guard is dead," he heard one of them say above the din of the bar. "… Taurlum injured him … cracked his skull … furious … the emperor says … last straw … Vapros …"

One of the soldiers noticed Neil listening. He nudged his comrades and whispered something that made them all look over at him. Neil waved and crossed the room to meet them. A few girls groaned in displeasure as he departed but most were too intoxicated to notice. He turned his attention back to the soldiers. "How are you gentlemen this evening?" he asked. The soldiers exchanged glances. None of them would meet his eye. "Come on, men. Why so glum?"

One of the soldiers threw back a shot exclaiming, "We're not in the mood to socialize, Vapros."

Neil flashed his famous, charming smile. "What's wrong? Bad day?"

The soldier suddenly became fascinated with his helmet on the table.

Neil tried again. "Must be hard to get comfortable in all that armor. Might that be the cause of your unrest?"

The soldier reddened and looked Neil dead in the eyes. "Listen, Vapros. No offense, but you are literally the last person on this earth I can discuss this with."

Neil raised an eyebrow. "Why?" he asked with genuine curiosity. "Is it something about my family? I'm sure we can handle any complaint you have. Something about the bar?"

The soldier sighed, rose to his feet, and started toward the door. The others followed. "Thanks for the drinks, kid," muttered one of them.

"Wait." Neil jumped up to follow them, starting to panic. He'd waited all night to pump these men for information. He couldn't let them get away without getting something out of them.

The largest soldier turned around and gave Neil a small half-smile. "Be careful, kid," he said sadly as he walked out the door.

Neil growled and curled his hands into fists. His father was right. He was a disappointment. Those soldiers had been hiding something, something huge, something that concerned his family specifically, and he'd let them get away. He slammed a small sack of coins on the counter for the bartender and started out the door to meet up with his brother. He gave one last wave to the girls before leaving. Maybe Rhys had had better luck tonight. Maybe he'd found his own group of soldiers to question at the masquerade ball . . . or maybe Rhys hadn't thought to question the soldiers, and he, Neil, could swoop in and get the information first.

Neil pulled open the door and stepped back into the bar. "You forget something, Mr. Vapros?" the bartender asked.

A smile was growing across Neil's face. "You don't happen to have a mask I can borrow, do you?"

Chapter Seven
Taurlum Mansion
Darius

Darius Taurlum had never attended the opera. Not only did he hate the music, but the operas performed at the Vapros Opera House were basically propaganda discrediting the other families. The most recent featured brutish clans of barbarians running across the stage dressed in red and gold before being vanquished. The allusion didn't escape the clever minds of the rich, and very few Taurlum attended performances there.

Tonight, Darius would be the exception.

The Taurlum boy dug furiously through the armory, searching for suitable armor. He slid a chain mail shirt over his shoulders, wincing as it chafed against the knife wound in his neck. They were going to pay.

Most of the time, members of his family didn't bother with armor. It was unnecessary; their skin was tough enough to prevent injury. In all his seventeen years, Darius had never felt the need to wear the full body armor that protected each of his pressure points. But choosing not to wear all his protective covering had almost cost him his life today, so Darius felt safer with his limbs shielded. He pulled on a breastplate over the chain mail and fastened it tightly. The armor was specifically built for Taurlum warriors, featuring a double layer of metal covering the pressure points. Nothing could touch him now.

Darius smirked a little as he lowered a helmet over his head. The Vapros brat wouldn't be wearing armor. His kind hardly ever did. It was too heavy for them. It slowed the weaklings down. Even the Celerius family was too frail to handle real armor. They had to build their own version out of leather. Only he, a great and powerful Taurlum warrior, was strong enough to protect himself completely. With strength like that, he knew, he could never fail.

The door to the armory heaved open while Darius was selecting a weapon. "I'm going to the market for some tail," said Michael. Darius grunted but didn't look up. "You want to come?"

"I'm going on a mission tonight," Darius replied, weighing a hammer in his hands.

Michael closed the door. "Dad gave you a mission? After what happened today?"

Beneath the helmet, Darius felt his face redden. "I asked him for one."

"Because you're embarrassed," Michael guessed.

Darius clenched his teeth together. "Yes."

Michael rubbed his stubbly chin thoughtfully and then moved to the far edge of the armory. He removed something from a chest and tossed it to Darius, who was still examining the hammers. It bounced off the back of his armor and hit the floor. "Darius," Michael complained, "pay attention, will you?"

Darius sighed. He didn't have time for Michael now. He had to focus. He felt guilty—not that he would ever admit it—about hurting the Captain of the Guard, and if he didn't take time to plan his every move

55

tonight, he might end up hurting more innocents. He turned to look at the object that Michael had thrown at him. It was a golden helmet, much heavier than the simple silver one currently on his head, but more regal. The finishing touch was the large pair of horns protruding from the top that would likely give the wearer the appearance of a bull.

Darius smiled. "Perfect. Thank you." He pulled the golden headpiece down over his face. Michael gave Darius a cocky grin before heaving the door open again. Darius could hear him whistling as he walked down the stairs toward the front door. Darius removed his cloak from a hook on the wall and draped it over his armored shoulders. He checked his appearance briefly with the reflection in a suit of armor propped up by the door. He looked like a warrior.

Tonight, the rich nobles of Altryon were going to the opera. Darius was not.

Darius was going to war.

Chapter Eight
Masquerade Ball
Neil

Neil entered the lavish masquerade ball silently and assessed the crowd, looking for his brother. Rhys wasn't easy to spot. He'd chosen to come to the masquerade dressed as a Taurlum, complete with a red and gold coat to match his mask. If Rhys's hair had been a little better hidden and if he had been a little taller, Neil would probably have been completely fooled. His brother stood among four other men who all seemed overly excited to be talking to one another. Neil wove his way through the waltzing couples and tapped Rhys on the shoulder. "So it looks like I'm not the only one with an ironic mask, huh, brother?"

Rhys peered out from behind his mask, with his jade eyes, and then grinned. Neil had donned a blue mask with gold stars: Celerius colors. "Excellent," he whispered. "Have you met the doctor's guild yet?" he asked in his normal tone, gesturing to the men with whom he'd been conversing.

Neil faked a smile. "I haven't had the pleasure." Neil had never liked doctors. They talked like they were members of a cult. "What's the latest in medical news?"

Rhys began to bounce with excitement. "We have a basic knowledge of where organs are located in the body and how they work."

Neil glanced over Rhys's shoulder, scanning the room for soldiers. "Uh-huh."

"And there's the nervous system, and we've discovered these chemicals that are produced by the brain and they actually control—"

"I hate to cut you off," Neil lied, "but did you manage to tell your friends about Quintus?"

Rhys waved his hand in the air. "Of course I did. So basically these chemicals can control—"

A doctor in a wolf mask had been eavesdropping. "I already knew," he boasted, cutting Rhys off mid-sentence.

"Knew what?" Rhys asked excitedly. "About the chemicals?"

"No," the doctor admitted, "about Quintus."

Rhys and Neil stared. "You knew about Quintus," Neil repeated.

"He's a patient of mine," the doctor informed them. "I've known of his ailments for months."

Rhys and Neil exchanged glances, and Neil tried not to smirk. They both knew the rumors about Quintus's drinking and marital problems were just that: rumors. They were entirely unfounded, just like all the other stories the Vapros family invented and spread around to hurt the reputations of their enemies. Inevitably, someone would pretend to have known about the rumor all along. It was incredible and terrifying to Neil how easy it was for rumors to gain false credibility.

The doctor moved on, and Neil grabbed Rhys by the back of his Taurlum cloak. "Come with me." They wandered away from the group. "First of all," Neil said, "brilliant costume." Rhys grinned. "Also, this could be nothing, but I talked with some soldiers this evening. They were acting really suspicious."

"Suspicious?"

"They wouldn't talk to me. They said something about our family. One of them told me to be careful."

Rhys nodded slowly. "I experienced something similar with an arms dealer about an hour ago. He said he couldn't talk to anyone in my family without jeopardizing some mission."

Neil furrowed his brow. "But you're dressed like a Taurlum."

Rhys's hand flew to his mask as if he'd forgotten. "You're right."

"So whatever's going on, it affects the Taurlum, too," Neil mused.

Rhys pursed his lips. "Do you think the Celerius are behind it?"

"I think so," Neil said. "The Celerius fill the ranks of the military. Where's your arms dealer friend? I'm dressed as a Celerius, maybe he'll talk to me."

Rhys shook his head noting, "You don't look like a Celerius at all. You have a blue mask, but look at the rest of your clothes. You're in black and purple. You look just like a Vapros."

Neil sighed angrily, "Damn. You're right. You're always right."

Rhys shrugged. The brothers sat in silence for a few minutes. "How'd things go with the girls?" Rhys asked.

"How'd you know about the girls?"

"You're Neil Vapros. There are always girls where you're concerned."

Neil smiled to himself. "Yeah, I talked to a few at the bar. All I learned was that Michael Taurlum is as bad as ever." He sighed. "I wish we had a Celerius," he said, catching sight of a soldier.

"Neil Vapros," a voice said from just behind them. Rhys turned quickly. Neil didn't bother. He knew that voice almost as well as he knew his own. "Fancy meeting you here."

"Bianca," he said, still not turning around.

"What, you're not even going to look at me?" He could almost hear her pouting. "I even put on a dress and everything." Neil let himself smile as he turned around. She swept a low curtsy. "How are you this fine evening, Mr. Vapros?" she asked, eyes twinkling. But Neil wasn't looking at her eyes.

Neil raised one eyebrow and Bianca saw his mouth twitch as he stared at her dress. Bianca stood in a noticeably extravagant dress, a voluminous ball gown that hugged her torso and then practically exploded into an avalanche of blue ruffles and lace. She probably didn't know it, but it even looked a little too extravagant for a party like this. She had an expensive-looking pearl necklace and matching pearl earrings. She had pulled her hair up into a twist and little blond strands escaped and hung endearingly along the sides of her face.

Neil pulled a handkerchief from his pocket and leaned over and wiped it across the edge of Bianca's forehead, where a smudge of ash had been overlooked. Bianca's eyes grew wide in surprise.

"What is this?" he asked as he looked at the handkerchief.

"Soot," she replied calmly.

"Why is there soot on your forehead?"

"Burned down a gang member's house," she said as she grabbed a glass of champagne from the table.

"That's hilarious," he sighed.

"It wasn't a joke."

"And may I ask where you got the dress?"

"This rich-looking girl and I traded clothes."

"Did she want to?" Rhys asked.

"I don't have to answer that," Bianca said with a grin.

"We'll address your crime spree later. But speaking of your dress," Neil said slowly. Rhys gasped and nodded.

"What about it?" Bianca tugged at the sleeves a little.

Neil grinned. "It's blue."

Chapter Nine
Vapros Opera House
Jennifer

Jennifer Vapros walked toward the Opera House arm in arm with her twin sister. "Any plans to meet up with you-know-who tonight?" she asked playfully as an usher wearing purple opened the front doors for them.

Victoria blushed. "I don't know what you're talking about."

"Oh, please, Vic," Jennifer sighed, letting go of her sister to tighten her ponytail.

"Don't tell Dad," Victoria begged.

"Don't meet up with that boy, and I won't have to," her sister fired back. "You have a duty." She started for the grand staircase. Victoria began to follow, but Jennifer stopped her. "I'm going to the second floor. You stay here. We'll meet up at the end of the night."

When Jennifer reached the top of the stairs, she scanned the halls for someone worth talking to. A cluster of giggling girls in large dresses walked by, but Jennifer ignored them. Their brand of gossip wasn't worth the effort. She leisurely approached the nearest balcony and peered out to watch how the opera was proceeding. She then remembered that this was her father's latest project: *The Birth of the Saviors.* Her father had overseen its conception over the last few months and had been anxious about how it would go over with the nobles. They never had a problem with lampooning the Taurlum, but this show had a heavier message; it was all about the legend surrounding the manner in which the families received their powers and the beginning of the feud.

From what she could see, they were still very close to the beginning of the legend. Four actors stood on the stage: one dressed as a Vapros, one as a Taurlum, one as a Celerius, and one in all black clothing. The lack of design that went into the fourth family was due to the fact that no one actually knew anything about the fourth family. Suddenly a horde of actors in furred clothing stormed the stage, these were the savages. They looked ready to attack the family members, but suddenly the dark and ominous music of battle slowed to a soft and pleasing melody. From the ceiling, a man covered with crystals was lowered by a few discreet wires. A light focused on him and he began to glow, shooting rays of light in every direction. He sang a few verses of blessing. She couldn't quite understand every word, but she got the gist: "Protect Altryon with the gifts I have given you."

This was the Man with the Golden Light. According to the legend, he had given the families their powers so that they could protect Altryon. The man ascended again into the rafters and the music returned to its rousing battle theme. A complicated fight scene erupted on stage and when finished, the savages and the family member in black lay dead on the ground. Jennifer turned away in disinterest. She knew everything that was about to happen. She spied a group of rich merchants by the window and allowed herself a slight smile. Perfect.

Jennifer moved like a well-oiled machine. Every action was deliberate and smooth, from complicated fight sequences to simple banter. She was, as her father often reminded Neil, a model assassin. She made a beeline for the merchants, her chest held high and a slight sway in her hips. "Not enjoying the opera, I assume?" she said when they noticed her coming.

One of the merchants nudged his neighbor. "It's a bit trite," he spoke up. "All of the 'enemy Taurlum' stuff, I mean. We've seen it all before."

"And it's . . . well, it's an opera," the merchant to her right admitted. The others laughed.

Jennifer leaned against the wall, arms folded. "I don't blame you," she said. "I prefer more . . . exciting pastimes." She unfolded her arms and examined her fingernails. "What would you be doing right now if you weren't here?" she asked idly. She could feel their eyes on her. "I know I'd be out on the town, maybe in a bar somewhere or at a party dancing with a handsome stranger." She knew exactly what to say to make them sweat.

"Yeah, a party sounds good," one of the merchants said quickly. "I know there's a masquerade tonight. If you want to get out of here, I can escort you there."

Jennifer smiled coyly. "Now, now, we hardly know each other," she chided. "It wouldn't be proper."

"Neither would dancing with a stranger," he pointed out. Jennifer met his eyes for the first time.

"Touché," she said finally. "I don't believe we've met before."

He bowed. "Clemens."

"Clemens," she repeated. "It's a pleasure."

"I know who you are," a new merchant said before she could introduce herself. "Jennifer Vapros."

She cocked an eyebrow. "My reputation precedes me, I see."

Clemens whistled. "So it is you," he said. "I thought it might be, but I wasn't sure." He looked her up and down. "I guess the rumors are true."

She glared at him but kept her cool facade. "Oh? And what rumors have you heard about me?"

The merchant countered, "Just that you're the most beautiful girl in Altryon."

Jennifer smirked and felt herself relax. "That honor belongs to my sister, actually."

"Aren't you identical?" asked a random merchant. Jennifer ignored him.

"I'm serious." Clemens said as he gave her a small smile. "They say every man who sees you falls in love."

Her eyes narrowed and she felt herself grow angrier than she should have.

"I've heard more," the first merchant jumped in. "I've heard she's an assassin."

Jennifer whipped her head around to stare at him. "Me?" she said. "An assassin? I'm just a young girl."

"That's right. They say men let their guard down around you. You draw them in, trick them into trusting you, and then kill them. They don't even see it coming."

One of the merchants nudged Clemens. "Be careful, Clem," he joked, "you could be next!"

Jennifer's hand twitched for her knife. She could feel her pulse quickening. "Not all rumors are true," she said finally. *Keep it together, Jen.*

"She's not an assassin," Clemens said sternly to his companion. "Leave her alone." He took half a step toward her. "So, how about that party?" He offered her his arm.

Jennifer let out a laugh. "With you? I'm flattered, but what would your wife think?"

Clemens looked shocked. The other merchants exchanged glances. "How did you know?" he trailed off.

"Your reputation precedes you as well, merchant," Jen said coldly. She knew she was destroying any chance of getting information out of these men, but she didn't care. This wasn't fun anymore. They had come too close to an awful truth. "I know all of you: Brock, Marques, Edgar." She glared at each one of them as she rattled off their names. "I'm a Vapros. We thrive on knowing everything about everyone."

The merchants looked like they wished they were somewhere else.

Jennifer planted her feet on the ground. "I suggest you all find your way back to your seats and watch the rest of the opera," she said in a low, menacing voice. "Unless you want your darkest secrets spilled over the streets of Altryon." The men, looking terrified, scurried down the hallway.

Jennifer kept a threatening look on her face until they were out of sight, and then sighed and leaned against the bar. She took deep breaths until her heart returned to its normal pace. She once again approached the balcony and saw that they were reaching an even more exciting part of the opera. Apparently, the three brothers had already fallen to infighting. She was always told that the head Taurlum had killed a Vapros child and this started the feud. This was no doubt the message this evening, although she knew the other families disagreed. Soon more Taurlum would arrive on stage and there would be another fight. Jennifer had never been too interested in operas and this one was no different. No longer in the mood to talk to people she didn't know, she darted downstairs to find her sister.

VICTORY LIES WITHIN
THE ASHES

Chapter Ten
Masquerade Ball
Rhys

The masquerade ball was in full swing. The noise level was increasing as the drinks flowed and patrons spoke louder to be heard above the band. Rhys watched his brother and Bianca cross the ball slowly. They had "borrowed" a large blue hat and Neil was tucking her last remaining strands of hair into it. She was actually starting to look like a Celerius. Hopefully, the arms dealer wouldn't notice that her eyes were grey instead of deep brown. Neil was quietly explaining to her what she needed to do. It was interesting to see the two interact. Neil had a customary way with women. He usually flashed his charming smile and his voice dropped to a deeper pitch; he leaned in when he talked and played it as cool as he could. But when he talked to Bianca it was different; it was almost as if they were dancing. Information flowed back and forth easily in a rhythm that had been established over years of communication and friendship.

Neil returned to Rhys's side and they watched from afar as Bianca approached the arms dealer. "I'm confused," Rhys said.

Neil reached for a drink from the table behind them. "It's simple. Bianca is wearing blue. The Celerius family wears blue. The arms dealer will think she's a Celerius and spill the secrets. You're a smart kid. How do you not understand this plan?"

"That's not what I meant," Rhys said indignantly. "I meant I don't understand you two."

"Us two?

"Yes. What is your relationship to her?"

Neil took a long gulp of his drink. "Friends," he said finally. "Just friends." Rhys nodded thoughtfully. "You don't look like you believe me," Neil said casually.

"It's just …" Rhys paused, "none of my friends have ever toppled titans for me."

Neil smiled briefly. "Don't refer to the Taurlum as titans. We don't need to fuel their egos. That's their job." He set down his drink. "Here she comes."

Bianca had made a beeline for them, her brow furrowed. "He wouldn't talk to me," she said when she was within earshot.

"What?" Neil looked over her shoulder. The arms dealer was nowhere to be seen. "He didn't say anything?"

"He just apologized. He wouldn't stop saying sorry."

"Did he say what he was sorry for?" Rhys prompted.

"No. He wouldn't even look at me."

Rhys frowned. "So the soldiers won't talk to any of the families?"

"Apparently not," Neil remarked as he searched the crowd for the dealer.

"Do you think it's something serious?" Bianca asked.

"I don't know what to think."

"I could try to talk to him as a commoner," she offered. "I'll change out of the dress. I have my armor underneath anyway." She grinned, trying to lighten the mood, but Neil was too lost in thought.

"We have to tell Dad," Rhys said, putting a hand on Neil's shoulder. They started toward the door.

"Wait!" Bianca ran after them. "You're leaving?"

"This can't wait," Rhys told her.

"Don't you want me to come with you? I'm the one who tried to talk to him."

"Sir Vapros won't want to talk to you," Neil said bitterly.

"But Neil!"

"You have to stay here, Bianca," he said sharply. "In case anything happens. You have to … keep watch."

"In case anything happens," she repeated. "You think something bad could happen? And you want me to stay here, to knowingly put myself in harm's way?"

"You have your armor under your dress," Rhys pointed out.

Bianca ignored him. "Neil Vapros, stop walking this instant!"

He didn't stop walking. She finally fell behind. "Fine!" she called after them. "But you owe me! For the second time today!"

He nodded back over his shoulder absent-mindedly which didn't seem to calm her temper. She huffed and turned to face the people and festivities once again.

Chapter Eleven
Vapros Opera House
Darius

Darius Taurlum gained access to the Opera House through the stage door. It was locked from the outside, but he'd pulled it straight out of the wall and walked in hurriedly before anyone noticed. There were probably better, less conspicuous ways of infiltrating, but visions of his impending revenge on the Vapros brat were clouding his thought process.

The backstage area was a maze of tiny hallways crowded with actors, stagehands, and set pieces. Nobody seemed to notice or care that he was there; they all just stepped around him without making eye contact. Looking around, Darius tried to assess the best way to cause chaos during the show. He could smash through the set with his hammer. Or, if he could find a match, he could set the curtain on fire.

A small man in a purple coat grabbed Darius by the arm and began to yank him toward the stage. Darius glared at him. "Your cue is coming up," he said in hushed tones. "Is that a new costume? It looks great."

"You want me to go onstage?" Darius asked, a new plan forming slowly in his mind.

"What do you think we've been rehearsing for? Of course I want you to go onstage! And don't miss your entrance! This isn't amateur hour."

Darius grinned. "Which side of the stage do I enter from again?"

Chapter Twelve
Nightlife District
Neil

The quickest route back to the Vapros home took them through the center of the nightlife district. Neil and Rhys had to weave between dancing villagers and try to avoid getting hit in the head with mugs of beer. It was slow going. Eventually, Neil ducked into an alley and led his brother to a quieter part of the district. The streets here were deserted; the bars closed early on the outskirts.

"Where are you going?" Rhys asked.

"We'll get there faster this way. There were too many people in the way."

They kept walking in silence. It had rained in this part of town. The streets were full of puddles and a few stray drops still fell from the sky. One of them hit Neil directly on the forehead. He found himself wishing he had his assassin's hood. In the distance, he heard drunken cheers from the part of the district that was still open for business.

"I hate when everything's deserted like this," Rhys mumbled.

"Why?"

"I feel like someone's going to jump out and attack me."

Neil smiled. "This isn't the poor district. Nobody's going to mug you. We're practically princes here. We do own every business you can see." But as he spoke, he reflexively reached for his knife. The villagers of Altryon had become increasingly restless lately. Some of the emperor's policies had left people desperately poor. Year after year, he had relentlessly increased taxes. There were whispers of uprisings. "And why would they attack you, anyway? You're Rhys Vapros. People love your quietness and gentleness. Who could hurt someone as adorable as you?" he mocked quietly. "You'd have more to worry about if you were the emperor."

Rhys shrugged. "I just don't like being out alone this late at night. I don't like the dark. It's an irrational fear. Don't ask me to explain it."

Neil slung his arm over his brother's shoulder. "You aren't alone. You have me—an assassin."

"An assassin in training," Rhys corrected, but he was smiling.

"Same thing," Neil countered as he sighed and looked up at the moon.

Neil and Rhys made it to the end of the alley and neared the center of the nightlife district. A large marble fountain stood in the center and the entire square buzzed with activity. Street performers, merchants, and young partygoers brought the street to life. The two Vapros boys wandered through the crowd and Neil's eyes settled on a group of kids. They were staring at him and whispering to each other. Rhys noticed and muttered, "This again?"

Neil smiled. "We sure do have quite the reputation." He took a few steps toward the group. "Sit tight," he called over his shoulder to Rhys. The group consisted of three boys and three girls, all of whom averted their eyes when Neil grew near. "You all seem rather skittish," he said with a grin.

"We're not supposed to talk to Vapros," muttered a boy who looked to be the eldest, perhaps Neil's age.

"Why not?" Neil came a little closer. "Because of the nursery rhyme?" Neil began to quote it:

"Billy was a good boy, who was never rude or sad.

Until he met the Vapros and then everything went bad."

"We aren't supposed to talk to you," the boy tried again, but Neil talked over him finishing the rhyme.

"They took him to their parties, they let him drink their ale.

The emperor came—they disappeared—and Billy went to jail."

"Exactly. If we trust you, we'll end up in trouble," one of the girls said.

"You won't," Neil said. "We are a good and noble people. It's just a story made up to scare you."

"Sorry, we aren't falling for your lies," the oldest boy said.

"Look, those stories aren't real," Neil said. "The emperor made it up to keep you obedient. Everyone goes through a Vapros phase and gets a little rebellious. It's normal." The eldest boy looked unconvinced, but the rest seemed interested. "Listen, if you all want a really good time, head down to the Liquid Ambassador. It's a pub a few blocks south of here. Tell them Neil Vapros sent you, and the food and drinks will be free." He patted one of them on the back. "Have a good night."

"That's exactly what happened to Little Billy!" the eldest cried, but the other kids were already shuffling off in the direction Neil had pointed. "Come on, guys," the boy pleaded, but they didn't stop, and with a glare at Neil, the boy ran after them.

"Ready to go?" Neil asked Rhys as he returned.

Rhys gave him an unimpressed sigh. "You shouldn't have done that."

"Oh, I'm just trying to help them have some fun. Don't tell me that the emperor's nursery lies don't bother you."

"What bothers me is that you just reinforced the stereotype."

"I did not!"

"You sent those kids to the bar," Rhys said. "They were told not to be around Vapros, and you talked them into going to one of our bars. If that's not being a bad influence, I don't know what is."

"They were in the nightlife district. You know they were already planning on doing something. I know the bartender at the Liquid Ambassador. Whenever I send him people around that age, he limits the amount of drinking they do. He makes sure they don't get into too much trouble. Of all the places in this part of town, that's probably the safest place for them to be."

Rhys thought for a second. "And you're a hypocrite, too," he added.

"What part of that made me a hypocrite?"

"You go on about not wanting to be a socialite, but here you are, socializing with every other person you come across."

Neil started to snap back, but a far-off voice suddenly called his name, "Vapros boys! Over here!"

Neil and Rhys turned to see a preacher standing on the edge of the fountain. He gestured grandly to the small crowd surrounding him. "The Man with the Golden Light bestowed his power upon the Vapros. They're the proof! Teleport for us! Show us your power!"

"Let's get out of here," Neil grumbled.

Rhys sighed. "Now you're against improving public image? This will be the best press we get tonight." He materialized a few feet away. Neil followed.

"The teachings of the First Church of Enlightenment are proven," the preacher cried. "Centuries ago, the Man with the Golden Light came forth from the heavens and bestowed upon you these divine gifts. And from these gifts, in turn, your feud was sprung." He turned to the boys expectantly.

Neil sighed. "I don't want to talk about the feud," he said to Rhys.

"Fine," Rhys said, "I'll do it." He positioned himself to face the crowd and spoke clearly, "We were given these powers by the Man with the Golden Light. Our descendants will have them, too. The Man with the Golden Light charged the families with protecting Altryon, and time and time again the Vapros have proven that we are the only ones capable of serving the people. We are the only family that does charity work. We are the only family building things for the people. The other families use their powers for selfish reasons—they monopolize the markets and the military. But we Vapros, everything we do, we do for you."

Rhys turned to Neil with a shrug. Before Neil could respond, the preacher boomed defiantly, "No! You were given these gifts for a purpose and you've squandered these blessings in a feud that has lasted for centuries while the people of Altryon suffer from your petty power struggle. You were charged to work together with the other families for the greater good. Instead, you each use these gifts for your own gain while the people suffer under this oppressive regime. Do you boys wear tattoos? Have you inscribed the souls of the dead into your skin?"

Neil countered, "Wait! We—" but his words were drowned out by the jeers of the crowd. Rhys grabbed Neil by the arm, and they slipped away down the street as the preacher continued his diatribe. Rhys pulled Neil into The Hideaway, a back alley pub owned by the Vapros family. As they entered the rustic tavern, Rhys locked the door behind him. It was closing time and the bar was empty except for the white haired, weather beaten barkeep wiping down the bar. Rhys and Neil plopped down on stools. "Alfred, we need a minute. Can you stay open for a bit?"

"Of course, Sir Vapros. It is in fact your establishment. Can I get you two something?"

"Yes, can we get some ale?" said Neil. As the barkeep turned away to grab mugs, Neil went off. "What was that? After everything we've done for the people of Altryon, this is the thanks we get? The ungrateful—"

Neil was interrupted by the barkeep.

"Your ale, sirs."

"Thank you, Alfred." Neil continued in a more controlled demeanor, recanting the event out loud. "You've run this pub for forty years, Alfred. Are we really that bad?"

For a moment, the innkeeper just looked at the two of them as if contemplating whether or not to respond. After cocking his head and scratching his forehead, Alfred slowly said in his gravelly voice, "It's not a question of being good or bad." This seemed to puzzle and even frustrate Neil. He began to say something as Rhys grabbed his arm.

"Continue," he said to the old man.

"It's not my place, sirs. I should stay quiet."

"No, please continue, Alfred. You know this town better than anyone. After all, you've run this pub forever. If anyone knows the people of Altryon, it's you."

"Well, it's no mystery we are far worse off under the emperor's rule than we were under the rule of the families."

Neil interrupted, "Then what's the problem?"

Rhys once again grabbed Neil's arm. "Let him continue."

Alfred cautiously began again. "Do you even remember what you're feuding about?"

"Sure," Neil retorted in the canned response that had become automatic.

The barkeep stared at Neil for a few seconds. "Well, that's a relief. It would be a shame if all this bloodshed between the families was for nothing. I hope it's for a really good reason, since it is coming at a great cost to the people." Alfred turned and resumed his cleaning.

Rhys stared at Neil. "Do we? Do we really know what this damn feud is about? Cause I sure as hell can't explain it."

Neil opened his mouth, ready to spew the propaganda he had heard his entire life, and then slowly shut it. He ran his hands through his hair, leaned his elbows on the bar, and rested his head in his hands.

Alfred said quietly, "I'm an old man and don't know much, but it seems to me whoever has you upset might have a point. Why were you given these powers? What is your destiny, Sir Vapros?"

Neil didn't have an answer. Alfred shrugged and moved into the back room. "I wonder how Victoria and Jennifer did tonight," Neil said quietly.

"They probably had an even less exciting time than we did." Rhys took a sip of his drink. "Nothing monumental ever happens at the Opera House."

Chapter Thirteen
Vapros Opera House
Victoria

Operas might be boring, but Victoria Vapros didn't care where her father sent her to socialize. Her love always seemed to find her by the end of the night. Even now she could see him across the room, smiling at her gently. It brought a blush to her cheek. She sent him a shy grin back, and he began to approach her. Victoria restrained herself from running to meet him halfway.

Robert wasn't of noble birth. Victoria couldn't have cared less.

"Hello," Robert said with a grin and a bow.

She suppressed a smile. "How do you always know where I'm going to be?"

He shrugged, eyes dancing. "I guess," he admitted, looking into her eyes. She loved those eyes, loved all of him more than she would ever tell Jennifer.

"Do you?" she asked breathlessly. "Well. You're quite good at guessing."

His face melted into the grin she so admired, and he started to say something, but a collective gasp from the people in the theater interrupted his train of thought. "Sounds like we're missing something important," he said, furrowing his brow in mock worry.

Victoria played along. "Oh, yes, I've heard this scene is visually outstanding," she said in the snootiest voice she could manage. "It's a shame we aren't in there watching."

Robert was looking at her mouth. "I don't mind, actually," he murmured. "I'm watching something else visually outstanding."

She giggled at that line, forgetting where she was as she began to lean into him, when a scream tore through the hall. She jumped away from him, cheeks burning. "What …" she began. Robert had already started into one of the boxes that overlooked the stage. She didn't hesitate to follow. The scene below them consisted of several actors dressed as Taurlum. One of the actors was taller. He held a comically oversized hammer like the rest, but as he raised it over his head, Victoria realized it wasn't a prop. She grabbed Robert's hand "We have to tell someone," she hissed. "That's a real Taurlum! We have to—"

She didn't have time to finish her sentence before chaos erupted on the stage.

<hr />

Darius had lumbered onstage after the rest of the actors and clumsily joined them as they formed a line. They began to sing a battle anthem. One of the men next to him nudged him when he didn't join in. Snarling, Darius caught a fistful of the actor's shirt and threw him out into the audience. The nobles in the first few rows shrieked; the others began to stand and run for the exit. Darius lifted his hammer and slammed it into the ground, sending splinters of wood in every direction. "This Opera House is closed in the name of the Taurlum family!" he roared, swinging the hammer over his head and down into the stage again. Screams broke out through the audience. "You will not make a mockery of us again!" A

Vapros guard charged at him, dagger drawn. Darius pummeled him to death with the hammer.

The Taurlum smashed through pillars and walls as he strolled offstage toward the back exit, only to find it blocked by a familiar figure. "Well, well, well," Jennifer Vapros said, examining her fingernails coolly. "Darius, we meet again."

Darius growled, "Out of my way."

Jennifer smiled savagely and cooed, "I can hear the rumors now: Darius Taurlum, beaten by two girls in one day. I don't think you'd be the Taurlum's 'Golden Boy' anymore."

He sighed and lifted his hammer and asked, "Are you sure you want to play this game?"

She raised an eyebrow and repeated, "Are you sure *you* want to play this game? You know what they say about playing with fire." She winked as she pulled a knife from somewhere in her dress. "Still have the scars from last time?"

He clenched his jaw. Jennifer Vapros, like most descendants of the original families, had developed heightened abilities—a feat which he, Darius, still had yet to accomplish. Everyone else in his family had some form of extra ability: Michael, for example, could create small earthquakes, and their father could turn his skin into actual steel. Nobody knew for sure how to coax out the extra power, but Darius had a feeling it had to do with experiencing some kind of trauma. It would make sense, after all. He himself had never gone through anything that left him feeling like he couldn't go on, but he knew Michael had been in some tough situations. And Jennifer Vapros, if the rumors were to be believed, had experienced her fair share of trauma.

Jennifer lifted her hand, as if in a wave and revealed her palm to him. The skin was red, like a glowing ember, and Darius knew, from their last meeting that if it touched him, it would burn like fire and leave scorch marks on his skin.

He had once been on a raid of one of the Vapros' parties with Michael. All had gone well until he decided to go after the only Vapros actually attending the party—Jennifer. He had only just caught her when she grabbed his arm and, eyes blazing, burned into his skin. The burn had since healed over, but his pride had yet to recover.

He charged at her, hammer in hand. She disappeared before his eyes and rematerialized just behind him. With a smirk, she thrust her knife into a chink in his armor. It didn't pierce the skin.

If she was frustrated by her failure, she didn't show it; her face remained as calm and collected as ever. Darius increased his grip on the hammer. "You're quick," he growled, "but you'll tire."

He swung quickly. Jennifer dodged the blow and reappeared in the air behind him and quickly pulled the helmet from his head. She materialized across the room, cradling his precious piece of armor. "Yes," she agreed, "but not before ending you."

"Jen!" a girl's voice cried, and Darius turned in time to see Jennifer's twin sister hurtling down the hallway. Behind her was a boy dressed sloppily in commoner clothes with what appeared to be a borrowed noble's coat. Grunting, Darius threw his hammer at the boy. It only nicked his shoulder, but it was enough to send him sprawling to the ground with a cry of agony. The girl rushed to protect him.

Jennifer redoubled her grip on her knife. "No helmet and no hammer?" she asked, arching an eyebrow.

"All I need are my fists." Darius charged her.

She ran at him with equal vigor. Before Jennifer could rematerialize behind him again, Darius was able to make contact with her. The force of the blow sent her crashing to the floor. Breathing heavily, he grinned at her. "Tired yet?" he asked.

She struggled to sit up. A few feet away, the sister was sobbing over her groaning commoner. Darius bowed mockingly to the fallen assassin and began to walk away. With a little cry, Jennifer leapt to her feet and caught his hand in hers. He felt the familiar burning sensation and shook her off, sending her flying into the opposite wall. It snapped apart at the impact, impaling her with splinters of wood. She didn't try to stand again.

Darius turned to Victoria. "Tell your boyfriend to visit a doctor," he said. "His shoulder's broken." And with that he swaggered from the Opera House, cloak billowing behind him. For the sake of his dramatic exit, he'd left the helmet behind, but Michael would understand.

He had only made it a few paces down the street when he heard the tell-tale clamor of horses making their way after him. As he turned around, he came face to face with what seemed like an entire army of Imperial troops. The soldier at the front lifted a parchment. "Taurlum," he said solemnly, "you are wanted for vandalism crimes against this building and the murder of the Captain of the Guard."

Darius's jaw nearly hit the ground. "He *died?*"

"By order of the Emperor, you are under arrest."

"Wait," Darius said, holding his hands out in front of him, "the vandalism charge. It's on the Vapros Opera House. You all . . . you never interfere in battles between the families."

"Times are changing."

Darius let out a stream of curse words and turned to see if he could run. More Imperial troops were flooding the streets, swords trained on him. Too late—he regretted not retrieving his hammer. He raised his arms in an enraged surrender as the troops moved in around him.

⚜

After she made sure Robert was stable, Victoria knelt over her sister. Wood stuck out of her back like spikes, but they hadn't gone deep enough to pierce any vital organs. She rolled Jennifer over, expecting the worst. "Jennifer?" she said timidly, shaking her sister's shoulder.

Her sister let out a groan of pain and brushed Victoria off. "I'm going to burn that bastard's face off."

Victoria sighed with relief and allowed herself to relax a little. "I'm sure you will," she said soothingly, "he deserves it."

Jennifer struggled to open her eyes. "You're not . . . supposed . . . to be with him," she accused, gesturing vaguely at Robert. Victoria paled.

A few Vapros guards rounded the corner, and Victoria jumped to her feet. "Get these two to a hospital," she barked. She didn't like giving orders, but this was important. "That Taurlum crossed a line tonight." As the guards reached for her fallen allies, Victoria felt tears swimming in her eyes. "This has to end," she whispered. "Soon!"

Chapter Fourteen
Celerius Estate
Lilly

Lilly Celerius rolled over in bed for the hundredth time that night and verbally cursed her insomnia. She should have been used to it by now. She hadn't experienced a full night's sleep since her brother Edward had been murdered unexpectedly in his bed three years ago. But tonight, the condition seemed especially merciless. She had been up all night, worrying about Anthony. She'd run out of tears a few hours ago, and now all she could manage was a dry hiccup once in a while. *It must be nice,* she thought bitterly while squeezing her eyes shut, *to be able to escape into dreamland for a few hours.*

Footsteps outside her door made her open her eyes. Who else was awake at this hour? Maybe Jonathan was coming to check on her. She closed her eyes, listening for voices. The footsteps stopped outside her door. "Jonathan?" she dared to whisper. The word died on her lips as the person outside her room began to speak.

"I think they're in the west end of the house," the low, gravelly voice said, and Lilly sat straight up in bed. This wasn't the kind, familiar voice of her caring servant. This was an intruder.

Another unfamiliar voice chimed in, "We'll have a better chance if we spread out." With a pang of fear, Lilly realized there was an entire group of intruders, as many as five or six, gathered outside her bedroom. She slid out of bed as quietly as she could and groped around in the darkness for her sword.

"Look for offices," one of the voices said. "Anywhere they'd keep legal documents." The other intruders grumbled in agreement. She heard the footsteps disperse and dared to relax. Then the doorknob turned. Her heart leapt into her throat as she whirled behind the opening door, sword held at the ready.

A man poked his head in. An iron mask shaped like a snake concealed his face. Lilly bit her lip hard. She recognized that mask. It bore the emblem of the Brotherhood of the Slums, a cult of bandits that had appeared when the empire had taken an economic downturn. The cult member sauntered over to Lilly's desk and began to rifle through its drawers, scanning each piece of paper quickly before tossing it aside. Summoning all her courage, Lilly moved through the darkness to stand behind the man. Quietly, she drew her sword. "Find anything?" she asked in a low voice.

The bandit whirled around with a yelp and moved to pull a dagger from his belt. Lilly slashed her sword across his neck, her expression cold and hard, in spite of her pounding heart. The man gasped as he fell, clutching at the cut in his throat. He did not get up again. Lilly wiped her blade gently against the dying man's grime-coated shirt, cleaning the blood away as best she could. Something told her she would need that sword again tonight.

As she raced down the corridor to sound the alarm, Lilly collided with someone in the hallway. She hit the ground, bruising her elbow badly.

She gritted her teeth and tried to ignore the injury. Luckily for her, nobody in the Celerius family felt pain for long. The figure she'd crashed into towered over her, leering from within his snake mask, and Lilly jabbed her sword upward, aiming for his throat. He dodged her blow and knocked the sword out of her hand. Lilly scrambled to retrieve it, but the bandit planted his foot on her wrist until he heard a tell-tale crack. The bones in her wrist began to repair themselves immediately, but Lilly screamed anyway.

"Come now," her attacker said soothingly, kicking her sword farther away from her groping hand. "Who are you? What are you doing out of bed so late?"

Lilly kept screaming. *Someone wake up!* she prayed. *Someone come help me!*

"Tell me who you are and I might let you live," the bandit offered.

"I'm a servant!" Lilly shouted.

"A servant with a sword?" The man cocked his head and gave her a small smile. "I think we both know that's not true."

"I took it from my master's room!" she yelled. Nobody could hear her. Nobody was coming.

The attacker leaned down and pressed his dagger to her neck. "I believe you," he told her, "but I can't let you raise the alarm." He pressed the dagger in hard and slit her throat. Lilly felt blood streaming down her neck and gasped for enough breath to let out a final scream, but all that came out was a weak moan. She closed her eyes. The murderer smiled, sheathed his bloody dagger, and walked away from the corpse.

As he neared the end of the hallway, he heard fast footfalls behind him. He whirled around just in time to see the girl he'd murdered inches behind him and wielding her sword. The cut in her throat had faded into a thin scar. "No," he said, eyes wide. "You're not a servant—you're—"

Lilly cut him down with one expert flick of her wrist. "I'm a Celerius," she told him as he died on the floor.

Lilly tore down the hallway and up the stairs into the guard tower. She heaved on the ropes to sound the bells. The bells rang so loudly she was sure everyone in Altryon could hear them. Someone would come now. She was safe. It was over.

One minute passed, then two. Nobody came. She pulled the bell ropes again. The house stayed quiet. Lilly's heart began to thud. She looked to the window of the guard tower and let out a gasp. The eastern tower of her family's estate was in flames. That's why no one was coming to help her. Down in the courtyard, two figures in iron helmets were sprinting for the exit. Jaw clenched, Lilly tightened her grip on her sword and flew down the stairs. She made it outside just before the bandits. "Stop!" she commanded, sword outstretched, barring the door.

The two men turned to each other, grinning. "What a brave little girl you are," one of them said, his voice raspy. "Coming after us in the middle of the night. You should be in bed," he snarled.

Lilly glared at them icily. "Find what you were looking for?" she asked angrily.

One of the men held up a few rolls of parchment and sneered gleefully. "We did, and now it's time for us to go. Step aside and we will let you live."

Lilly didn't budge. "Do you two know what lies beyond Altryon?" she asked stonily.

"Nobody's ever been outside these gates," the taller one scoffed. "Move aside, girl."

"My brother has been outside!" Lilly shouted. "He goes outside every day to fight the savages and protect everyone within the city—even you two. And this is how you repay him? You rob his family? You burn his house?" She was breathing hard. The bandits looked nervous.

"Just move aside," the one holding the parchment said angrily. "Don't make me hurt you."

Lilly scoffed. "You couldn't hurt me if you tried," she spat. "Know this about my brother, the one who protects you. Before he became the leader of the military, he taught me how to fight." She flipped the sword expertly. "My name is Lilly Celerius; you will yield."

Without warning, the shorter man charged at her. She leaped aside and flicked her sword with lightning swiftness as he ran past. He landed on the ground with a cry. "Ready to join your friend?" Lilly asked the remaining intruder, cleaning her sword on his comrade's shirt.

The bandit reached for his pistol and fired a shot straight into her shoulder. She didn't even flinch. The wound bled for only a few seconds before the skin laced back together. The only evidence that the shot ever occurred was the smoking gun in the bandit's hand. He dropped his pistol and turned to run. He didn't make it far. Lilly's cold steel sliced into his back after only two steps. She could thank her Celerius speed for that. He fell to his knees and dropped the documents into the mud. Lilly walked around him and positioned her sword under his neck so she could look into his frightened eyes. She leaned in close. "Who sent you here? Why did you come?" she growled.

The bandit spat in her face. His saliva was mixed with blood. He gurgled, "I'll tell you nothing."

Lilly raised her sword in a high arc and brought it down hard on the man's neck. His head rolled into the mud after the parchment. Kneeling, Lilly wiped her sword clean and then began to gather the documents. It only took her a moment to realize what she was staring at: the architectural plans of the Celerius house, documents about banking and finances, figures she couldn't comprehend. The bandits had been after everything that made the Celerius estate run smoothly.

She looked back at the house and saw the fire under control; people had finally awakened, apparently. She pulled the snake-like helmet off the bandit and went inside, lost in thought. It was time to find her father.

"Lilly," Sir Celerius said, looking down at the papers spread across his desk, "I know you're worried, but this isn't anything to be concerned about."

"No?" Lilly sat in the high-backed chair in front of her father's desk and twisted her hands together. "I think it might be."

Sir Celerius shook his head. "We should just count ourselves lucky that the thieves didn't get away with any of our valuables. Or our lives," he added, smiling at his only daughter.

Lilly licked her lips. "That's what I don't understand," she said. "Why didn't they try to take our valuables?"

"I'm more concerned with this rumor about your brother." Sir Celerius sighed and lowered his head into his hands. "Tell me again what you heard?"

Lilly swallowed. It wasn't the first time she'd relayed the story, but that didn't make it any less painful. "They're going to execute Anthony. They want someone else in power, someone who isn't from our family, so they're going to kill him in order to send a message: the families aren't as powerful as the empire. And if he tries to resist, they'll come here and kill us instead."

Sir Celerius's eyes were blazing. He shouted, "They won't get away with this. I will make sure of it. It isn't right. It isn't honorable. How sure are you that this is legitimate?"

Lilly paused. "We've had scares like this before, what with the Vapros and their rumors. It could be a trick to get Anthony not to trust his men, or to distract us, or Anthony could be overly paranoid… but I'm not sure."

Sir Celerius nodded angrily. "Either way, I'll have some spies in the military get closer to this. I'm willing to go to war with the emperor over it."

Lilly focused very hard on the documents on her father's desk. "I'm scared, Dad," she said quietly, even though Celerius never admitted they were scared. "I'm really, really scared."

"It'll be all right, Lilly." Sir Celerius stood and walked around the desk to embrace his daughter. "It'll be all right."

VICTORY LIES WITHIN
THE ASHES

Chapter Fifteen
Imperial Palace
Neil

The following morning Neil paced the floor outside the emperor's throne room, wishing desperately that he were somewhere else. Last night had been a whirlwind of confusion. A few minutes after he and Rhys made it home, Victoria burst into Sir Vapros's office in tears. Apparently there had been a scrape with Darius Taurlum at the Opera House, and Jennifer was in a hospital with minor stab wounds. Sir Vapros had pressed her for details, and Victoria let it slip that she'd been with her lover, and the rest of the night had been yelling and tantrums. When Sir Vapros calmed down enough to focus on the matter of the Imperial soldiers, he sent Rhys to spy in the markets and Neil to schedule an audience with the emperor himself. And so, Neil found himself here, pacing the halls of the palace.

He pivoted on his heels and faced the giant throne room doors. They nearly reached the ceiling and were made of what appeared to be ivory with gold embellishments. Neil remembered that this was the same

91

palace where his ancestors had originally ruled, and if legend were to be believed, it was also where they were gifted with their powers. Neil focused on the empty space in the room and tried to picture a glowing deity floating in the air. He could almost see the Man with the Golden Light. Shining. Radiant.

The door to the throne room opened loudly and Neil's heart leapt to his throat. The emperor was unsettlingly cold, and he had a cruel sense of humor. Neil would give anything to be in the markets with Rhys. "Sir," he said, bowing hastily, but as he looked up, he realized with relief that he was looking at the empress and her personal guards. "Your highness," he amended, bowing again.

"Neil," she said, with a careful smile, hurrying toward him. The empress may have been a noble, but she was still a woman. Her hair bounced around her face in loose curls as she curtsied and welcomed him. Suddenly, she halted as if she remembered not to get too close to him. She took a step back. "How are you? How is your father?"

He smiled hesitantly, noticing her reservation. "We are well, thank you."

"I assume you are here to see my husband?"

"I am. We have matters to discuss regarding the city."

The empress looked at him, a newfound interest sparkling in her eyes. "The city? How ... interesting," she commented. She seemed to be choosing her words very carefully.

"It's just a passing rumor," he said trying to keep his voice free of suspicion. "Nothing too monumental."

She gave him a smile that didn't quite reach her eyes. "It's always something monumental with your family." She invited him inside the throne room. "Remember, Neil," she said thoughtfully, running her hand over her husband's golden throne, "you can never be at peace if a few sparks set your world on fire."

Neil nodded in agreement, but he had a feeling this was more than just a "few sparks." In addition, she was acting strange. Never before had a rumor concerned him like this. "If it were up to me," he said with a smile, "I'd be in the markets."

The empress looked up at him. "Chatting with the ladies?" she asked knowingly.

"Is there anything else to do?"

She threw back her head and laughed. "Not for a boy your age, I suppose." She turned and began to walk toward the door. She stopped and looked back at Neil for an uncomfortably long time, a strange expression on her face, before finally hurrying away. "I'll tell the emperor you've arrived," she said, pulling the door shut behind her.

Neil was sorely tempted to try sitting in the great golden chair before him. The empress would probably have let him do it if he'd asked, but she'd seemed so distant today that he hadn't bothered. Normally she was always jovial and excited, but today something clearly weighed on her mind.

The door opened again, and Neil whirled to bow. "Been waiting long?" asked the slow voice of the emperor. He strode toward his throne, followed by a trembling servant.

"No, your highness," Neil said. "I'm here to discuss some concerns."

The emperor reached his throne and sat without making a sound. The servant sat beside him in a small wooden chair. Neil glanced over a few times, but the servant wouldn't meet his eyes. His arms and face were covered in large purple bruises and he peered at the floor from behind his dark, matted hair. Neil felt a surge of sympathy for the poor man. It was a well-known fact that the emperor beat his servants.

The emperor leaned forward slightly and examined Neil. Neil tried not to stare back, but he couldn't help but scan the emperor's face a few times. It had no wrinkles, no discolorations, and no marks of any kind. It was as if he had been fashioned out of the purest marble. That face was both fascinating and terrifying.

"I wonder," the emperor said, running a long finger down the arm of his throne, "what it is about me that repulses you so?"

The question caught Neil off guard. "Excuse me?"

The emperor laughed once. "Look at you, Neil Vapros. You've been gawking at me since I walked in. I disgust you." He tapped his chin with a slender forefinger. "Is it my face?" he asked, eyes boring into Neil's. "Do I look ugly to you?"

"No, sir. I'm here about—"

"Is it my voice?" the emperor interrupted. "Do I sound like some sort of monster? You're looking at me as if I jumped out of one of your nightmares."

"I don't think you're a nightmare," Neil said uneasily.

"Come, now," the emperor chided. "You're afraid of me, I can see it in your face. You want nothing more than to run from my palace and never look back. Isn't that right?"

"No, sir," Neil said, but it was only partly true.

The emperor sighed and laced his fingers together. "You're lying to me, Neil Vapros. But I forgive you. I understand. There are certain times when it is wiser to lie."

"Yes, sir," Neil said. "Um, about the city—"

"For instance, if you were to tell me I looked ugly to you, or that I reminded you of a nightmare, I might be offended. I might become . . . angry." He let his gaze drift to the servant at his side. "I can be unpredictable when I'm angry. Can't I, Saewulf?"

The servant shuddered and nodded.

The emperor continued, "It's because I'm a man with power. And when a man with power becomes angry, you never know what he might do. He might throw you in a dungeon. He might have you exiled. He might use his power to destroy you—all because you made a mistake."

The servant inched away from the emperor's throne.

"But I'm a patient man, Neil Vapros," the emperor droned on. "I won't get angry because of one mistake. I won't even get angry about two mistakes. But when the mistakes begin to pile up, I'm afraid I lose control of myself." He looked pointedly at Saewulf, who was shuddering visibly. "So please, for everyone's sake, try not to make mistakes, Neil Vapros. Now, let's get down to business. Why are you here?"

Neil glanced at the servant once more before answering. "I came here to talk to you about some concerns I have about the city."

The emperor heaved a sigh and leaned back into his throne. "The city," he said uninterestedly. "The city your ancestors were sworn to protect until they threw it all away."

Neil forced himself to remain quiet. The emperor raised his eyebrows, silently egging him on. "They couldn't handle that kind of power, I suppose. Not strong enough. Not worthy. It's not their fault. Some men weren't born to be great."

Neil clenched his jaw. "I have some concerns, sir," he repeated.

The emperor grinned. This was his game. Pushing Neil, testing him, seeing if he could get him to sweat. "It was this very room, if legend is to be believed."

"Yes, your highness."

"Savages broke through those very doors and stormed this hall, and then according to your little 'myth,' a deity came down and made you 'godlike' in your own way."

"I know the story, sir."

The emperor's face suddenly twisted into a violent sneer. "I'm sure you know it very well, Vapros," he hissed. "I'm sure you tell yourself that story every single night. I know it would make me feel less guilty if I believed there was some god justifying my actions. For how can you feel bad about stomping on the rest of us when it's 'his will.'"

Neil didn't quite know what to say. The emperor grinned when he noticed Neil's attempt to form a sentence. "Yes, sir. But I'm not here for that. I'm here because of our concerns about the city."

The emperor gave in and queried, "What sort of concerns?"

"I've been hearing strange rumors about the Captain of the Guard," Neil began, but the emperor cut him off.

"The Captain of the Guard," he said, "the one who died of a broken skull thanks to a *family member?*"

"Yes," Neil interjected. "Because of a *Taurlum* family member."

"But the Taurlum was only there because he was chasing a *Vapros*, isn't that right?" the emperor asked, raising one eyebrow.

Neil swallowed hard. "I'm not the one who threw your soldier into a wall."

"I didn't say you were."

"There are rumors," Neil pressed on, "that you are planning to retaliate for what happened. People are saying you're going to target the family members. I just wanted to know, sir, if there's any truth to those rumors."

The emperor blinked slowly.

"I just—I don't think my family deserves to be punished for something a Taurlum—"

"Have you ever heard of the legacy phase, Neil Vapros?" the emperor asked.

"I, um, yes." Neil was trying hard to hide his frustration. "When a family's bloodline is threatened, the head of the family sort of . . . panics, I guess. He feels a responsibility to keep his family line from dying out. So he makes it a priority to produce more offspring, to pass on our powers to as many children as possible."

"And how many offspring inherit the powers, Neil?"

"All of them," Neil explained. "Our powers are always passed on. That's why we all still have powers."

The emperor smiled. Neil didn't like it. "So it is perfectly normal in your family to have one parent with powers," he said slowly, "and one parent without. That's what happened to you, in fact, is it not?"

Neil nodded. "That's how it is for everyone in my family."

"Who is more powerful, your mother or your father?"

"My mother is dead, so my father."

"Ah, that's right. Such a pity." The emperor looked off into the distance as if picturing something from the past. "I remember your mother: gorgeous woman. Your parents were treated like royalty. The people adored your mother. There was always a lot of nonsense about her clothes, what party they were attending. People actually referred to them as 'Altryon's first couple.'" He nearly spat the words. "The empress was quite upset when she heard that one. Really, people made such a fuss."

Neil swallowed. His father rarely talked about his mother. Neil hung on every word, not knowing if he wanted him to stop or continue. The emperor went on. "Your father adored her. He must have been completely devastated when she died." His eyes returned to Neil.

Neil felt his cheeks burn. He felt goose bumps up his arms, but didn't understand the conflicting emotions: outrage at the emperor's underlying scorn, pity for his father, a longing for the mother he never knew. Before he could sort through it all, the emperor interrupted his thoughts. "Anyway, back to the original question. Before your mother died then, who was more respected, more important in your family, your mother or your father?"

"I don't know. My father, I suppose."

"Why?"

This conversation didn't make sense. "He's a direct descendant of the Vapros line," Neil said finally.

"There it is." The emperor stood while declaring, "A direct descendant.

97

You and your family members, you think you're all so much better than the rest of us. We ordinary people, we're *nothing* to you. We are *ugly* to you." He ran a hand across his marble chin and continued. "You throw us into walls, break our bones, bend our laws, because once upon a time there was a leader who had powers and you are his direct descendant." The emperor wasn't shouting, but Neil still felt deafened by the words.

"Your majesty, I don't—"

"A Taurlum killed my father twenty years ago," the emperor said, trapping Neil in his gray glare. "He didn't agree with some of his new laws so he *murdered* him. This defiance of authority is not new to our city, and it will not be tolerated much longer. That I can assure you."

Neil shifted his weight from foot to foot for a tense moment of silence. "My family would never intentionally defy you, your highness."

"Of course not," the emperor replied, waving a hand dismissively. "It was the Taurlum, as you said before." He looked into Neil's eyes again. "You have nothing to worry about. Frankly, I'm surprised you bothered to come speak to me at all. It was so kind of you to converse with an ordinary person like me."

Neil opened his mouth to protest, but at the last second caught sight of the beaten servant, shaking his head very, very slightly. "It was a pleasure to meet with you, sir," he said as politely as he could. "I'm sorry for taking so much of your time."

"An apology," the emperor exclaimed as Neil walked away. "Did you hear that, Saewulf? How polite it is for him to apologize. You could learn a thing or two from Neil Vapros."

As Neil left the palace, he turned toward home and began to run. He had to see his father. Despite what the emperor had said about having nothing to worry about, Neil wasn't convinced in the slightest.

Upon returning home, Neil found his family convened in the Vapros war room. He took an empty chair next to Rhys and leaned over to ask what he'd missed, but stopped when Sir Vapros began to speak. "Now that we're all here," he said, looking pointedly at Neil, "we can begin."

Neil wanted to shout at him that he was only late because he'd been visiting with the emperor, something Sir Vapros had ordered him to do. While he was at it, he wanted to ask why he always had to do the worthless jobs and, more importantly, why he had to learn about his mother from the emperor?

He still had an uneasy feeling about that whole conversation, but kept his mouth shut. Throughout Neil's life, it was as if his father had always been wary of him. Uneasy around him, as if he wanted to be close, but there were barriers. Neil had always wanted to ask why. However, he couldn't do that. And he already knew why, anyway. He'd been born.

Sir Vapros nodded at Neil and he gave a quick summary of his conversation with the emperor, leaving out any mention of his mother.

Sir Vapros made eye contact with each of his children while noting, "Something is very wrong in our city. We have seen worrisome behavior among the Imperial Guards. Rhys had a troubling encounter with an arms dealer."

Neil scowled. His father hadn't mentioned his contribution, or Bianca's. Sir Vapros began to review the recent suspicious activity. "Today, two business partners have chosen to end their affiliations with our family. Meanwhile, Darius Taurlum has been arrested for attacking our Opera House, which means the emperor isn't turning a blind eye to our actions anymore. And last night, the Celerius house had a break-in and an attempted robbery. The culprits were members of the Brotherhood of the Slums." An uncomfortable murmur went up. "They tried to steal worthless documents," Sir Vapros continued a little more loudly, " and why they chose papers when they could have gone after jewels or money, we can't be sure."

"How is all of this related?" asked someone from the other side of the table.

"This is not just about our family," Sir Vapros said. "It concerns the three houses. For the first time in three hundred years, we may have a common enemy."

The room fell silent. Finally, Rhys spoke up. "The Celerius are moving a carriage today. I heard they are transporting something important away from their house, in case of another attack. I want to take Neil and Jennifer to raid it. See what they're so concerned about."

Neil was touched that his brother wanted him to accompany him on the mission, but Sir Vapros shook his head and said, "We can't risk any illegal activity, particularly when the Imperial Guards are arresting family members."

Neil looked over at Jennifer. She seemed slightly relieved. She'd come away from the fight with Darius with nothing more than a few bandages wrapped around her torso, but Neil suspected she wasn't eager to jump back into action quite yet.

"We'll ambush them in the orchards," Rhys insisted. "It's neutral territory. We can hide in the trees until we see them. A sneak attack. We'll be in and out before they can do anything about it." He was getting excited. Rhys loved to plan battle strategies. "I can put them to sleep. They won't even see us."

Sir Vapros relented. "Fine. Proceed." Out of the corner of his eye, Neil saw Jennifer open her mouth, but then she closed it and arranged her face in her trademark smirk. "The rest of you should be on the lookout for more information. Spread no more rumors. Just listen." He stood. "This meeting is adjourned." Rhys jumped up and ran to prepare for the coming carriage raid. "Remember, Rhys, heart or head." Rhys nodded and darted out the door. The rest of the family funneled out of the room behind him. Sir Vapros was reminding his son of the fact that the only way to kill a Celerius was to damage their heart or their brain. This was another detail that Neil had known from the time he could walk.

Neil slumped in his chair and groaned. "How did things get so messed up?"

"Things always get messed up," a cold voice said from the other side of the table.

Neil looked up to realize he was alone with Jennifer. She slumped in her chair too, moodily examining her knife. He wanted to get up and leave, but Jennifer stopped him with a hard look. "Sure you feel comfortable going along with us?" she asked lightly, staring at him with icy eyes. Neil felt like prey caught in a hunter's trap. "After all, your powers haven't evolved at all."

A surge of anger coursed through him. How could Jennifer be so different from her twin sister? Victoria was kind to Neil. She encouraged him and helped him. Jennifer goaded him, mocked him, all the while knowing she was safe because she could kill him with one twist of her wrist. "Are you sure you feel comfortable going along with us?" he mimicked. "After all, dear sister, you did have half a wall pulled from your back last night."

Her eyes widened, and then narrowed. She materialized in front of Neil, her knife an inch from his eye. "Care to repeat that?" she snarled.

Neil materialized to his feet behind her. "You seem a little sensitive," he said, resting his hand on his own knife.

Jennifer's eyes began to burn. "People don't talk to me like that."

He saw her hands begin to heat up and knew it was time to go. "Maybe they ought to," he said with a mocking bow, and then he was out the door and materializing down the hallway as fast as he could. He reached the strategy room in record time. Rhys hardly took notice of his presence. He was pouring over a map and muttering to himself.

"We're not going to lose anyone on this one, right?" Neil asked, collapsing into one of the padded chairs positioned around the table.

"No. I've taken nearly every variable into consideration," Rhys replied without looking up. "The Celerius family is small. The only possible threat is Lilly, the daughter, but she doesn't have any advanced powers, so I've ruled her out as a danger. Her brother is the General of the Imperial Army, but he doesn't have time to sleep, let alone escort a convoy. Other than that, they're all either off on military business or powerless servants."

"Lilly doesn't have advanced powers?" Neil asked.

"No, not yet."

That struck Neil. He knew the Celerius girl was a year older, seventeen. If Rhys thought there was hope for her powers to develop, maybe there was hope for his.

"I'm a little concerned about the youngest brother," Rhys said and pointed at his right temple. "He reads minds. He might be able to see us coming. And he's decent with a sword. They all are. If he shows up, Jennifer and I will double-team him with our powers. So he'll either end up asleep or Jen will burn him until he surrenders." He finally looked up. "I think we should be on our way soon. We've only got about two hours to prepare."

Neil noticed that Rhys was squinting at his documents on the desk. "You need spectacles," he said.

Rhys shook his head. "Father won't allow it. He thinks it'll show weakness if we wear things that show our flaws."

Neil ran his fingers through his hair. "That's one of the dumbest things I've ever heard. You're practically an inch away from the paper and you're still squinting."

"Neil, I can't," Rhys sighed. "Will you tell Jennifer to get ready?"

"She's ready to slit my throat. You'd better tell her." He started toward the door, and then stopped. "Rhys," he said, a smile starting on his face, "would it help if I brought along a friend?"

Rhys nodded. "As long as you can meet up with us quickly. The Celerius carriage is probably already on the move."

Chapter Sixteen
The Orchards
Jonathan

Jonathan grasped the door handle as the carriage jostled over another Taurlum pothole. He sighed and looked at Lilly. Jonathan always did his best to keep Lilly happy. It was his job, of course, as her personal servant, but he also cared for her deeply. Today, he was worried about her state of mind. Not only had she recommended a convoy full of the Celerius personal documents to be sent far away for safekeeping, but she had also insisted on accompanying it herself. He kept his eyes trained on her face, hoping to see an expression besides her usual troubled glare. He couldn't blame her for feeling shaken up. Last night she had killed four men. She had all the right in the world to be moody and quiet.

"It's cramped back here," Lilly complained, breaking the silence for the first time.

Happy for a bit of conversation, Jonathan energetically responded, "Yeah!" She raised an eyebrow at him, and he quickly amended, "I mean, yeah. It looks like we have about ten boxes."

"Yes," she said. "This is only the important stuff."

Jonathan wanted to respond, but his mistress didn't seem in the mood to talk. He leaned back in his seat and hummed quietly. The carriage rolled on.

❦

"When most boys invite me out, they don't take me to sit at the top of a tree and ask me to bring my knives," Bianca said conversationally.

Neil sharpened his knife and began testing it on a nearby branch. "What can I say? I'm not most boys."

She grinned and winked. "On that, we can agree."

Ambushes were usually boring, especially when remaining quiet was part of the criteria. Neil and Bianca had long ago given up on silence, and Neil was surprised at how quickly the last hour had passed. "You know you're going to stick out with your hair like that," he informed her.

She touched a strand of her ivory hair. "What do you mean 'with my hair like this?'"

"Well, we all have our black masks and hoods. We blend in. But you—"

"Have beautiful shining hair?" she supplied, tossing her head.

"Yes," he said rolling his eyes, "you have beautiful shining hair."

She smiled and checked her reflection in her knife and offered, "Do you think your siblings are having an equally interesting conversation in the other tree?"

"No," Neil said immediately, "absolutely not. Rhys is probably enforcing the silence over there. And Jennifer doesn't like talking to us, anyway."

"Your family is so close," she said, a light, teasing sarcasm in her voice.

Neil scoffed. "We're a military unit. Not a family."

Bianca looked like she felt sorry for him. Neil wanted to defend his family's arrangement, to proclaim that it was fine how it was, but he said nothing. His family was far from perfect. Rhys and Victoria felt like family, but the others were allies, nothing more. His father didn't like him; Jennifer detested him. The older cousins didn't give him the time of day, and the younger ones were fidgety nuisances. His aunts and uncles were unapproachably aloof. His mother was dead. He made sure not to complain too loudly when he was with Bianca. He knew that she hated talking about her parents, or lack of parents.

Once he'd met a girl in a bar who had told him the Taurlum family ate and drank together every night, and for the first time in his life he'd been jealous of the brutes. He knew the Celerius family treated family customs with honor (but with them, everything was about honor. They got dressed with honor, ate with honor, went to the bathroom with honor and tied their boots with honor). He hadn't realized that even the barbarians had closer family ties than the Vapros. The closest thing they had to an event like that was the tattoo ceremony, and even that was a celebration of their progress in the feud. However, there was never any real progress. They took steps forward and then steps back.

As if reading his thoughts, Bianca said, "Do you remember when we were kids?"

"Of course."

"There was that one thing you wouldn't tell me." It wasn't a question, but he knew she wanted an answer.

"How my mother died?"

She nodded. "You never talk about it." He looked at her silently, hoping she'd rescind the question, but she didn't. "You do owe me one ..." she whispered quietly.

He took a deep breath and shrugged. "Childbirth," he said finally, looking down.

Bianca blinked. "Oh. That's not what I thought it would be at all."

"No?"

"I was expecting some kind of ... I don't know, horrible assassination or attack or something. Not just . . . an accident."

"Well, now you know."

Bianca put her hand on his shoulder. "I'm sorry," she said sincerely, "but at least you had a few years with her."

Neil shook his head. "She died giving birth to me."

Bianca's brow furrowed. "But Rhys—"

"Rhys is my half-brother. When she died, my father had this big revelation. He realized we're all mortal, you know? And he was afraid that if he died, he wouldn't have enough heirs to keep our family going. He wanted more kids, more security for our family line." Neil fiddled with the knife absently. "Rhys's mother was a waitress from one of the taverns my father owns."

Bianca's mouth fell open.

"It's called the legacy phase," Neil explained bitterly. "He thought he had some kind of responsibility to pass on our powers to as many children as he could have. Because, I guess, he didn't have enough faith in the kids he already had."

"Oh."

"Anyway, that's why my father doesn't exactly cherish me," he continued dully. "Because I took his wife away." He looked at Bianca with a small shrug.

Bianca grabbed his arm and said, "But you have to know that your mother . . . it wasn't your fault."

Neil laughed cynically. "Next time you come for family dinner, we can tell my father that. I'm sure it'll convince him."

She looked like she wanted to hug him but held back. "Where is Rhys's mother now?"

"She's dead. She came to a Vapros event when Rhys was five. The Taurlum raided it and killed her. He was there. I think that's why he wants to be a doctor so badly, because he didn't know what to do. One small consolation, he developed the ability to put people to sleep shortly after watching his mother's murder."

Before Bianca could respond, they both looked toward the road at the sound of hoof beats. "Here they are," Bianca murmured, poking his arm. The lavishly decorated carriage rolled down the road toward them, completely unsuspecting. The blue and gold carriage was a sitting duck.

"Ready to go?" Neil asked, unsheathing his knife.

"Born ready."

Neil prepared to materialize down the tree, but before he could move, Jennifer was already upon the driver. Neil watched, mildly disappointed that he hadn't made it there first, as she burned him to death and hurled his body to the ground. Neil materialized to the ground and Bianca landed next to him. Jennifer was smirking. "A little slow today?" she asked. A stream of smoke ascended from the driver's body.

Rhys appeared next to them and charged for the door, materializing every few steps. Neil never grew tired of seeing his family members appear and reappear. It looked as if a person had dissolved himself into ash, and then an entirely new person not too far away reformed himself out of the same ashes. The ability was gloriously beautiful. Rhys performed it effortlessly, barely taking notice of his change in location. Materializing was just like taking another step to him.

Rhys then threw open the carriage door, brandishing his knife calmly. He was wise to prepare for an attack. Lilly Celerius herself lunged from the cabin, swinging her rapier viciously. With a little surprised gasp, Rhys materialized out of range of her weapon. She lunged after him. He jumped back, luring her away from the carriage. "Lilly!" Neil called, trying to help.

Breathing heavily, she turned to Neil, weapon at the ready. "I'd address you by your name," she snarled, "but you're too much of a coward to show your face."

Neil pulled down his mask. "This ends better for you if you give up now," he said. "Hand over what you're transporting."

Lilly shook her head, eyes blazing, and hissed, "Neil, right?" He nodded, surprised that she knew his face. "I've heard of your stupidity and arrogance. Seems I was not misinformed."

"I'm not arrogant," Neil argued, but he was grinning as he added, "I'm self-assured. I have every right to be. Look around you. I have three allies. You're alone. What's so stupid about that?" He kept inching backwards toward Jennifer and Bianca, hoping she'd follow. She didn't take the bait.

"What is stupid is not your numbers," she said, feet planted. "It's the fact that you attacked our carriage with no idea of what was inside. Is it worth risking lives to you, Vapros?"

Rhys cut in. "You seemed rather eager to move it. I calculated the risk. It's worth it, if the bounty is important enough."

Lilly shrugged, still looking at Neil. "I think you will return home disappointed."

Bianca moved forward. "Let's see what you're moving then, shall we?"

Quick as a whip, Lilly swung her arm around so her sword was pointed at Bianca. "Take another step and lose your head," she spat through her teeth. "I make that promise to you, street girl."

Neil was slightly surprised by the off-handed insult, but Bianca took it in stride. She palmed her knife and prepared to throw it. "Speak to me like that again and lose your eye," she said calmly. "I make that promise to you, rich girl."

A tense silence stretched over the entire forest as the two girls stared each other down. Jennifer smirked and folded her arms, but Neil was nervous. Suddenly, a small figure jumped down from the carriage and darted to Lilly's side. Neil couldn't help but chuckle as the tiny man waved around a tiny sword. "Jonathan," Lilly declared. "Are you prepared to fight for the honor of the Celerius family?"

Jonathan gulped. "Yes."

Bianca whipped her knife at Lilly; she sliced it out of the air with a flash of steel. Bianca looked surprised. "All right," she muttered, "you're fast. I'll give you that."

Bianca hurled a few more knives and was greeted with the same result. Neil tried to take Lilly by surprise, but she seemed to sense exactly where he planned to rematerialize and swiped at him, nearly slicing his throat. He staggered backwards, gasping, heart pounding from the close call. "Amateur," Jennifer said to him with a smile. She jumped into the fray and lunged at Jonathan, her glowing hands outstretched. The diminutive servant closed his eyes and swatted blindly with his blade. She ducked around his weapon and struck him across the face with the back end of her knife. He yelped and hit the ground. Lilly turned at his cry and Rhys, seizing the opportunity, materialized behind her, grabbed the back of her neck and closed his eyes. Lilly's eyes rolled back into her head and she collapsed into Rhys's arms.

"See?" he said, lowering her to the ground gently. "Not even a little risky."

Neil walked over to the fallen servant, who had his hands clamped over his cheek. He was groaning and rolling from side to side. "You'll pay!" he cried as he saw Neil coming. He struggled to sit up, but ultimately failed and fell onto his back. Neil planted his foot on the servant's chest. "Is Lilly …." Jonathan asked fearfully.

"She's alive," Neil assured him, "but she's napping. However, you and I need to have a little chat."

From the back of the carriage, Neil could hear Rhys's voice: "Common documents? Architectural plans? Bills? Why was there so much fuss over this?"

Neil repeated the question to Jonathan, "Why so much fuss over these documents, servant? You were moving them quickly. Why are they important?" Jonathan tried to squirm away. Neil pushed down harder with his foot and called out, "Jennifer, come here. He doesn't want to talk." Jennifer would never take orders from her younger brother, Neil was well aware, but Jonathan didn't know that.

Jonathan let out a squeak. "Keep her over there," he cried. "I'll tell you! I'll tell you!"

"Good choice." Neil smiled a little. "I don't like to deal with her either," he said as if it were a big secret. The humor escaped Jonathan.

"Last night we were attacked," Jonathan said. "By the Brotherhood of the Slums. They were after our documents. Lilly managed to kill them but we found this on one of them."

He pulled a small paper from his coat pocket and tried to hand it to Neil. Neil looked at him skeptically for a moment, then met him halfway to retrieve the parchment. As he began to read it, his expression shifted from curiosity to confusion to fear. "Rhys!"

Rhys materialized next to them. "What is it?"

Neil handed the paper to him. "We have a problem."

Rhys squinted and brought the paper close to his face. Neil sighed. The kid needed spectacles. Rhys gasped. "Yes, we have a problem."

Chapter Seventeen
Imperial Military Outpost
Carlin

"We have a problem," Carlin said, slamming his fist against the table. The soldiers sitting closest to him jumped as the noise echoed through the war room of the Imperial Military Outpost. "The situation outside the wall has become dire, and …." he trailed off. Nobody was listening. He coughed loudly to regain their attention, but everyone at the table was either staring at the general or at the floor. "We could be outnumbered in the West! One thousand men are too many to ignore!" Carlin said loudly. One of the soldiers glared at him; the rest remained motionless. A palpable tension hovered over the table like a thick fog, and Carlin eventually stopped trying to break through it and resorted to muttering under his breath every few seconds.

Finally, General Anthony Celerius cleared his throat. "Dismissed," he said shortly.

Nobody moved. One of the smaller men raised his hand slightly. "Sorry, sir?"

Anthony met the man's eyes and offered him a small, weary smile. "You are all dismissed. This meeting is adjourned."

The men rose and filed from the room, sneaking glances over their shoulders at their general. Carlin stayed in his seat. "I said you are dismissed, Carlin," Anthony said with all the conviction of a man who has given up hope.

"Forgive me, sir, but I think you and I have more business to discuss."

"Then discuss it."

"You and I have private business," Carlin amended, shooting a glare at the corner of the room where a single soldier remained.

Anthony met the eyes of the man in the corner and barked, "Virgil. I already dismissed you."

Virgil Servatus, third in command to Anthony and only one rank below Carlin, removed his golden helmet and shook out his shoulder-length brown hair. "I will not let this happen," he said.

Anthony looked at him for a long time with an expression Carlin couldn't quite read. "I don't know what you mean," he said finally.

"Don't lie!" Virgil cried, turning to Carlin in a rage. "Carlin, we've been friends. This is wrong. There are other ways!"

Carlin scoffed. "You don't know what you're talking about."

"Virgil," Anthony pleaded, "just go. It'll be okay. Trust me." He looked at the man with wide eyes.

Virgil dropped his helmet on the table and let the sound resonate through the room. "Are you really going to pretend this isn't happening?" he shouted, taking a step toward Carlin.

Anthony held up a hand for silence. "You know your orders," he said firmly, "and you know your place. Don't worry about me. This is not the end. I will say it one more time: you are dismissed."

Virgil gave Anthony a long look. "Forgive me," he whispered, scooping up his helmet and storming from the room.

Anthony watched him go. "I do," he whispered.

Carlin stood and drew his sword. "Well, General," he said with a smile, "that was a touching little scene. The temporary loyalty that these men have shown you is inspiring. It's almost tragic."

Anthony sipped his wine and traced a river on the war map with his fingertip. "If I let you do this … my family will be safe?"

Carlin nodded. "You have my word. The emperor is just looking for a shift in power."

"I can see into your soul, Carlin," he said tiredly. "And it is lost."

Carlin leaped forward and pointed his sword between Anthony's eyes. The general didn't flinch. "Don't give me that bullshit," he hissed, "I know you mighty Celerius think you're impressive with your advanced abilities, but all you can see is what's on the other side of a wall. You know nothing of my soul."

Anthony met the other man's eyes and addressed him quietly, "I don't need advanced abilities to know you're lost, Carlin. Your actions alone are enough to prove it."

Carlin narrowed his eyes. A moment later, the smug smile was back in place. "It's truly flattering that you're so concerned with my soul's well-being, General," he said casually as he lowered his sword to the level of Anthony's heart. "But you don't need to worry. I don't have a soul. Neither do you. They don't exist, you know." *Argue with me. Tell me I'm wrong. Go on. Give me a reason.*

Anthony bowed his head slowly as he whispered, "I pity you."

Carlin's smile twisted into a maniacal sneer of rage as he plunged the sword forward. The blade slid easily between the general's ribs and came out on the other side, piercing the chair. With a gasp, Anthony snapped his head up and instinctually groped desperately for his own sword. It was as if he suddenly realized that giving up was a mistake, as if there was something else he could do. Skewered against his chair, he couldn't quite reach the hilt. Carlin pulled his sword out and began to wipe it clean of Celerius blood. "Long live the Emperor," he said quietly, walking away with a calm little smile as Anthony slumped forward over the table, knocking over his glass and spilling wine across the war map.

Chapter Eighteen
The Orchards
Lilly

Lilly Celerius's first thought upon waking on the side of the road was that she had never experienced such a deep, peaceful sleep in her life, and she probably never would again. Her second thought was that the Vapros brats had undoubtedly stolen her precious cargo. She jumped to her feet. "Jonathan!" she cried, peering inside the carriage. To her relief, all of the boxes appeared to be inside. "Jonathan?"

A loud cough came from the other side of the carriage. "I'm here," he said, flat on his back and desperately trying to dust off his oversized military jacket.

"What was the point of all this?" Lilly wondered aloud. "They didn't even take anything. And why would they bring that . . . that poor girl with them?"

Jonathan tried and failed to stand up, but managed to ask, "Do you know her?"

"She sneaks into parties a lot. I didn't know she could throw a knife."

Jonathan finally made it to his feet. "Just because she's poor doesn't mean she's useless," he said quietly. "I'm from the slums, too."

"You don't live in the slums," Lilly said with an eye roll. "You live in my guest house." She rifled through the papers. "I think everything is here."

"Not everything," Jonathan admitted. His face grew red. "I gave him the paper."

Lilly whirled around. "Who's him, Jonathan?"

Jonathan tried to fight his tears. "Neil Vapros."

Lilly pulled her rapier from the ground. "Well, now they know." She swung a few practice arcs through the air. "Stop crying, Jonathan. It's all right. It won't do them much good anyway. Unless we truly are at war."

Chapter Nineteen
The Markets
Michael

Michael Taurlum had no trouble weaving his way through the crowded marketplace; people saw him coming and dove out of the way. He swaggered down the street, dressed in a tight red and gold shirt that clung to his skin and showcased his muscles. He kept his eyes peeled for women to occupy his time.

A group of giggling girls caught his attention as they made their way into a shop. Grinning, he made his way across the street and fumbled with the doorknob for a moment before heaving his way into the store. His head swayed dangerously near the ceiling. "Hello, ladies," he said casually. The storekeeper winced as Michael nearly tore the door off its hinges.

The girls whispered to each other nervously. One finally said, "I'll do it," and separated herself from the group. "Hello, Taurlum," she said. "How are you today?"

He grinned at her. She was tiny, but everyone looked tiny to him. "I'm fine," he answered. "And better, now that I've had the pleasure of seeing such a beautiful woman."

The other girls giggled, but this one wasn't fazed. "I'm just surprised to see you here," she said, the beginning of a laugh on her lips. "Considering this is a woman's hat shop."

Michael froze. The other girls were laughing uproariously. "I know," he said, trying desperately to save face. "I just owe the owner some coin."

"Why?" the girl asked, biting back laughter. "Did you buy a hat from him earlier and forget to pay the bill?"

Michael slammed a few coins down on the counter. One of the girls let out a little scream, followed by an eruption from the others. "The hat was for my sister," he invented. Michael turned away from the girls and leaned toward the storekeeper. "Play along," he hissed, and the keeper nodded. "Anything these ladies want," Michael said more loudly, "is on me."

The girls squealed and began running up and down the aisles of hats. One of the girls didn't join them. "That was generous of you," she said, offering him a smile. She wasn't the most beautiful of the bunch, Michael noted, but her face wasn't difficult to look at.

"I'm a generous man," he replied, subtly raising his arm in a stretch that showed off his bicep and his bracelets at the same time.

The girl's eyes widened as she saw his jewelry. "You have a lot of bracelets," she said. "You must be very wealthy."

He grinned. "Oh, these?" he said haughtily. He pulled off a bracelet and threw it to her. She caught it. "I have thousands at home," he bragged. Then he looked at her thoughtfully and offered her a wink. "I can show you, if you'd like."

She slipped her wrist through the bracelet. It stood out radiantly against her shabby coat and worn shoes. "You want to take me home with you?" she asked.

Michael grinned and flexed again. "Why not?" he said lazily. "I can give

KYLE PRUE

you a tour. We can see the private bathhouse ... my bedroom ... you know, all the best parts of the Taurlum mansion."

She bit her lip and gazed up at him from beneath her eyelashes, all while asking, "Won't the other Taurlum mind?"

Michael scoffed. "I'm allowed to bring poor people inside," he said. "It's my house."

The girl looked hurt for a moment, but she covered it up quickly. "Of course," she said flirtatiously, touching the gold band on her wrist. "I bet no one in your family controls you, do they? You're too strong for that."

Michael liked this girl. "Come on," he said, turning toward the exit. "Tell your friends you're leaving. I really want you to see my room."

The girl touched her new bracelet again and waved to her friends before hurrying out of the shop and following in the Taurlum's wake toward the mansion.

Chapter Twenty
Imperial Prison
Darius

Darius tried to move for the ten-thousandth time, but before they'd thrown him in the dungeon the Imperial Guards had fitted him with a wooden collar that bore down on his pressure points. With every shift in position, he could felt it dig into his skin and leech his strength. He had gone over every single member of his family, wondering which one was most likely to break him out. His father would be far too busy. His mother, only a Taurlum by marriage, was too frail. His sister Cassandra might show up, if she felt like it, but Darius eventually came to accept that his best chance was, unfortunately, Michael—the Nose, his idiotic, womanizing brother.

Sweat began to drip down his face as he tried not to struggle. Each movement was painful. They'd anchored his hands to the floor, and he could easily have broken the shackles if they hadn't been designed to hit him at the pressure points in his wrists. He was immobilized, powerless, and for a Taurlum, that meant he was nothing.

He heard footsteps coming down the hall, and he hoped it was his dinner. Last night, the guards had served him some sort of pig slop, spoon-feeding him because he could not move his arms, and he'd held eye contact with the guard for the whole meal, a vengeful fury brewing in his expression. The guard seemed terrified. Darius loved it.

The footsteps reached the door. Darius gurgled through his collar, "I think the chains are getting loose, buddy. Hopefully, I don't break free while you're feeding me." The person behind the door didn't answer. "Hello? I'm getting hungry," he prompted.

A tiny key shot through the crack at the bottom of the door and landed close to his hands. Darius grabbed at it clumsily and maneuvered it into the lock on his handcuffs. They sprung free. "Michael?" Darius asked. "Cassie? Is that you?" No answer. He felt at his collar, searching for the keyhole. To his surprise and relief, the same key unlocked the cuff around his neck. "Lazy bastards," Darius muttered with satisfaction. He wrenched off the collar and let it clatter to the floor. "Look out, Imperial Guards," he said a little louder, lumbering to the cell door and tearing it off its hinges. His strength was back. The abrasions on his neck and wrists were fading already. "The beast has escaped!"

His triumphant smile disappeared as he realized the person waiting on the other side of the door was not one of his siblings. It wasn't even his father. His savior was dressed in leather armor and camouflage green, jet-black hair pulled back out of her face, and a mouth set in fierce determination. She wielded a long chain with a single spike fixed to the end, and she had an unyielding expression on her face. "Who are you?" Darius asked.

The girl blinked her dark, slanted eyes, but didn't answer. He repeated his question more forcefully this time. She gave him a small smile and then hurled her spike straight into the vulnerable part of his stomach.

He stumbled back, impressed at the skill of the throw, but also furious that the foreign girl was not here to free him. He pulled the spike out of his navel and gave it a strong pull; she lost her balance and stumbled toward him. He prepared to club her to death with his arm, but she anticipated the blow and abandoned her weapon to barrel roll underneath it and into the cell. Darius felt his stomach begin to bleed. "Listen, sweetheart," he said, raising his giant fists into fighting position, "you're thin as a stick. Give this up before I snap you like one."

She smiled. "Poor baby," she cooed with a thin accent as she unsheathed a spare knife. "Scared and bleeding, so he has to make idle threats."

Darius replied, "Idle threats? We'll see."

She darted forward and carved a long cut into his arm. It began to bleed. Darius couldn't help but feel a little nervous. She was obviously well-trained. He knew better than to underestimate her based on appearance; he had learned that lesson from Jennifer Vapros. "You broke me out of prison to kill me?"

She grabbed her spike on a chain from the ground and answered, "Couldn't open the door. It was too thick and I couldn't find that key. So I needed some help."

"You're welcome."

She hurled the spike at his neck, but he saw it coming and jumped out of range. She narrowed her peculiar eyes. "You're quick. I was not told that you would be quick."

"What can I say, I'm full of surprises." He swung his arm out, sending her flying into a wall. With a cry, she dropped her knife and chain. He grabbed her by the throat and lifted her into the air with his remaining strength. "I ask again," he said, loosening his grip enough so that she could speak. "Who are you?"

She glared at him. "Anastasia," she spat.

"Anastasia," Darius lowered her to the ground, but kept his grip on her neck. "You clearly don't work for the Imperial Army."

"No," she said carefully. "I'm not a soldier. I'm an assassin."

"Oh, really?" Darius said sarcastically. "Is that so? I hadn't noticed." He examined her attire. "Where are you from?"

Anastasia tried to scoff. The effect was ruined by the fear in her eyes. "You wouldn't believe me if I told you."

"You look like a savage. I'd guess you have come from the outside."

"When did this become a casual conversation?" she growled.

"Fine. Let's get less casual." He lifted her off her feet again. "Why did you come to kill me?"

She laughed. "Because I was paid."

"Who paid you?" It came out as a snarl. He was getting impatient.

"A good assassin never reveals her employer."

"A good assassin wouldn't let me catch her." Darius threw her against the wall again. She fell to the ground, harder this time, and when he picked her up he saw she'd been knocked unconscious. He thought about killing her, but he was running out of time to escape. He left her limp body on the ground and hurtled out of the dungeon. He was alive, but someone wanted him dead badly enough to hire an assassin from some unknown place.

A pair of guards rounded the corner. One of them held a bowl of the slop they'd been feeding him for dinner. He dropped the bowl, stunned, when he saw the prisoner. Darius grinned and cracked his knuckles. "Who's first?"

Chapter Twenty-One
Taurlum Mansion
Michael

Michael Taurlum's eyes flickered open. He recognized the ceiling of his bedroom and instantly realized something horrible: he was cuddling. There was some girl latched onto his arm, sleeping peacefully. Without thinking, he quickly brushed her off, then winced as his Taurlum strength sent her over the edge of his bed and onto the floor. She squealed as she fell. Michael tried to resist doing the same. "What the hell was that, Michael?" she groaned, stumbling to her feet and wiping the sleep from her tired eyes.

Michael hopped out of bed and tied his red and gold pajama bottoms tighter with his ringed fingers. "You tell me," he breathed, heart pounding. "Why were you in my bed?" He grabbed a glass from a side table and filled it with wine.

The girl shrugged and self-consciously adjusted her corset. "I fell asleep—so what?"

Michael drained the glass and poured himself another. "I prefer to sleep alone."

"Oh, really?" the girl remarked and moved to sit on the bed, but she backed off when he turned to glare at her. "Michael Taurlum, afraid to share his bed? I find that hard to believe, given your reputation."

"I'm not afraid," he insisted. "You're the one who should be afraid. It's dangerous to sleep near a Taurlum. If I rolled over, I could have crushed you."

She snorted. "Like you care about what happens to me," she muttered. "Do you even remember my name?"

He turned away from her and began to pour another drink. The girl sighed and put a hand on his shoulder carefully. "Something tells me that isn't the only reason you're upset," she said soothingly. "Was it something I did?"

"It has nothing to do with you."

"Some other girl then?" she tried. "You can tell me. I'm a good listener."

"Leave it alone," Michael warned. He pulled away from her hand and dropped back onto his bed, throwing his empty glass carelessly across the room. It shattered. The girl winced.

"If you leave now, you can make it home by sundown. I think. I don't know where you live."

She stood over him. "Come on, Michael. You can tell me. You're strong on the outside, but I can tell there's something making you weak on the inside." She ran a hand down his bare shoulder. "Tell me. I'll help make you big and strong again."

She was trying to appeal to his ego. He saw right through her game, and part of him wanted to toss her out into the street, but instead he sighed and rolled up on his side to look at her. "The last woman who shared my bed was my fiancée," he said bluntly. The girl's eyes widened, and Michael quickly added, "She's gone now."

The girl didn't seem to understand and asked, "Where did she go?"

He laughed humorlessly. "Turns out, she was also sharing a bed with another man."

"Oh." The girl nodded. Her eyes had strayed from Michael to the extravagant tapestries on the wall behind him. "So you kicked her out." This room was so much nicer than the little shack she called home.

"Not exactly," Michael replied, leaning back into the pillows and closing his eyes. "The other man was a Vapros."

The girl's eyes snapped back to the Taurlum. "Yeah," she said slowly, "those Vapros, so … immoral." They were nearing dangerous territory. The feud was a sensitive topic among the families. One wrong word could set him off like a bomb. "Is she with him now?"

Michael chuckled darkly, opened his eyes and answered, "You could say that."

The girl looked uncomfortable. "Maybe we should talk about something else?" she suggested, but Michael wasn't paying attention to her anymore.

Michael reminisced, "I confronted her, and she lied to my face. That was the first time I ever created an earthquake. It wasn't intentional. And it wasn't a very impressive one, compared to what I can do now. But it was enough." He heaved himself out of bed. The girl stood, too, and backed away a little. "I'm not even sorry," he said, "I was going to give up so much for her, and she couldn't even be faithful. Look around you. I was about to leave all of this for her. She deserved what she got."

"Of course she did," the girl soothed. "Of course she did …"

"I tracked down her lover and killed him, too," Michael continued. "It's my favorite death to date."

The girl was trembling. She attempted a smile. "You're a warrior," she whispered, more to herself than to him, as if she were trying to justify something.

Michael grinned and spoke with pointed sarcasm, "Thanks for bringing those memories to the surface. You've been very helpful." She attempted to sit back down on the bed, but he shook his head and pointed to the door. "Now get out."

"Are you sure, Michael?" she asked. "I can help you. If you just opened up to me a little more, I could—"

"Get *out!*" His volume shook the room.

She let out a little scream and ran, pausing only long enough to snatch her dress off the floor. Michael sighed and settled back into his giant bed. At last, he was alone—just the way he liked it.

Chapter Twenty-Two
Celerius Estate
Lilly

illy paced around the Celerius training room, sizing up her adversary, and trying to shake the carriage fiasco from her mind. She lunged outwardly with her wooden sword and her brother blocked it easily. Thomas back-peddled a few paces and smiled. "You know you'll never be able to land a hit, Lilly." He grinned, brown eyes twinkling. "I know what you're going to do before you do it."

She sighed and swung her sword again, and once more he blocked it expertly. "I'll hit you eventually," she said with another swing.

He parried and hit her hand. She winced and felt a cracked bone reset. "Sorry," he muttered.

She leapt forward and swung as quickly as she could, but he didn't try and block this time. The wooden sword collided with the side of his head, but he didn't even seem to register the blow. His eyes were closed in quiet concentration. "Thomas," Lilly said as she moved forward. "Are you trying to read my mind?"

He shook his head. "People are screaming inside their heads. They're crying out in pain," he whispered.

"Knock it off," she sighed. It wasn't unlike her brother to pull stupid pranks with his powers.

He opened his eyes and tears leaked out. "Anthony," he whispered.

A blood-curdling scream pierced the stillness. Lilly stared at Thomas for a moment and then she dropped her sword. She dashed through the hallways and made it to the front door faster than she had ever run anywhere. Her father stood at the door holding a small wooden box. Her mother was on the ground sobbing. There was an Imperial messenger on the ground bleeding from his throat. "What …." She couldn't form any other words.

Her father turned to face her and she noticed his face was as red as it had ever been. She took a step forward and opened the box hesitantly. It was filled with ashes. She looked up at her father with disbelieving eyes, "Is it …."

He shook his head and tried to choke out a few words. After a few seconds, he was able to manage, "It's Anthony."

Chapter Twenty-Three
Vapros Bunker
Neil

"Who the hell is Carlin Filus?" Sir Vapros shouted. They were all crammed in his office, describing the events that transpired with Lilly Celerius and the carriage. Sir Vapros stood behind his massive desk drumming his fingers, his piercing green eyes staring pointedly at his children. His sleeves were rolled up, and it was possible to see more of his tattoos. Neil couldn't help but think about how many lives they represented. There was one in the shape of a broken sword on his forearm and Neil was willing to bet it had come from a Celerius.

Neil shifted uncomfortably in his seat and finally said, "He's the second in command in the Imperial Army. Or, he was, until the general was murdered. Now he's number one." The Vapros network of informants worked swiftly and efficiently.

"He has power," Jennifer said. "He can get around certain laws."

Sir Vapros sighed and sat down in his black leather chair, rubbing his hand thoughtfully over his black and grey stubbled chin. "So what does this mean?"

Neil seized his opportunity. "The Celerius servant gave me this," he said, pulling the crumpled piece of paper from his pocket and passing it across the table. "It's a document Carlin wrote up. It authorizes all crimes committed by the Brotherhood of the Slums."

"Only crimes against the families," Rhys corrected.

"So their attack on the Celerius house that night was legal," Neil finished hurriedly.

Sir Vapros was quiet. He held the document in both hands and scanned the lines several times. "Crimes against the families," he repeated slowly. "*All* the families?"

Rhys nodded. Sir Vapros let out a snarl of fury and turned his hands to smoke, consuming the paper and turning it to ash.

"We're going to be next," Jennifer drawled, looking at her fingernails. "The Celerius were robbed and there's a Taurlum in the dungeons. We're the only ones who haven't been touched yet."

"We have been touched," Sir Vapros said. "Our records keeper was murdered. They found his body this morning."

"Records," Neil said thoughtfully. "That was what was in the Celerius carriage: boxes of their records. That's what the Brotherhood tried to take."

Sir Vapros looked at Neil for the first time. He really looked at him and seemed to truly appreciate his son's contribution to the conversation. "It's a legitimate connection," he said. "What would this Carlin want with family records?"

Rhys frowned slightly and joined in. "I have a theory. What if Carlin wants to study us? Track our habits, find out about our businesses and discover how we go about our daily lives. But he hasn't actually attacked us. What if he isn't the main threat? What if he's a spy for someone more important?" He turned to Neil. "You said the emperor was acting strangely."

Jennifer interrupted. "There's no motive," she said flatly. "The emperor is already the most powerful man in Altryon. What can he gain by starting a war with us?"

Rhys shrugged. "Maybe he's afraid we'll try to take over again, like the old days."

Sir Vapros turned to Neil. "You talked to him. Did anything seem out of the ordinary?"

Neil ran his hand through his hair. "I don't know, he was incredibly creepy," he admitted. "He acted cold, but that's not unusual for him. He played games and clearly had been beating that poor servant. He tried to make me uncomfortable." Suddenly, a memory tugged at his brain. "But his wife acted distant, too, and that's unusual for her. He did say he was going to retaliate against the Taurlum; it's not unreasonable to assume we could be next."

"Rhys," Sir Vapros said suddenly, "I want you to look into the Taurlum records. See if anything's happened to them."

Now that missions were being assigned, Jennifer, who was much more interested in the discussion, asked, "Why don't we have someone gather information on the Brotherhood? I can find out how Carlin got them in his pocket."

"He probably offered them food," Neil said. "Things are so bad in the slums now—"

"Neil," Sir Vapros snapped. "Enough." Neil sighed and closed his mouth. "I care about my family, not the poor. If the emperor decides to make an enemy out of the Vapros family, then we will strike him down and leave his throne in ashes. I hope he's not that stupid." Sir Vapros left the room. Jennifer followed.

Neil leaned over and whispered to Rhys, "Do you actually think we have a chance of defeating the emperor?"

Rhys thought for a moment, and then slowly shook his head. "Not alone."

Chapter Twenty-Four
Imperial Palace
Sir Celerius

Sir Celerius had always been one for following procedure. He tried his utmost to do everything as correctly and politely as possible, without breaking rules or endangering his honor. Reputation was, after all, the most important thing for a man to protect. Bodies died, but reputations lived forever.

Today, all formalities were abandoned. No one had ever barged in on the emperor before; Sir Celerius made himself the first.

"You bastard!" he screamed, charging into the throne room without even so much as a knock.

The emperor didn't even look up from his chessboard. "Check, Saewulf."

"You had my son murdered!" Sir Celerius shouted. The emperor raised a hand for silence, but his enraged visitor ignored it and continued ranting. "You invaded my home and put my daughter's life in danger. Are you trying to destroy my family? After we have been nothing but loyal to you for all these years? I heard the rumors, but I never thought you could be this ruthless."

The man called Saewulf moved his queen diagonally a few spaces. The emperor pondered a moment, hovering his hand over a few different pieces as he tried to decide on a move. "Have you met Saewulf?" he asked calmly.

Celerius knocked the chessboard across the room. "You killed my son!" he roared. "You had his ashes sent to my house in a box!"

Sighing, the emperor finally looked up at the furious man. "Saewulf is my humble servant," he explained. "He looks different, doesn't he? We've realized how special he is. We've gotten him all cleaned up, and I'm starting to look at him in a new light. I used to play chess with myself, you know."

Celerius, breathing hard, looked at Saewulf. His body was unmarked by the bruises that usually covered servants around here. He had orange hair that had been pulled back away from his face. His skin looked rough and tan as if from constant work in the sun. Celerius snarled, "I don't care about your servant." He drew his sword. "I'll kill you both. I'll kill you myself! You're unarmed and unguarded. It will be easy. It will be a pleasure."

The emperor gazed at him with an expression that almost looked like boredom. "Is this a genuine threat?"

Sir Celerius made a sound halfway between a laugh and a sob and lunged with his sword.

Suddenly, he was in the air, suspended as if from unnoticeable wires. He struggled to break free, but the most he could do was swing his sword harmlessly three feet from the emperor's head. "What's happening?" he screamed.

The emperor nodded toward Saewulf. The servant had his arms raised, palms facing Celerius, holding him immobile with some invisible force.

"What's happening?" the emperor echoed vaguely as Saewulf silently held Celerius in place. "What's happening indeed, my dear Celerius? I've been wondering exactly that. What's happening behind the closed doors of the families? Are they planning to overthrow me and climb back to the top? Are they plotting ways to kill my Captain of the Guard? Who will they hurt next with their ambition? Me?" He looked pointedly at the sword still dangling from his prisoner's hand. "That would be a shame."

Sir Celerius dropped his sword with a clatter. There were tears in his eyes.

"A shame, indeed," the emperor said. Saewulf's eyes had turned frighteningly black. "I'll take care of your family once you're gone," the emperor promised. "Don't you worry."

Saewulf punched straight through Sir Celerius's chest, destroying his heart so thoroughly that even his ability to heal was not quick enough to save him.

The emperor rose and walked over to the body, which Saewulf had let fall to the floor. "What a pity," he said softly, nudging the corpse with his toe. "Saewulf, gather the chess pieces."

His servant obeyed. "I was about to beat you, too," Saewulf complained in a raspy voice as he set up the pawns with bloodied hands.

The emperor smiled and gestured to Saewulf to make the first move. "We should try to get through this game before the siege," he said methodically. "There won't be much time afterwards."

The servant moved a pawn forward two spaces. "We'll have to finish quickly," he said. "It all begins tonight, after all."

Chapter Twenty-five
Vapros Bunker
Neil

Neil lay on his back in the bunk bed he shared with his brother, staring up at the mattress over his head. He'd been lying here for hours, unable to fall asleep. "You still awake?" he whispered to the darkness.

"Yeah." The mattress shifted, and Rhys's head appeared over the side of the top bunk. "Do you really think the emperor is coming after us?"

Neil sighed. "I hope not."

"But do you think it's likely?" Rhys's eyes were wide with something close to fear. It was an expression Neil hadn't seen since he was five years old, when Rhys had still been afraid of the dark. Neil had always let him crawl into bed with him, acting like a tough older brother, but secretly a little scared himself.

"I think it's likely," Neil said, wishing he had a different answer.

"Do you think he'd kill us?"

Neil wanted so badly to say no, but chose, "I don't know. He never seemed all that evil before, but people wear masks." The man made of marble wasn't ruthless or tough the way the Taurlum were, but he had a cold, inhuman kind of mercilessness according to his enemies. If his plans were to destroy the families, he would not hesitate to murder everyone in his path. "If he attacks us, will you stay and fight?"

Rhys didn't answer.

"I think I would run," Neil said to break the silence. "I don't stand a chance against the emperor's forces."

"What you're describing is desertion," Rhys said quietly.

"Is it, though?" Neil sat up and whispered, "We were born into this. We never took an oath. We never made any promises. Everything we've done so far was out of loyalty, hatred, or revenge."

Rhys sighed. "I'd leave, too," he whispered. "Going up against the emperor is suicide. I'd go with you." He gave a little, disbelieving laugh. "We're talking about abandoning our family, Neil."

Neil's thoughts flashed to Darius Taurlum, who got to drink with his family every night, and then to Bianca, who didn't have any family left to abandon. "To be honest, we aren't exactly the closest knit family around," Neil said.

Rhys looked at him. "You think?"

"I've gathered a few clues over the years." Neil fiddled with the edge of his comforter. "So it's decided? If this turns into a war, we run?"

"We run," Rhys confirmed. "And then we'd live in the slums, I guess."

Neil closed his eyes for a moment, and then opened them as wide as he could to stave off sleepiness. "What about . . . beyond the wall?"

Rhys scrunched up his eyebrows and recited:

"There is no story sadder than that of little Billy.
He thought he'd have adventures if he could leave the city.
He made it through the wall and quickly lost his head-
For the savages were waiting and they cut him up instead."

"Don't quote the emperor's nursery rhymes at me," Neil sighed.

"You know what's beyond the wall ... desert, desert, and savages. Why do you think people who are exiled are forced to leave the wall? Because it's certain death, Neil, certain death."

"But where did the savages come from?" Neil pressed. "They have to be from villages. They have to have families. Otherwise, they would've died out. We can't be the only city out there."

"Even if there are other cities, we'd die of hunger—or stab wounds—before we made it anywhere. Altryon is in the middle of a wasteland. It's a fact. I've read about it. It's essentially suicide."

"Staying here is just as much of a suicide, if this turns to war. At least out there, we'd have a chance—"

"No, Neil, there is no chance."

"But if there was, just think about it for a second. What if there are other civilizations? And what if there are civilizations where they've never heard of the Man with the Golden Light, or the families, or the feud, or any of it?"

Rhys shrugged. "It's a nice thought. I'd love to leave behind the feud. I get the feeling Dad sort of likes keeping it alive. He adds fuel to the fire sometimes. Like when he sent you out to kill a Taurlum. It wasn't necessary. It was just to rile them up." He yawned. "It's all part of his hatred. I'd like that to go away, I think. No more assassinations. No more strategizing. No more plotting."

"I thought you loved to plot, Rhys."

"I do. But sometimes, I wish I didn't have to." There was a long pause, before Rhys spoke again. "We should bring Victoria."

"Yeah, of course," Neil said as he buried his face in his pillow. "She'd love a world like that."

Rhys let out a yawn. "So it's decided. If a war starts, we get the hell out of here."

"We get the hell out of here," Neil confirmed quietly.

Chapter Twenty-Six
Celerius Estate
Lilly

Lilly felt like this horrible day would never end. Her carriage had been attacked by those meddling Vapros, and then she had returned home to the horror of seeing her brother's ashes hand-delivered in a box. Her father had raced out to heaven knows where in a blind rage.

Lilly made a habit of refusing to drink. She hated alcohol, hated its taste and its side effects and the headache it caused the next day, but tonight was an exception to the rule. Her brother was dead. Anthony, who had long ago promised to protect her no matter what, was gone, just like the rumors had said he would be.

It didn't even feel real yet, maybe because they only saw each other on special occasions. If she tried, she could almost convince herself that he was still alive and well at the military base. But the truth always settled back in like dust over her skin, and never again would she see that big, toothy grin he reserved just for her, or hear his belly laugh, or feel his strong embrace. She was already forgetting the color of his eyes.

She poured herself another glass of wine. She was being silly. Death was just a part of life. She'd lost people before. Before today, the one that had hit her the hardest was her brother, Edward, victim of an assassination a few years ago. He had been found dead in his bed; they never did find out who was behind the murder. His death had crushed her. But time had eased that pain; this loss was fresh, new, agonizing. And this time, she knew exactly who had taken the victim away from her.

"Miss," Jonathan said quietly. "I think you've had enough."

She looked right at him and drained the glass, daring him to speak again. "They sent my brother's ashes in a box," she said hoarsely, refilling the goblet and wishing her house had something stronger than wine. "Killing him wasn't good enough. They had to burn him and scoop him into a box and send him home." She was out of tears. She gripped her glass and whispered, "I can't believe I have lost another brother."

"No more wine," Jonathan said quietly as he reached for the bottle.

She said something under her breath.

"Pardon?"

She made eye contact and said with steely resolve, "He dies."

Jonathan touched the buttons on his coat nervously and asked, "Who?"

Lilly threw her full glass against the fireplace. It shattered. "Carlin, and I'm going to cut out his black heart and burn it to ash, same as he did to Anthony."

Jonathan was quiet for a moment. "Good," he finally replied.

If Lilly had been able to feel anything but fury and numbness, she would have been surprised. Jonathan was not the vengeful type. "He will regret the day he betrayed my family."

Jonathan went to fetch another glass from the cabinet. He filled it halfway with water and offered it to her. "I'd love to be there when it happens," he said.

She ignored the water and took a gulp of wine, straight from the bottle. "I want everyone there."

A fire of rage ignited in her chest, working with the alcohol to dull her pain. She promised herself she wouldn't extinguish the flame. She would let it burn.

Chapter Twenty-Seven
Vapros Bunker
Neil

Neil was dreaming about being chased. He dodged through the market streets, materializing around corners and tearing down alleyways to get away from the stampede of people following him. He finally ducked behind a fruit stand, hugging his knees to his chest and listening to the thudding footsteps of his adversaries as they raced past.

"Neil! Wake up!"

Neil blinked a few times. "What?" he mumbled groggily.

Rhys was standing over him. "Do you hear that?"

"Hear what?"

"Listen!"

Neil sat up. Overhead, on the floor above them, he could hear footsteps running in all directions. "People," he said stupidly.

"A lot of people," Rhys said urgently. "How many people live in this house?"

"I don't know. Thirty?"

"I hear a lot more footsteps than that."

Neil listened again and then everything clicked: the raid they had feared was happening—tonight, right now. He jumped out of bed and threw on his assassin cloak. "We have to go now," he said, suddenly wide-awake. Rhys ran to get his things. As they barreled out into the hallway, they nearly crashed into Jennifer and Victoria. "You heard?" Neil asked, pointing up at the ceiling.

Jennifer nodded. "We were just coming to get you." She and Victoria were both wearing their battle cloaks. The latter looked extremely uncomfortable. "Never been so glad to be sleeping on the bottom floor," Jennifer said.

"We don't have time to talk," Rhys said. The four of them started for the stairs. "We should find Father first," Rhys decided. "He's the strongest. He's the best equipped to deal with this."

"Taurlum?" Victoria asked, pulling her hood over her head.

"I don't think so," Rhys said. "The footsteps aren't loud enough to be Taurlum. And our hallways are too small for them to fit."

"Celerius, then?"

"Doubtful. It's not like them to make the first move. And they wouldn't cut us up in our beds. It's not honorable."

"Then who?" Victoria and Jennifer asked together.

Rhys and Neil shared a look. "I think I know," Neil said. "It's the—"

"Look out," Jennifer hissed, throwing out an arm to stop her siblings from proceeding. "We have guests."

At the end of the hallway, unaware that they'd been spotted, were three soldiers clad in Imperial armor and some sort of mask. "I'll take the one in the middle," Jennifer said from the side of her mouth. "Rhys, you get the guy on the left. Neil, you can have the one on the right."

As soon as she finished giving orders, they were sprinting down the hall toward their adversaries. Jennifer reached her soldier first, burning straight through his mask with her palms and sliding a knife across his throat. Neil hit his target next, materializing behind him and stabbing his heart through his back. Rhys brought up the rear, calmly putting his man to sleep before throwing his limp body to the ground.

Victoria finally caught up with her siblings. "Why are they wearing masks?" she asked, looking a little pale. She had never admitted it, but killing made her sick to her stomach.

Rhys bent down and removed the mask in fascination. "I could be wrong, but it looks remarkably like an apparatus for protecting against asphyxiation via smoke inhalation."

The other three stared at him blankly. "Talk like a person," Jennifer grumbled.

Rhys slid the mask over his own face experimentally. "It's a gas mask," he said, voice slightly muffled. "If there's a fire or something, this can help you breathe through the smoke."

Jennifer ran her hand across the man she'd just killed and cremated him. "How do you know all this stuff?" she asked, picking up the gas mask from the pile of ash.

Rhys pulled off his gas mask, looked at it and spoke thoughtfully. "I think I invented it." The other three stared at him. "I mean," he clarified, "I think I talked to the guy who wanted to invent them. I helped him work out some flaws in the design. It was supposed to help save people. He told me he was part of the doctor's guild and was a philanthropist."

Jennifer narrowed her eyes. "And now the army has them." She tightened her ponytail and grumbled. "The same army that wants to go to war with us. Good going, Rhys. You practically handed them their victory."

Rhys stared at the floor. "You're right. I'm sorry. I didn't know."

Neil glared at Jennifer. "Leave him alone."

In a flash, Jennifer had her knife in her hand. "Don't tell me what to do."

Victoria stepped between her sister and brother. "So the soldiers have gas masks," she said, trying to guide the conversation back to the matter at hand. "So they were going to set fire to our house?"

Rhys shook his head. "They wouldn't have come all the way down here just to start a fire." He began fishing through the fallen soldiers' pockets. "Ah," he said quietly, pulling out a small canister filled with a pin on the top. "Of course. I've seen these before. It all makes sense now."

Jennifer exhaled heavily. "Are you going to enlighten us?" she asked with exaggerated patience, "or just talk to yourself?"

"These canisters have gasses inside that make people fall unconscious or suffocate," Rhys explained. "It doesn't usually kill them, just puts them to sleep for awhile. It would be a good way to capture us because we need air to materialize."

Neil waited, but Rhys didn't continue. "So?" he prompted gently.

"So they don't want us dead," Rhys elaborated. "They want to take us prisoner. They were going to find our bedrooms, release the gas—they'd be safe because of the gas masks—and bring us to ... well, wherever they want."

Victoria tried to look calm. "So here's the new plan," she said as forcefully as she could. "We get out of here. We'll warn people on the way when it isn't too risky, but above all else, we have to escape."

Jennifer grinned. "Taking charge," she said, patting her sister on the back. "I like it." She stood. "You heard her," she said to Rhys and Neil. "Let's go. Run."

"Wait." Neil knelt to pick up the masks from the fallen soldiers. One of them had a giant hole burned through it from Jennifer's hands, but the other two were still whole. "Put these on," he said, offering them to Victoria and Jennifer. "Just in case."

Victoria took hers and slid it over her face, but Jennifer waved hers away. "You wear it, Neil," she said with a foreign kindness. He was about to thank her when she added, grinning, "After all, you need all the help you can get."

Scowling, Neil handed the mask to Rhys, who pulled it on without hesitation. The four Vapros started down the hallway, pounding on doors and yelling about the invasion as they went. Jennifer kept her knife in her hand at all times.

They rounded a corner and found themselves face to face with a large group of masked soldiers. Jennifer lunged at one of them, sinking her knife into his arm and yanking his mask off his head and onto her own. Victoria hung back, holding a knife in her hand just in case, but Neil knew she had no idea how to use it. He jumped into the fray, stabbing and dodging and materializing out of the way as the Imperial soldiers swung at him. He wondered desperately where the rest of his relatives were. Maybe the soldiers had already gassed them. Maybe he, Rhys, and the twins were the only ones left.

"Look out!" screamed Victoria. Neil turned just in time to see one of the soldiers pull the pin on a canister full of the foggy vapor. He groaned. He was the only one without a mask. Holding his breath, Neil materialized behind one of the soldiers and tried to pull off his mask. But fighting without breathing was hard work, and the man was struggling hard. Any second now Neil knew he'd have to take a breath.

Just as his lungs began to burn, something heavy was shoved against his face. Neil gasped against his will. Instead of breathing in the toxin, however, he found himself inhaling clean air. He pawed at the object against his face. He pulled it the rest of the way over his head, quickly finished off the soldier, and looked around for his savior. The only one in his vicinity was Jennifer. "You?" he called to her over the noises of combat.

"Thank me later," she yelled back, burning through the masks of two soldiers at once. The holes she made rendered their masks useless, and after three seconds of breathing in the gas, both soldiers were lying motionless on the ground. He looked around for more men to fight, but there was nobody left standing other than his siblings.

"I think we beat them," he started to say, but stopped himself. Waiting on the stairs in a stiff formation stood more soldiers. The room was silent except for the heavy breathing of Jennifer, Rhys, and Neil. One of the new soldiers stepped forward and approached them. "Vapros children," he said in a cold voice, "surrender now. We will not harm you unless you resist."

"Go to hell," Jennifer said through her mask, throwing her knife directly into his stomach. The soldier hit the ground screaming. The group on the stairs began to file down, swords outstretched, and Neil prepared to charge them. Suddenly, a scream went up near the top of the stairs. The soldiers paused. More screams joined the first one, and then the soldiers were gone and Sir Vapros appeared on the bottom step. The stairs behind him were littered with small heaps of ash.

Victoria paled. "How many did …?" She couldn't finish her sentence.

"I consumed about ten," he answered. "We're leaving. Now! It is no longer safe here."

Victoria pulled a mask from a body on the floor and offered it to her father, but he shook his head. "There's a gas," she started to explain.

"The gas cannot harm me," he assured her. "I am smoke." He let his body transform back into a giant cloud and glided up the stairs. His family followed, watching in horror and awe as he enveloped every soldier they met and turned them into little piles of dust.

When they reached the second highest floor, Sir Vapros took human shape again. "We met much less resistance than I expected," he mused. "The emperor sent a rather weak—"

Before he could finish, he was lifted off the ground by an invisible force. A figure emerged from the shadows, eyes an otherworldly black, hands outstretched. He had a familiar face, but Neil couldn't quite place it. Victoria let out a scream.

Sir Vapros materialized out of the man's hold, but before he could revert back into smoke the invisible force had taken hold of him again. The man clenched his outstretched hands into fists; Sir Vapros went flying into a wall headfirst. He landed on the ground with a thud and didn't get up.

Neil ran to his father's side. Sir Vapros's chest rose and fell slightly, but his head was bleeding badly. "Who are you?" Neil demanded, standing to face the intruder.

The man looked at Neil, an odd smile playing at his lips. "You don't remember me?" he said in a raspy voice. "I'm insulted. We've met before. I suppose I looked a little different."

Neil squinted, trying to remember. It came back to him in a sudden burst. "You're the emperor's servant," he said. "The one he beats. You were there when I went to see him."

The servant bowed. "Saewulf."

Saewulf looked strikingly different. Apparently when clean, his hair was actually a burnt orange color. It was pulled away from his face and lapped down near his shoulders. His ragged servant-wear had been exchanged for well-made, tight-fitting, black clothing.

Victoria couldn't take her eyes off her father's unconscious form. "What are you?" she asked, with her voice catching.

He turned his gaze to her. "Not a student of history, I see."

Jennifer stepped forward. *"Answer her."*

Saewulf laughed. The sound sent chills down Neil's spine. "You know the legends that surround your family. You tell me."

Before any of them could respond, Saewulf whirled around and stretched his arms out toward Rhys. Neil's brother was lifted into the air. He flailed and began to scream. Before Saewulf could do anything further, Neil and Jennifer were upon him. Saewulf dodged Neil's blade, but Jennifer was able to nick him with her red-hot hands, and his concentration was broken. He dropped Rhys, who materialized to the other side of the room and sprinted up the stairs. His siblings followed. As they materialized through the small door and pulled off their gas masks, Neil could hear Saewulf charging after them. "Split up," he said, panting. "Meet at the Opera House later."

"But Dad," Victoria began.

"He's alive," Neil assured her. "He was breathing. Split up!"

For once, nobody argued with him. They headed out into the night, dematerializing to avoid being seen. Neil had made it onto the rooftop when he heard the iron door being ripped off its hinges. Saewulf swung his arm and it clattered into the darkness. Neil turned to flee, but he heard his sister scream. He looked down to see Victoria, who had almost escaped, being lifted into the air. Saewulf dragged her back to the entrance of the house using his invisible force. "Surrender or she dies!" he screamed into the night.

Neil whipped his head around to look at Jennifer. For the first time in his memory, he saw real fear in her eyes. She took a halfstep back toward their house. "Don't do it, Jen," Neil cautioned. She looked at him, trembling, and he could see the conflict in her face.

"It's your last chance!" Saewulf yelled. "I'll kill her in front of your eyes!"

Victoria wasn't screaming, but she looked out of her mind with terror. Jennifer made eye contact with Neil. "I'm sorry," she mouthed and then materialized to the ground. "Don't touch her!" she shrieked, running toward her sister. "I surrender! Let her go!" After a moment of internal struggle, Neil materialized to the ground and followed Jennifer up the street. He didn't see Rhys. His brother had probably made it far away before Victoria's capture. "Jen!" Victoria cried. Her voice echoed oddly, as if she were trapped in a giant bubble, "Don't do it! Run!"

Jennifer stopped a few yards out of Saewulf's reach. She was crying. "I'm not leaving you." She turned to Saewulf, her knife drawn. "I'm here," she said. "You have me. Let her go."

Saewulf didn't drop Victoria. She struggled to dematerialize away the way her father had, but she didn't have enough energy. "Jennifer," she begged, "you have to get away. Find Robert. Tell him . . . tell him I can't meet up with him."

Jennifer's face was bathed in tears. "You're going to get out of this. We all are. I'm here, Saewulf. Put her down."

Saewulf smiled. He pulled Victoria in closer, keeping her suspended. "Something you should know about me since we only have just met," he said lazily. "I'm a liar."

He pulled Victoria in so close that he could reach out and grab her. He caught her neck in his glowing hand. Jennifer and Victoria screamed together. With a quick flick of Saewulf's wrist, Victoria fell to the ground, neck twisted at an unnatural angle, eyes wide and blank.

Jennifer let out a snarl of rage and pain as she materialized in front of Saewulf faster than Neil had ever seen a human being move. She wrapped her hands tightly around his throat, and Neil swore her entire body glowed red as she burned him. With a yell, he threw her off; she landed in the street next to Victoria's body. With a shuddery gasp, she gazed into her twin's eyes and then began to sob uncontrollably. Neil ran to help her to her feet. "We can't win this," he gasped. Saewulf had his hands clasped around the raw skin on his neck, howling in pain.

Jennifer let Neil hold her. "He dies right now," she vowed through sobs.

"He'll die," Neil promised, "but not now. We have to regroup first and then get stronger."

Jennifer groped for her knife. "Now," she snarled. Her hair was coming down from its ponytail, but she didn't reach up to fix it. Neil let go of her. This was not a Jennifer he'd seen before. Gone was the poised assassin; this Jennifer was wild, like a savage, like an animal.

"Please, Jen," he begged. "Not tonight. We have to get out of here before he calls in reinforcements. We'll die."

"I don't care if I die!" Jennifer screamed.

"Victoria would care," he insisted.

At the name of her sister, something in Jennifer collapsed. New sobs filled with anger and pain racked her body as she sheathed her knife. "He will die," she whispered to Victoria as she placed her hand on the back of her sister's neck. They spent a few precious seconds watching the ash float away into the distance as Victoria dissolved. Then with one final look back, they ran into the darkness.

~❦~

The empty Opera House was ominous, Neil noticed, but his siblings didn't seem to care. Jennifer had run out of tears hours ago. She turned her knife over and over in her hands, sniffling and hiccupping. Rhys wept silently in the corner, head buried in his cloak. Neil was still in shock. No tears fell from his eyes because none of this felt real. It was all a dream, just a continuation of the nightmare he'd been having a few short hours ago. Any second now he'd wake up in his room and Victoria would be fine.

"So we're on our own now?" Jennifer asked bitterly.

"I think we're the only ones who escaped," he answered.

"Do you think they'll kill the others?" Rhys asked.

"No," Neil said. "Why bother using gas to knock us out if the plan was to kill us? They want us alive."

"We have to save them, " Jennifer said. "We have to overthrow that bastard."

Rhys laughed humorlessly and muttered, "You really think the three of us can topple the strongest man in Altryon?"

Jennifer shook her head. "We're going to build an army. We'll start with Robert."

"Robert?" Neil asked.

"That boy from the slums—the one who followed Victoria everywhere."

Jennifer closed her eyes and took a deep breath. "She was in love with him. She never told me but I could tell. They were going to run away together. She never told me that either. But I know they were planning it. I saw how they looked at each other." Jennifer wrapped her arms around her chest, as if she were physically coming apart. "If anyone will fight to avenge her, Robert will."

"Who else can we find?" Rhys asked.

"I don't care who we team up with," Jennifer said stonily. "I don't care who we have to convince or what we have to do. Tomorrow I'm starting a revolution. Saewulf and the emperor are going to die."

Neil and Rhys exchanged a glance. "I know we talked about leaving, but ...." Rhys trailed off and gestured at their sister.

Neil pushed a hand through his hair and sighed. "I know, we can't." He stood up and walked backstage, searching for bottles of alcohol. He grabbed a large one and threw it to Jennifer. "To Victoria Vapros," he said as she popped open the top and took a long drink. She passed it back and he followed suit. "It's in her name that we start this revolution."

Rhys had already begun strategizing. "They had those canisters specially filled with hazardous gas," he said thoughtfully. "They could only have gotten that kind of weapon from an arms dealer. There aren't too many dealers around here. I could track him down. We know it wasn't the Celerius."

"And you already know the man who sold them the gas masks," Neil reminded him. "You said you helped him out."

Jennifer traced the rim of the bottle with her finger. "I say we start from the bottom and work our way up until the empire is in ashes." She reached up to tighten her ponytail, the familiar determined gleam back in her eye. "We ravage until the emperor is entirely alone."

Chapter Twenty-Eight
Celerius Estate
Carlin

Carlin stood at the top of the hill overlooking the Celerius estate. Across the city, he knew Saewulf had already begun the siege on the Vapros bunker. "Virgil, get the men in formation," he commanded. "And then I'd like to talk to you." He examined the estate, taking note of all of the exits. Not a single Celerius would escape him tonight.

"We are prepared, sir," Virgil said a few minutes later. "Rifles loaded, men in position."

Carlin grinned. "Just think, tonight every single Celerius in Altryon will be dead or a prisoner. It's a beautiful thing."

Virgil didn't budge. "You wanted to talk to me, sir?"

Carlin turned from the house. "Will you look at me, please?" Virgil made eye contact with the new general. "Look," Carlin said, putting a hand on Virgil's shoulder, "I know you were close to Anthony. I'm sorry I had to kill him. I had my orders. There was nothing I could do."

Virgil didn't say anything.

"I'm in charge now," he continued, as he straightened his red cloak proudly. "And as my second in command, I hope you will put aside your emotions and act with professionalism."

Virgil finally spoke up. "My allegiance lies with this army and whoever leads it. That was the oath I took when I enlisted. I tried to save Anthony because it was my duty. Now my duty is to protect you. I don't blame you for being the soldier that the emperor instructed you to be. Emotions have nothing to do with it, sir. If you'll allow me, I'll cut down the Celerius myself."

Carlin smiled and patted Virgil's shoulder. "Good, excellent," he said gruffly as he turned his sights back to the house and raised his sword. "Time to interrupt a funeral!" he cried and led his army down the hill with Virgil at his heels.

Lilly was on her fourth glass of wine and showed no sign of stopping. Jonathan, who was on glass number three, was having trouble staying awake. "I'm too small to drink as much as you, Miss," he slurred. He'd taken off his military coat and attempted to drape it across the back of his chair, but it had fallen onto his lap an hour ago and he'd accidentally kicked it onto the floor. It lay in a heap at his feet.

Lilly tilted her glass and sent a river of wine down her throat. "I don't care how much you drink," she muttered. She wished she could feel as intoxicated as he looked, but grief kept finding her through the alcohol. "I should stop. It's not even helping."

Jonathan tried to sit up. "It would be rude to keep drinking alone," he said as formally as he could manage. "I should stop, too." He let out a small burp and then turned bright red. "Forgive me. I . . . excuse me."

Lilly cracked a smile. "You look terrible," she said, polishing off her glass.

Jonathan rubbed his eyes. "I feel terrible."

"Don't we all."

They heard footsteps coming down the hall in their direction. Jonathan jumped out of the chair and then toppled over, his feet tangling in the jacket he'd left on the ground. "Allow me to hide your glass," he panted, trying to stand.

Lilly waved her hand. "Don't bother. This is the least of my worries."

"It's just . . . drinking with one's servants—it's not—"

"Proper?" Lilly interjected with a humorless laugh. "Anthony is dead. Being proper is not important any more."

The door swung open. Jonathan began to bow and then let out a cry of surprise. An Imperial soldier burst into the room and struck the servant across the face with the butt of his rifle. With a cry, Jonathan hit the floor. Lilly jumped up, reaching for her sword. She grabbed the hilt clumsily, finally feeling the effects of the wine and rolled behind one of the cabinets for cover. She held her sword up from behind it as steadily as she could. "Lilly Celerius," the soldier boomed, "we have orders to capture you. If you come quietly, you will not be harmed."

More soldiers gathered in the doorway. Lilly redoubled her grip on the sword and tried not to sway into range. Why was the alcohol kicking in now? "Who gave you your orders?" she asked, fixing her eyes on the leader. "The same person who told you to stand by and let Carlin murder my brother?" Tears stung her eyes but she willed them away.

"Put down your sword," the soldier ordered, but Lilly didn't move. Jonathan lay unconscious at her feet. For a terrifying second she thought he was dead, but then she heard him snoring faintly.

"I will die before I go anywhere with you," she spat.

The soldier reached down to draw his weapon, and Lilly noted with dismay that they were all equipped with powerful rifles. Her heart sank. She couldn't outrun a gun or dodge a bullet.

"I'm hard to kill," she said quickly. "People have tried before. I can heal from any wound. Think about that before you waste your ammunition."

The soldier shook his head. "I know how to kill you," he said, grinning. "All I have to do is hit your heart or your head. You can't recover from that. And I'm more than capable."

Lilly took a deep breath. "Shall we test that theory?" she asked and before any of them could respond, she rolled out of her cover and was upon them. She swung her sword wildly at the leader, slicing cleanly through his neck. His body hit the ground almost a full second after his head. None of the soldiers were prepared to face someone so fast. One of the soldiers behind him panicked and shot his rifle. The shot went wide, and the bullet buried itself in her shoulder, but a bullet was nothing compared to losing Anthony, and by the time she'd killed the shooter, her arm had already expelled the bullet and healed over into a scab. The other guards had clearly not expected this much resistance. As they began to fumble to load their guns, Lilly cut them down like weeds.

Gasping, Lilly sank to the ground and began to sob. "Anthony," she whispered, sword slipping from her hand, "help me …."

A low chuckle came from the doorway. One of the soldiers, in spite of a large gash across his chest, had failed to die. "You'll be with him soon," the man gurgled, lifting his rifle as best he could from his position on the floor, and Lilly was almost glad that it was about to be over.

As the soldier put his finger against the trigger, a large vase sailed through the air and connected with the side of his head. His body went limp. Lilly looked around in confusion and saw Jonathan, grim-faced, struggling back into his military coat. "Are you all right?" he asked, helping her to her feet.

Lilly wanted desperately to hug him, to sob into his shoulder and let him tell her she would be okay, but she refrained and declared, "I'm fine. Thank you."

"It's just my duty, Miss," he said humbly, bowing and stumbling a little.

A group of Celerius guards entered. "We heard a shot," one of them said. "Are you all right?"

Lilly nodded. "Are there any more of them in the house?" she asked.

"We've been fighting them off in the courtyard," a guard answered. "It's nearly the entire Imperial army. We can't keep up with their guns. I'm sorry, Miss Celerius, they've captured your mother. She's unharmed, but I'm afraid your brother Thomas is dead."

Lilly's heart stopped beating. "Thomas?" she whispered. "How?"

The guard bowed his head. "Your brother fought hard," he said, "but swords are no match for rifles."

Lilly couldn't breathe. "Who killed him?"

"I didn't see. None of us did. We just found the body in the main hallway."

"Maybe he wasn't dead," she insisted. "Maybe he was still recovering."

The guard shook his head. "His heart was gone."

She blinked. "His heart was …."

"Someone cut it out of him. It looked like a wide blade, maybe a broadsword."

She was going to be sick. "They cut out his heart?"

"Probably to make sure he was really dead," a guard supplied.

Lilly closed her eyes. "Carlin," she growled. "He's behind it; I know he is. With Anthony gone, he's the leader of this army." She opened her eyes. They were blazing. "He will bleed for what he's done."

"Do you think he's here?" Jonathan asked.

She hadn't thought of that. "I'm going after him," she said, retrieving her sword. "He won't be on the front lines. He's probably inside somewhere … looking for the real challenges. I'll destroy anyone who stands in my way of killing that bastard." Her brain no longer felt fuzzy. Anger destroyed the dull calm she'd tried to weave earlier. "You prepare the horses," she commanded, addressing the guards. They began to file away. "Wait!" They paused. "Half of you get to the treasury. Empty it. We will not be returning." The guards obeyed.

"Me, Miss?" Jonathan asked.

She barely looked at him. "Go with them."

He looked disappointed, but he ran to catch up with the guards, nearly tripping on his coat.

Lilly strode down the hallway as fast as she could without running, throwing open every door she passed. The first room was empty. The second had an overturned dresser partially blocking the door but nobody inside. The third room: Lilly clamped both hands over her mouth to hold in a scream upon seeing the bodies of two servants stabbed through their hearts. She nearly retched when she recognized them—Jonathan's parents. *Don't think about it,* she told herself. *Not now. Not yet.* She closed the door and moved on to the next one, her father's bedroom. Inside was a troop of four men, headed by Carlin himself. They were rooting through drawers and overturning furniture, laughing cruelly. Lilly kicked in the door. "Carlin," she roared, swinging her sword.

He jumped at her voice and turned to her. His face cracked into a dangerous smile. "Oh my," he laughed, "you came right to me."

She let out a wordless snarl. "I am going to kill you for what you did to me."

Carlin unsheathed his broadsword. Against her will, her eyes strayed to the blade. It was caked with the dried blood that she knew belonged to her brother. "You sound so upset," he said delightedly. "It's adorable."

"There is nothing adorable about this," she said coldly. "No more politics. No more deception. This is pure unadulterated revenge."

His men looked uneasy and shifted uncomfortably. Carlin chuckled. "I bested your brothers," he reminded her. She bit down hard on her tongue to keep from screaming at him. "They weren't quite … fast enough. So what is it that makes you think you can escape my blade?"

Lilly's face stretched into a savage grin. "Trust me," she said viciously. "I'm fast enough." With a blur of movement, she lunged at one of his men and sliced through him. Carlin jumped forward and tried to cut her legs out from under her, but she whirled out of the way and stabbed his remaining companions before he could suck in a breath to gasp.

"So you're fast enough to defeat these pathetic fools," Carlin spat as he kicked a half-alive body to the floor at her feet. "Have a go at me."

She laughed without humor. There were tears in her eyes. "My pleasure."

She swung, ready to cut his arrogant throat, but her sword collided with steel, and with a shock she realized he'd blocked her blow. That had never happened to her before. He lashed out at her, and it took everything she had to twist out of the way in time. He swung his sword like a maniac, and she let out a cry as she realized she wasn't strong enough to block him every time. His weapon nicked her side, making her bleed, and she stared up at him in fear. "You're ..."

"Faster?" he supplied. He knocked the sword from her hand. "Stronger?" He missed her neck by a fraction of an inch. "Better?"

She dropped to the ground and dove for her sword. He kicked her hard and trapped her neck beneath his boot. Flipping her onto her back, he positioned his broadsword against her heart which pounded so fast she could barely breathe. "Yes," he said. "I am."

An arrow came flying out of nowhere and embedded itself in Carlin's hand. He howled in shock and let the sword fall; it left a shallow scratch just over Lilly's heart, which healed over before she even felt the pain. Carlin hit the floor. Gasping hard, Lilly jumped to her feet and fled.

As she raced down the hallway, thankfully deserted, she allowed herself to glance over her shoulder to see if Carlin had begun to pursue her. The corridor behind was empty, but Lilly put on a burst of speed just in case, threw herself around the corner and ran directly into a tall Imperial foot-soldier holding a bow and arrow. She gasped in surprise as she collided with his armor and started to fall backwards, but he caught her and held her arm firmly until she regained balance. She couldn't see his face through his helmet, but she felt his eyes on her. With a grunt, she twisted out of his grip and reached for her sword before realizing she'd left it back in her father's room.

Lilly backed away down the hall, eyes on the bow in the guard's hand, waiting for him to fit an arrow into it and shoot her. He remained motionless. When she was halfway down the corridor, she turned and bolted. The soldier didn't chase her.

Lilly was puzzled. Other than Carlin, that soldier was the only one on this floor and he was definitely the only person she'd seen all night carrying a bow and arrow. He must have been the one to shoot the arrow into the room. No doubt he was aiming for her and had only hit his leader by mistake. But that was quite a mistake. She'd been on the ground at Carlin's mercy. There was no need to shoot an arrow at her if she was already about to die. And why hadn't he finished her off just now, when she was clearly weaponless and vulnerable?

She reached the back door of the house and stumbled out into the night. The Celerius guards had loaded the horses with bags of the family treasure. Lilly mounted one of the steeds hastily and urged it to turn around so she could face the men. "Carlin is still alive," she admitted. "He's strong. I need to get stronger before I can face him again." She took a deep breath. "Too many people have died. It cannot be ignored. I am fighting for the memory of my brothers and for the guards and servants who fell tonight." She fought back tears, exhausted. This was too much. She needed sleep, or at the very least more wine. "I, Lilly Celerius, will lead this rebellion against Carlin and the emperor and every one of the Imperial bastards who attacked my family. Who will ride with me?"

Jonathan urged his horse to the front of the group. His cheek bore a large black bruise, but if he was in pain he hid it well. "I will, Miss," he promised.

The Celerius guards echoed his vow, and Lilly let herself smile. "Follow me," she cried, turning her horse and nudging him into a gallop. "The Emperor of Alytron will fall."

Chapter Twenty-Nine
The Taurlum Mansion
Michael

Michael sat in his bed, groaning and rubbing his temples. *Was it possible to be hungover during the middle of the night?* Apparently, it was. Waking up had been a mistake. He crawled out of bed and walked over to his side table with a groan that was almost a roar. He heard a few family members singing a drinking song downstairs, but he didn't care to join them. He grabbed a bottle of gin and poured a glass. "Are you my best friend or worst enemy?" he asked the bottle with a small grin. "Bit of both," he decided with a sip.

He drained the glass and had it refilled within a minute. It was funny how alcohol was the only thing that ever made him feel any sort of pain. At the same time it was the only thing that granted him a bit of peace. It was as if every time he held the cup he was holding a loved one's hand. In recent months, his drinking schedule had changed. Formerly, he would drink in the Taurlum dining room with his father. Things were different since the night he barged into his father's office and told him he was leaving. The glass exploded in Michael's hand and he realized that he had been clutching it a little too tightly. That wasn't a problem. He had others.

He heard the drinking song cease suddenly. That was odd. It wasn't like the Taurlum family to leave a song unfinished, no matter how drunk they were. The silence was quickly followed by loud crashes and Michael's ear perked up in interest. *Did they all pass out drunk at the same time?* He closed his eyes and waded through his sheets into the center of his bed. Suddenly the smashing grew louder and echoed down his hallway. *What the hell was that?*

Then he heard the racket closer to his bedroom and a rifle being fired. He threw his sheets off and leapt to his feet. These noises were not an after-effect of his family's antics. Someone was in the house. He threw open his door and was instantly greeted by a volley of fire from a small squad of Imperial soldiers.

He stumbled backwards and toppled to the ground. One of the soldiers pulled a pin on a canister and threw it at his fallen body. As he staggered to his feet, Michael noticed that the canister expelled smoke at an alarming rate. He knew not to inhale, even in his intoxicated state. While holding his breath, he grabbed a bottle from his side table and chucked it at one of the Imperial guards. The bottle flew so straight and swiftly that it knocked the guard off his feet. Michael grabbed the table by one of its legs and charged at the soldiers. One managed to reload his gun and fire in time, but the bullet ricocheted off Michael's chest and found its way into the soldier's vulnerable neck. Michael followed up that manuever with a swing of the table. The two remaining soldiers were knocked clean off their feet in an explosion of splinters, glass, and alcohol. Michael wearily teetered back and forth in the doorway, furious and confused. *Why were they here?*

He stepped out fully into the hallway, holding one leg of the table that had broken off. He heard a soldier on the floor groaning so he stepped on him. Michael tiredly turned to his right and realized he was staring at nearly ten Imperial soldiers who were trying very quietly to load their rifles. "Oh," Michael said quietly as he dropped the leg and turned to face them head on. They were about thirty feet away and standing in front of a giant glass window.

The silence was nearly unbearable as they tried to load their guns with care. Michael picked up one of the unmoving soldiers by the foot and with a mighty roar, he hurled the body at the throng. One or two soldiers fell, but that was only the distraction. Michael began his charge. He barreled at full speed down the hallway before the soldiers even had a chance to regain their formation. He was going too fast to slow down, but that was okay. Michael didn't want to slow down. One second he was running and the next he and three soldiers were falling from the third story window. He hit the pavement on all fours, crushing a soldier in between his iron skin and the street.

He stood up and looked back to see a few soldiers gathering by the broken window staring down at him. He vaguely remembered somehow being involved in a similar situation earlier that week. He turned to see the three soldiers in a broken mess on the street behind him. He scoffed and thought to himself: *Good. That's what they get.*

He took a moment to readjust to the change in scenery. Glancing around the side of the house, he could see what looked like half the Imperial army leading members of his family into a wagon. They had some kind of strange collar around their necks. Michael wanted to race to their aid, but he was grossly outnumbered and still hadn't escaped the rifle fire. A few bullets bounced off his back and he began to run in a panicked fashion. He glanced back at the mansion one last time, then bolted off into the markets for shelter.

⚜

Darius kept his head down as he pushed through the crowded streets.

He'd only been out of prison for a few hours and he wasn't looking to go back. The markets were usually deserted after sundown, but tonight the alleys were packed with civilians. Maybe there was a riot. He readjusted the cloak he had stolen to cover his golden hair. If anyone here recognized him, he'd be thrown back in the dungeon for sure.

The Taurlum mansion was barely visible in the distance. Darius took a long look at it and sighed. There was no way he'd be able to live there anymore. He was a fugitive now. He'd have to hide out in the slums, or worse, the sewers. Never again could he enjoy the bathhouse with Michael, or have a drink with his father, or even feel the adrenaline rush of holding a hammer above his head.

"Hey!" someone shouted, and Darius turned to see someone running toward him holding a weapon. For a split second, he was sure he'd been discovered, but then realized the person charging at him was none other than Michael Taurlum.

"What the hell's wrong with you?" Darius exclaimed, putting up his hands to stop his brother.

Michael stopped in his tracks. "Darius?" He looked confused. "Is that you?"

"Of course it's me!" Darius pulled off his cloak and revealed his hair. "Who did you think it was?"

"I don't know," Michael offered, looking weary. "You shouldn't walk around here with your face hidden like that. People will be suspicious. There's been an attack." He was still looking at his brother skeptically, as if he wasn't completely sure Darius wasn't a threat. "I thought you were in prison."

"I made it out," Darius quickly explained. "There was an attack?"

"Yeah." Michael looked up at the mansion as he spoke. "The emperor. He brought an army. I think he got everyone except me. And you, apparently."

"Everyone?" Darius gasped.

"They're not dead," Michael reassured him. "I saw them being taken away, probably to the dungeon."

Darius slammed his fist into a building. The bricks shattered loose with a crunch. "Why would someone do this?" he yelled, attracting the attention of everyone around him. An Imperial soldier at the other end of the street turned his head toward them and began shoving through the crowd.

"Darius," Michael hissed, yanking his brother's cloak back up over his hair. "Run!"

He didn't need to be told twice. The brothers took off down the street, shouting and waving to startle people out of the way, diving around corners and zigzagging through alleys, trying more to lose the soldier than to actually get anywhere. Their noise attracted more attention, which in turn attracted more soldiers. Arrows began to fly; one of them bounced off the back of Darius's head, missing a pressure point in his neck by inches. "We have to hide!" he screamed, putting on a burst of speed. Michael roared and slammed his ringed fingers into a building, effectively blocking the alley with a good amount of debris.

Michael was falling behind though. "Where?" he yelled back.

"Orchards!" Darius replied and pointed to the grove of trees a quarter mile down the road.

"Why there?" Michael panted.

"Trees!" Then Darius was out of breath. He couldn't manage more than the one word, but Michael understood. Trees were easy to climb, easy to hide behind, easy to use as shields. They raced for the orchards, Imperial soldiers hot on their heels. A volley of arrows slammed into Darius's back. He reached around, still running, to feel for blood, but his impossible luck held out and the arrows missed his vulnerable points.

They reached the edge of the orchard. "I want to try something,"

Michael said, slowing to a stop.

Darius dove into the forest gasping and pulled himself up into a tree. "What are you doing?" he hissed. Michael had knelt to the ground and pressed his palms against the dirt.

"I just want to try."

Darius realized what was going to happen only a second before it occured. "Have you been practicing?" he shouted. "Michael! Can you control it?"

Michael grinned. "Nope."

The earth began to shake. Fissures erupted in the ground, beginning where Michael's hands touched the soil. Darius's tree shuddered. The soldiers came closer, almost there. They were going to catch them—

And then a cavern opened in the ground and swallowed the guards. Michael's earthquake ripped through the ground, sending trees toppling into the chasm, crushing the Imperial soldiers. Darius held on tightly to the branches of his tree, praying it wouldn't fall.

Then it was over. The earth closed up, and Michael, sweating profusely, dusted off his hands on his cloak. "There," he said casually, as if he hadn't just killed a handful of men.

"Damn, Michael," Darius said, sliding down from his tree. "That was insane."

"I don't think I could do it again," Michael admitted. "It took a lot out of me."

Darius pulled off his cloak and sighed. "We can't stay here."

"I know."

"Where can we go?"

Michael shrugged and suggested, "The sewers, maybe? Like Uncle Nicolai did?"

Darius snorted. Nicolai Taurlum, according to legend, had attempted to murder the previous emperor. He'd been successful, and when the

168

soldiers pursued him, he'd escaped into the sewers where he had supposedly been living ever since. "You know that's just a story, right?"

Michael shrugged. "What do you think happened to him?"

"They probably caught him and killed him. He's not living in the sewer. That's ridiculous."

Michael shook his head noting, "They never caught him. He's still at the top of the most wanted list."

"Then he died some other way. You can't survive in a sewer for twenty years. It's not possible. We're not hiding there," Darius said sitting on the trunk of one of the fallen trees. "We have to save everyone else. That assassin girl, she broke me out in less than a day."

Michael leaned against the trunk and closed his eyes. "So go find the assassin girl," he suggested wearily. "I'll wait here."

Darius snorted. "I don't need her. If she can do it, I can do it. I'll have them out by the end of the week and then we'll leave. We'll go outside the wall. Start a new life far away from here. Live in the savage's tribe or something."

There was no answer from Michael other than a faint snore. Darius sighed and pulled his cloak up over his head. "Fine," he muttered. "Sleep for now. But tomorrow we have a family to rescue."

Chapter Thirty
Imperial Palace
Carlin

Saewulf pushed open the large door with his mind and stepped back to allow the emperor to enter first. "I swear you do that just to show off," Carlin muttered, bringing up the rear.

Saewulf smiled serenely. "If you could do what I do, you'd show off, too."

Carlin shrugged and put his feet up on the large war room table. "Yeah," he admitted. "Probably."

The emperor stood at the head of the table and contorted his face into a grin. It made Carlin wince. "Tonight was a success," he announced to his panel of soldiers. "There were a few holdouts, a few—mishaps—but on the whole, I am very pleased."

Every eye in the room flickered to Carlin's bandaged hand. He scowled and hid it under the table. Saewulf nudged him. "Did you ever find out who shot you?" he asked.

Carlin repressed a growl. "No, and I don't intend to search. It was just an accident."

Saewulf smiled slowly. "Of course. An accident."

Carlin clenched his teeth. "Are you suggesting it was not an accident?"

The servant shrugged. "I don't presume to know anything about your army."

"What if it wasn't an accident?" someone asked. Carlin whipped his head around. His eyes widened as they found the man who had spoken.

"Virgil? I ... what do you mean?"

Virgil stood. "Every man in this army took an oath to protect the emperor," he said. "But none of them took an oath against the families. The Celerius did good things for Altryon. One of them formerly led this army." He paused. "Some of the soldiers have loyalties to the families. Maybe one of them wanted to protect the girl you were trying to kill."

Carlin looked down at his bandaged hand. "You think we have a traitor?"

"I do. And I hope you will let me uncover him."

Carlin looked thoughtful. "Find this traitor," he told Virgil. "Interrogate every man who was there that night. And if none of them seem suspicious," he added, glancing at Saewulf, "we will know it was only an accident."

Virgil took his seat, and the emperor regained control of the room. "Only a few people escaped us last night," he said. "They are all children. Three of the Vapros, two Taurlum, and the Celerius girl."

How do you like that, Saewulf, Carlin thought bitterly. *You let three of them get away. I only lost one.*

"We have the houses in our possession," the emperor continued. "We are seizing control of their assets. The plan is working. The families are no longer a threat to my rule." A light applause went up from the table. "And as for the ones we failed to capture, they will be hunted. They will be caught. They will kneel before me, and they will be killed."

The emperor addressed the men at his right. "Saewulf and General Carlin, you will track down the rest of the children. When the final one is executed, we will have not only eliminated the families, but their legacy as well. They will be scrubbed from the history books. No one shall ever speak their names again." The gruesome smile stretched across his face again. Chills flew down Carlin's spine. "Their time playing God is over."

Part Two

Six Months Later
The Fugitives

Chapter Thirty-One
Home of Quintus
Neil

Neil was about to push his hand through his hair and groan in frustration when he saw it—an open window. He smiled and nudged his brother. "Look who decided to enjoy the night air?" he whispered, nodding at the opening in the wall. The window was small and a little too high to climb through, but it was enough.

"Thank God something's open," Rhys said. "I've never tried to materialize through a solid wall before."

Neil poked his head around the corner and waved to catch his sister's attention. "We found a window!" he mouthed, and she abandoned her post and materialized next to her brothers. Smiling, Neil looked up at the window. "Six months since the raid on our house," he said fondly, "and see how much our army has grown!"

He turned to face his army, which still consisted of only Rhys and Jennifer. "You're hilarious," she said with an eye roll. "Has anyone ever told you you're hilarious? Because you are."

Neil bowed. "Okay," he said seriously. "Recap time. When we get inside, we take out the guards. Once they're taken care of, Jen and I will provide Quintus with a necessary show of force." Jennifer reached up to tighten her ponytail. "Rhys, you get to the front doors as fast as you can and let our friends inside. Don't let them out of your sight. They'll ransack the treasury and split the money with us." He looked at Rhys and repeated, "Make sure they split the money with us." Rhys nodded. "I'll find Quintus and have a conversation with him." Six months of spying, bribery, and trading rumors had revealed that the emperor's advisor had played a major role in the attack on the Vapros bunker. "Rhys, when you're finished in the treasury, meet back up with us by this open window. We won't leave until we're all together." He pulled up his hood. "Got it?"

Jennifer nodded. Rhys whispered, "Yes."

"Then let's go. Good luck, everyone." Neil materialized up to the roof and then, with a deep breath, jumped off. He kept his eyes fixed on the tiny open window. Just before he fell past it, he materialized through the opening and appeared inside with a light thud. Jennifer followed a second later. She hit the floor soundlessly, landing in a crouch like a cat. Rhys was not quite so graceful. His landing made the loudest noise of all, echoing down the hallway and startling a sleeping sentry to his feet.

"Who's there?" the watchman slurred groggily. Neil slid a knife into the nape of his neck and neatly severed the spinal cord. The sentry died without another sound. Jennifer reached out and gently closed the guard's eyes before turning his body into dust. She'd become less ruthless since the night her sister died. All her life, she'd been trained to look at her targets as just that—targets. *But now,* Neil thought, *now she couldn't help seeing them as human beings who could breathe and laugh and hurt, just like Victoria.* Gone was the merciless assassin whose eyes blazed when she killed. The only thing filling Jennifer's eyes nowadays were grief and revenge.

"Are there any more?" Rhys asked, looking up and down the hallway. It appeared to be deserted, and Neil told him so. "I'll go open the doors, then," he whispered and started down the hallway, materializing every few steps. Neil watched him go.

"Quintus's door," Jennifer reminded him. He turned. She pointed at an extravagant double door made of marble. He reached for the handle. Jennifer opened her mouth and then quickly closed it.

"What's wrong?" Neil asked.

She sighed. "Nothing," she said. "I'm just wondering how many guards are on the other side."

"Probably none," Neil said. "He had a sentry. He has no reason to expect an attack, except for the obvious reason."

"Right." Jennifer still looked troubled, but she pushed past Neil to throw open the doors.

As Neil predicted, there were no guards in Quintus's bedchamber. The emperor's advisor sat up when the doors opened, then stumbled out of bed in his nightgown and tried to flee. "Quintus!" Neil cried jubilantly, "It's been too long!"

"Guards!" he shrieked as he frantically searched for an exit.

Jennifer was across the room in an instant. Quintus desperately flailed out at her, but she dodged his attack and clasped her hand around his throat. He started to struggle but instantly stopped when he felt the intense heat coming. "Your guards can't hear you," she cooed as he fell to his knees. Her grip remained strong. A shadow of the old bloodthirstiness crept into her eyes.

"What do you want?" Quintus sputtered as he tried to avoid being burned alive. "I don't have any way to save your family."

Neil walked to Quintus's bedside table and selected a bottle of wine from his vast array of bottles. "You know," Neil said, "the night right before my family was imprisoned, we were spreading rumors about you, Quintus. We told everyone you were an alcoholic. I thought it was just a rumor, but look at this. You have an entire cellar right next to your bed." Neil's ease was all an act, but it was necessary. Interrogation relied on a show of power.

Quintus growled and attempted to shift his position, but Jennifer held him in an iron grip. "Letting your brother make all the speeches?" he spat.

She smiled and her hands grew a little hotter. "I don't mind. I like my current job well enough."

Quintus glared at Neil and spoke as slowly as he could. "Why are you here Vapros? To kill me? For what? All I am is an employee of the emperor. I had nothing to do with the capture of your family."

Neil shook his head and dropped the wine bottle. It shattered as it hit the floor. Wine splashed onto one of Quintus's extravagant rugs. Quintus winced. "You don't give yourself enough credit, my friend," Neil said as he took a step closer to him. "In recent months, I've learned a lot about you. Mostly because a lot of fingers seemed to be pointing clearly at you when we asked who planned the attacks."

"Why don't you get your sister off me so we can converse like gentlemen?" Quintus groaned as a portion of his neck became visibly discolored.

Jennifer glanced at Neil who nodded. She dropped Quintus, who fell to the ground, panting. "Fine, let's talk," Neil said, his theatrical voice fading away and turning to one of anger. "I want answers, and you're going to give them to me. Otherwise, Jennifer will melt your throat and you'll choke on the flesh."

Quintus patted his ginger curls into his usual hairstyle. "What do you want to know?" he asked, clearly attempting to maintain a bit of dignity.

"I know one thing for sure: the emperor didn't imprison us because we're a threat to the people. He did it for some sort of personal gain. That's why he took over our businesses and our money."

"Well …." Quintus's eyes narrowed as he spoke and a bead of sweat dripped down his face. "As you probably know, based on our pasts, I'm not exactly pro-family. Neither is the emperor. He's wanted you out from the moment he took the throne. But who is he to change two centuries of tradition? He had to let you live. He had no choice.

"But then he found that new servant, Saewulf, and the two of them started speaking about the issue behind closed doors. It was like he started to actually consider wiping out the families. He made plans, discussed tactics . . . I, of course, was against all of it."

"The truth, Quintus," Neil snarled as he pulled his knife from its sheath.

Quintus sighed. "I wasn't against it, but I knew it would be difficult. You all owned so many businesses, and Anthony Celerius was leading the military. You had too much power. People actually *liked* you, despite your childish fighting. We needed a way around all that. The general was easy to dispose of, but the business part was a trickier challenge. We couldn't just overtake businesses without knowledge of how they worked. It would cause an economic disaster."

Jennifer's eyes were narrowed. "So you decided to study up on us."

Quintus gulped. "We made plans to steal documents, study how your assets operated. That was my contribution. It was supposed to be a gradual takeover. Then the Captain of the Guard was killed and the emperor snapped. He felt the manslaughter was an act of defiance. He wanted to speed things up."

"So you put your little plan into action?" Neil asked.

"We had already planned to get rid of the general. Now we had a reason to go after the families. We had a reason that the people could understand, anyway. So Carlin killed the general and I collected the documents. Then Sir Celerius tried to kill the emperor, which was when we decided to act that night."

Neil stared at Quintus. "That was a lengthy explanation," he said warily, "but I'm not sure I believe all this. What did we ever do to the emperor?

Where did all this hatred come from?"

Quintus started to snicker, but stopped when nobody else joined in. "It's obvious, isn't it? He lost his father to a Taurlum. That's not something you ever forget."

For once, Neil allowed his icy expression to melt as he glanced at Jennifer. Having an enemy who wanted something from you was one thing, but having an enemy who despised your entire being was something completely different.

The doors burst open, and for a split second Neil thought another guard had discovered them. Then he recognized his brother. "I know this wasn't part of the plan," he said, "but we heard some yelling and thought we'd investigate." He ushered in about a dozen men from the hallway. Each man was armed to the teeth and bore helmets designed to look like snakeheads.

Neil smiled. Good old Rhys. "You're familiar with the Brotherhood of the Slums, aren't you, Quintus?" he said cheerfully. Quintus didn't move, but Neil continued anyway. "Yes, these men are crooks and mercenaries, but tonight we have hired them to help us carry off your valuables." He swept a bow. "Thank you for your donation to the cause."

Quintus opened and closed his mouth rapidly. "Please," he said finally. "Please don't kill me. I'm sorry. I'm sorry!"

Neil laughed. "Kill you? No. We aren't barbarians. We've spread rumors about you, robbed you, dealt with your guard out in the hallway, and told everyone you're unfaithful to your wife, but we would never kill you. By the way, I've noticed you're sleeping alone. I hope we can take credit for that. From experience, we know there are fates worse than death." He saw a shadow pass over Jennifer's face. "We just want your money to finance our revolution and to feed the people starving in the streets because of your laws. But don't feel too bad for the poor people, Quintus. Soon you'll be one of them."

Quintus stared at him in shock throughout the entire speech. "You're not going to kill me?" he stammered.

"No. Just leave you penniless."

"Don't, don't do this to me," Quintus said, but he looked relieved.

"You did this to yourself," Neil said carelessly. "Goodnight, Quintus." Jennifer let go of his arms and planted her foot in his back. She kicked, sending him sprawling across his bed. He didn't get up. The Vapros children, flanked by the Brotherhood, left Quintus's room and shut the door behind them.

"Did you get the treasure?" Neil asked Rhys as they marched back to their open window.

Rhys nodded. "It fills three carts."

"Did you run into any trouble?"

"Ten guards who are all asleep downstairs."

Neil smiled. "Good work."

"What now?" Jennifer had caught up to her brothers.

"We have to pay the Brotherhood, of course," Neil said. One of the Brothers grunted. "We promised them half. And then we have to take the rest of the money to the safe house."

"Anything else?" she asked.

"No." He looked at her. "Why? Did you have something in mind?"

The old glint was back in her eye. "I want to give this house a proper send-off."

"A send-off?"

She held up her hands. They were glowing red.

"We can't," Neil told her, sighing. "Quintus is still inside. Didn't you listen to a word of my speech. I promised not to kill him."

"We'll get him out," she said. "He's unconscious anyway. I kicked him pretty hard." She looked at her brother. "Let me do this, Neil, for our sister."

Neil pushed his hand through his hair. "Fine." He looked around and picked the smallest Brother. "Take Quintus outside," he instructed, "and leave him across the street." The man grunted and turned back toward the marble doors. "The rest of you, get out of here." When the hallway was deserted, he nodded to Jennifer. "Go."

Grinning, she seized a curtain in both hands. It ignited immediately. She materialized down the hall a few feet and grabbed a tapestry, and then ran her hand along a long velvet couch. She stooped to touch a carpet. The entire hallway was in flames. Neil materialized out through the window, expecting Jennifer to follow, but it was several minutes before she finally appeared. "Where were you?" he asked. Smoke billowed through the open window.

She grinned and pulled him a few yards down the street, away from the heat of the building. "I had to hit every floor." She tightened her ponytail. "Why, were you worried about me, little brother?" she teased.

Rhys came around to meet them before he had time to answer. Two Brothers trailed behind him, dragging carts full of rubies and gold. "Got the money," he said. "We divided it all up already. I can't believe you burned down his house."

Neil reached into one of the carts and pulled out two gold rings. He handed one to each of the Brothers. "For your trouble."

The Brothers exchanged glances and grinned within their helmets. "Pleasure doing business with you," one of them said, pocketing the ring.

Neil bowed. "The pleasure was all ours." The mercenaries disappeared into the night.

"Now what?" Rhys asked, eyes locked on the carts.

"You two go home," Neil answered. "I'm going out."

"Out?" Jennifer had already started dragging a cart down the road. "Out where?"

"Socializing," Neil said as he grabbed a sack of coins and walked away. "I'm going to make us some new friends."

Chapter Thirty-Two
The Powder Barrel Pub
Neil

Neil walked into the bar feeling nervous. He had never been in a bar outside the nightlife district, much less a bar in the middle of the markets. The markets weren't Taurlum territory anymore—the emperor had taken over everything in the aftermath of the attacks—but it still made him uneasy to walk through these streets. He always had a faint suspicion that Darius Taurlum was waiting around the corner, hammer raised, ready to pummel him. But Darius was long gone. All the Taurlum were.

Neil poked his head inside the bar and looked around for Imperial soldiers. In the old days, finding a soldier in a bar was lucky, but now it was a death sentence. He relaxed slightly when he didn't find any guards and sauntered up to the bartender. Reaching into his pocket, he pulled out a few gold coins he'd snagged from the carts at Quintus's house. "I'd like to buy a round," he said, dropping the money on the table.

The bartender raised his eyebrows. "For whom?" he inquired.

Neil smiled wistfully. He missed the days when bartenders knew exactly what he meant when he put money on their counters. "For everyone."

The bartender slid the money off the table and into a pocket of his apron. "Everyone!" he called out. "Next round is on this guy!"

His announcement was greeted by total silence, and then a disbelieving cheer from the patrons. This clearly wasn't the norm around here. Neil ducked away from the counter as the customers rushed toward it and went to sit in the back and eavesdrop. He didn't take a drink himself. He needed a clear head tonight.

A large bearded man was having a heated discussion with his table. Neil caught the word "emperor" and shifted a little closer.

"… Never been worse!" the bearded man was saying. "I haven't had a job in months. My children go to bed hungry. This nation used to be great! The emperor ruined us." He took a long swig of brandy and raged on. "If it weren't for that stranger, I wouldn't even have been able to afford a drink tonight."

A smaller man sighed. "This kind of thing used to be common," he reminisced. "Remember the old days? Go to the nightlife district, wait around for one of the you-know-who to come buy a round of beer and then head off to the opera?"

Another man nodded knowingly. "I was there the night Darius Taurlum stormed the Opera House. I wish I'd known it was the beginning of the end. I might've stayed a little longer." His companions laughed.

"The families were generous," the bearded man said. "They made sure we had jobs. They were generous to people. Not so much to each other, but to us, they were kind."

Neil decided this was the best opportunity for him to join the conversation. "The families were kind," he said, pulling up a chair. "I remember those times well. They cared. Not like the emperor. He's supposed to be a leader. He's supposed to protect us, but he doesn't give a damn. We should do something about it."

The bearded man looked skeptical and glanced around the bar for soldiers. "Since you bought me a drink, I'll humor you. What do you suggest we do?"

Neil smiled. This was his favorite part. "The emperor decimated the families and told you all it was for the good of the people. Do any of you feel better off? People are starving in the streets. The emperor has failed us, and a man who fails his people doesn't deserve to keep his position." People at other tables were listening now, leaning in as inconspicuously as they could. But it wasn't enough. Neil stood on his chair and began to speak loudly. "The emperor doesn't deserve to reign!" he cried. "He deserves to lose his head. I suggest revolution!"

The bar fell silent. "You can't say things like that," the smallest man whispered from the back of the bar.

"I do not fear him," Neil lied with a cocky smile. Nobody scared him like the emperor.

"Those are big words," the bearded man said finally. "Who's going to start this revolution? You?"

Neil rubbed his hand through his hair. "You still don't know who I am, do you?"

"Enlighten us," the bartender spoke up.

"Look at my hair," Neil said patiently. "Look at my eyes." He felt everyone in the bar studying him. People began to gasp. "Need another hint? I bought you a round. Who does that sound like, I wonder? This cannot be this hard for you."

The bearded man's eyes grew wide. "My God," he breathed. "We could be beheaded for talking with you, Raven."

He whispered the Vapros nickname as quietly as he could. Neil smiled and extended his arms. "Yet, here you are."

"Which one are you?" asked the small man from the back.

"Neil.

The bartender pointed to a sign tacked to his wall. "According to my wall, you're one of six remaining family members."

Neil nodded. "There are only three Vapros left," he confirmed. "We can't win this war alone. We need help."

A woman at a nearby table asked, "How did you escape?"

"We heard them coming and ran," Neil said. "We left behind our family. Some of them died that night. Some of them are in the emperor's dungeon. We will do anything to get the remaining ones back."

"So you don't care about us," the bearded man declared. "You just want your family back."

Neil shook his head. He'd been prepared for this. "I've spent the last six months on the streets. I have been hungry and scared and homeless. I have gone to sleep wondering if I will survive to see the sunrise. Nobody should live like that. I love my family," he emphasized, "and I want them to be free, but I want all of you to be able to eat first."

That seemed to do the trick. Neil could see the fire of inspiration in every pair of eyes in the pub. "I'm not saying I'm interested," said the bearded man, "but if I were willing to join you, how would I begin?"

"For now, it's all about waiting for the right time. Stockpile weapons. Spread the word. Lay low." He couldn't keep the grin off his face. He had them. "Just remember: we were beaten, but we have not been defeated. When you see us revolting in the streets, I hope you will join us. Goodnight gentlemen." He stepped down off his chair and the bar began to buzz with conversation. He was almost out the door when a voice stopped him.

"So, I've been searching for you for months and all I had to do was give up and go to a bar? You have truly impeccable timing, Neil."

Neil closed his eyes. Even after six long months of absence, that silvery voice was just as familiar as it had always been. And tonight, it sounded furious. He pivoted on his heel and faced Bianca. "It's been awhile," he said lamely. He was struck by how much older she looked. Her ivory hair was unchanged, but her eyes had an intensity he'd never seen before.

"We need to have a conversation," she said. Her eyes didn't leave his.

Neil sighed. "Yeah, I know."

He reached for a chair to pull up to her table, but she shook her head and stood. "Not here." She wouldn't stop looking at him. "Follow me."

He followed her out of the bar, pausing to throw a pouch of coins on the counter before he left. "Make sure everyone gets some food and another round." The bartender nodded and Neil followed Bianca out into the dark night. They walked in tense silence. "Are you going to kill me?" he asked, trying to sound like he was joking but genuinely afraid to hear the answer.

She stopped and looked at him for a few seconds. "I haven't decided yet," she admitted, but she didn't look quite so dangerous anymore and resumed her quick strides down the street. Exhaling with relief, Neil followed her through the dark streets.

Chapter Thirty-Three
The Slums
Robert

Robert kept his hands shoved in his pockets. He clenched his fingers hard around this week's wages, making sure the coins didn't hit each other and make noise. Walking through the slums with full pockets was dangerous, especially now that the Brotherhood was recruiting. With every passing day, Robert saw more snake helmets patrolling the streets and preying on the vulnerable. They'd tried to convince Robert to join several times, and each time he'd genuinely considered the offer, but in the end something always stopped him—Victoria. She was gone, she'd been gone for what felt like ages, but it was as if he could still hear her voice in his ear. She would have hated him for giving into the Brotherhood's corruption. She would have stopped loving him if she knew he spent his nights causing suffering and pain. And so, he declined every offer. Nothing was worth hurting his love, even though part of him knew she was beyond being hurt.

The smoky air began to clear as Robert walked farther away from the factories and neared the dingy shack that was his home. He stepped inside, dropping his coat and cap to the floor and shaking curly brown locks from his eyes. His hair sorely needed cutting, he knew, but he couldn't be bothered. Who was going to see it? He'd stopped sneaking into fancy parties. He had no one to impress.

He stumbled to his closet and yanked it open. Without even looking, his hand closed around his nicest outfit. With a quick jerk, he pulled it to the floor and sank down next to it. The long green coat and vest were gifts from Victoria, back when he had to pretend to be a noble if he wanted to see her. He'd give anything to have those days back.

Trembling a little, Robert slid his arms into the vest. He hadn't worn these clothes in so long. He'd forgotten how heavy the coat was on his shoulders. It felt foreign and nostalgic and part of him wanted to tear the outfit off and never look at it again, but he had to endure it. Tonight was important.

When he was dressed, he carefully avoided his shoulder, which had been healing for the last few months. He kneeled down in front of his only desk and pulled a large pouch from its hollow underside. He opened it and slipped the coins he'd earned this week inside. The bag was getting full. It might finally be enough.

He heard a knock on his door and hurriedly shoved the coins back into their hiding place. He approached the door cautiously and kicked the bottom three times; he was answered by four more kicks. Robert opened the door and ushered the three men inside. "I have the money," he said, pulling the bag back out of concealment. "What about you?" The other men produced similar pouches.

"Do you think it's enough?" one of them asked.

Robert examined the contents of each sack. "Yes," he said thoughtfully. "We have enough to hire a contractor. The Imperial workshop will be gone before we know it."

The men exhaled in relief. "Good job, Rob," one of them said, patting him on the back. "Time to celebrate. We brought drinks."

Robert was already gathering the pouches. "I'll join you after I find a middleman to send this out." He stuffed the coins into the inner pocket of his green coat and left, trying to ignore the inexplicable mixture of happiness and pain in his heart.

Chapter Thirty-Four
Bianca's Apartment
Neil

"This is where you live?" Neil asked as he followed Bianca into the small but nice-looking apartment. They were on the third floor of a building in the working district. He had no idea how she was able to afford something in this part of the city.

"We are not going to discuss my living arrangements," Bianca said shortly as she took a seat on her couch. Neil sat beside her. "We are here to talk about why I shouldn't kill you."

Neil sighed. "I'm sorry about everything that happened over these past months. I don't know what else to say."

Bianca nearly growled. "You don't know what to say?"

"That's not what I meant," he backtracked. "Listen, you have to have some sort of idea of why I—"

"Abandoned me?" she offered. "Left me an emotional wreck as I wondered whether or not you were alive?"

"I was just going to say left, but that works too," he said sheepishly and brushed the hair out of his eyes. It had gotten longer since they had been on the run. "The situation's been complicated."

"Complicated? The situation's been complicated? I have been worried sick, not knowing if you were dead or alive, and you say it was complicated? No note, no nothing? You just vanish without a trace and that's your answer?" Her voice was hard, but tears burned her eyes. She took a breath and stared down at her hands as she said softly, "You were my best friend, Neil. How could you just disappear like that?"

Neil swallowed and bit back emotion as he took a finger and used it to lift her chin. She looked at him with those sad, grey eyes. "Bianca, I watched my sister die and practically my entire family was arrested and thrown into a dungeon. You've been my best friend since I was six. I don't know what I would do if I lost you, too. Look, I only have three people left in this world that I care about: Rhys, Jennifer, and you. I can't lose you too. I didn't want to put you in danger. Anyone who knows or cares about me is in jeopardy. I couldn't risk leading them to you. I thought maybe when all of this was over I could come find you then."

"You couldn't have sent a note?"

"I couldn't risk it. You had to have seen the 'most wanted' signs and at least known I was alive and that they were hunting for me."

She nodded reluctantly. "I hoped and I heard rumors." She looked at Neil for a long moment and then squeezed his hand. "What about Victoria? You saw it happen?"

Neil winced. He still felt the pang of Victoria's death like a knife through his heart, but he tried to maintain his calm expression and said slowly, "The emperor's servant, Saewulf, killed her in cold blood."

Bianca's expression softened. "I'm sorry."

He shrugged as he replied, "Don't be. Sorry doesn't bring people back."

"Saewulf." Bianca turned the name over on her tongue. "He's the psychic everyone's talking about. The one who can torture you without touching you, the emperor's new favorite."

Neil nodded. "Sounds like him. He's the most terrifying human being I have ever met."

"How's Jennifer?" Bianca asked with trepidation.

Neil shook his head. "She doesn't think we notice, but we do. She's broken. She tries to hide it though." That was a very subtle way of saying it. Jennifer wasn't just broken. She spent nearly every night alone and sobbing.

Bianca sighed and closed her eyes. "What have you been doing for all these months?"

"As much as we can without going against the empire directly. We raid the homes of city council members who approved laws against the families. We stockpile weapons. We've been working with the Brotherhood of the Slums, but now we're starting our own group down in the poor district. We take out Imperial Guards. We go to bars at night and try to get people fired up. In the beginning, we eliminated arms dealers but the emperor has the Celerius's assets; he doesn't need them."

"What about the other families?"

Neil shrugged. "I don't know much about them, actually. I guess Lilly Celerius is living with some guards and a servant. She took out a military outpost, but that's all I've heard. The two Taurlum are still alive. Darius tried to free his family, but he failed. He's a complete drunkard. I don't know how he's been avoiding capture if he's spending all his time in a stupor."

Bianca opened her eyes widely and stared at him. "You're all idiots," she said bluntly. "You have the same goal as the other families, and you haven't thought to ask them to team up with you yet?"

"Of course I've thought of it," he said, mildly offended. "There's no way it would work. The scars of this feud are too deep. We'd kill each other before we ever got to the emperor."

Bianca shook her head. "You can't disregard them. You're the only ones who have any advantage over the emperor and his guards—your powers. You have to reach out to them, or the whole thing is hopeless."

"Part of me knows that," he said reluctantly, "but the other part of me is having trouble accepting that my enemies since birth could help me save my family."

Bianca countered, "The old legend says your families have to protect Altryon—together. This could be what the prophecy was talking about! You have a duty."

"Maybe," he mused quietly. Neil sighed and leaned forward, placing his hands on his knees. "I'm going to have to go. Rhys and Jennifer will be worried. Life as a fugitive keeps everyone a bit on edge. Are we good?"

She smiled a little and stood up. "Do I get a hug?" she asked. "I've missed your stupid face, Vapros."

He leaned in and hugged her tightly; he felt a sudden rush of emotion as they embraced. It had been far too long since he had experienced a sincere moment. He almost felt a sense of peace with his arms wrapped around Bianca's signature black leather armor. It, too, had changed slightly since he saw her last. It was trimmed with some kind of fur. "What's with the fur?" he asked.

As they separated, she glanced down as if she had forgotten. Her eyes lit up. "I've been planning a trip," she said excitedly.

Neil raised a questioning eyebrow. "What kind of trip?"

"The kind no one in all of Altryon believes is possible." She was grinning.

"Oh great, you're being cryptic," he said with an eye roll. "I see. I'll play along." He cleared his throat. "What kind of impossible trip, Bianca?"

She laughed, but still didn't give him a straight answer. "I met someone in the slums who said he was from somewhere very interesting."

"And where did he say he was from, exactly?"

"Oh, nowhere." She was drawing this out on purpose. "Just . . . beyond the wall."

Neil leaned in slightly and dropped the act. "Tell me more." In spite of the revolution he was trying to start, he'd never quite forgotten the plans he and Rhys had made to escape it all on that fateful night.

"Well," she said, shaking out her ivory hair, "he told me what's on the other side of the wall."

Neil could hardly contain himself. "Well? Desert and dead earth or . . .?"

She smiled. "Cities—villages—civilization."

Neil exhaled. "Impossible."

She nodded. "Neil, we have been so sheltered. Everything we think we know is a lie. Altryon is just one city. There are villages outside the barrier. Some of them are at war with us—most of them, actually. Our city is fighting a war within itself, but it's also fighting a war with several villages full of other people. The empire has been lying to all of the people about what really goes on out there. We think it's a wasteland but it's actually not."

Neil's world began to spin. He let himself sink into the couch. "Who was this guy? How do you know he's telling the truth?"

She remained standing and began to pace excitedly. "He found a way to sneak through the barrier. He has proof. He showed me documents that represented five different villages. Five! And all of them are outside the wall."

Neil raked his hand through his hair. "How the hell did you get this guy to tell you all of this?"

She paused. "Well," she admitted carefully, "I might have done some interrogating."

Neil sighed. "Why am I not surprised?"

"I really wanted to know!" she said defensively. "He let something slip about life outside the wall and I couldn't let him stop there."

"Do you realize how incredible this is?" Neil said. "I've been trying to start this revolution for months, but there's already a war against Altryon! And there are several villages involved! If we could join them, if we could make it past the barrier somehow …." He trailed off, lost in thought.

Bianca was getting excited. "We could bring the other families," she suggested, and Neil groaned. "I know you don't want to, but it's our best bet. You need them. They're strong. We already know at least one of them is stronger than you," she finished with a wink, and Neil knew she was remembering the time she'd saved him in the markets.

"I'll admit I've been thinking about it for awhile now. I just don't know if they'll go for it." Bianca batted her eyes and waited. She always knew exactly how to wear him down.

"They might not want to end the feud," he said stubbornly.

"Is that any excuse not to try?" she persisted. "Getting through the wall would really help if we had a Taurlum's strength."

Neil rubbed his eyes and tried to focus. "Okay, you could be right. And speaking of Darius Taurlum, I guess I'll track him down first. He's the one who needs the most help."

"When will you go?"

"There's no time like the present. I'll check a few places on my way home. How much time do we have before you were planning to leave?"

"Not a lot. I was planning to leave in less than a week."

He stared at her for a moment. "What if you had left and I didn't know where you had gone." His stomach dropped at the thought.

"Unlike you, I had planned to leave a few clues that only you would have understood."

Neil's eyes widened in surprise. "Really? Ok, you can tell me about that later," he said as he ran his fingers through his hair. "For now, give me details. Everything I need to know."

She quickly explained and he listened intently. When she finished he smiled. "I think we can make this work. But I've got to leave now. We don't exactly have a ton of time." He turned to leave in a hurry but stopped. He turned back to Bianca and wrapped her in a tight hug. "Thanks."

She smiled. "You're welcome. Now go try and end your stupid feud."

Chapter Thirty-Five
The Fallen God's Pub
Darius

Darius staggered into the bar and hobbled over to the bartender. "Hello," he slurred. "A glass of ale, please, Mr. ...." He trailed off as he tried to remember the bartender's name.

The bartender shook his head. "You've got about seven tabs you need to pay first."

Darius grinned at him. "Why don't we try for a record?"

The bartender sighed. "You set the record two tabs ago. You can't drink here. Either you pay or you get out."

Darius grumbled a string of creative curses under his breath and hobbled into the street. He looked around, remembering simpler times when he was allowed to show off his impeccable strength to all the civilians. It had been a long time since he had been able to cause unbelievable amounts of property damage. He hummed a few off-key bars of his favorite Taurlum drinking song. He wasn't worried about being recognized. He hadn't showered in about a month and his usual blonde locks had become matted and dark with filth. His usual upright posture had been abandoned for a heavy slouch and his body had thinned from months of eating sparsely.

A small commotion was happening at a nearby stand. Unwilling to be left out, Darius half-ran, half-stumbled across the street to join the crowd. A vendor was attacking someone who had tried to steal from him. Darius raised his fist in the air. "Let me take care of this!" he shouted.

The shopkeeper glared at Darius. "Go home, drunk," he said. "Let me handle my own problems."

Completely undeterred, Darius plucked the crook out of the vendor's grasp with one hand and hurled him into the wall. He beamed at the crowd, ready to be praised. He was greeted instead by uneasy silence as the people in the crowd started to back away from him. Through his intoxicated haze, Darius realized that using his power had probably not been his wisest option. *No*, he thought moodily as he turned to sulk off into an alley, *the wisest option would have been to sit quietly in the bar and drink another ale. Why didn't I do that? Because you can't pay for it.* He sank to the ground and rested his cheek against the pavement. Oh, how his head ached.

"Well, you've certainly handled your change in circumstance well," the voice came from the entrance to the alley.

Darius didn't lift his head. "If you're here to kill me, do it before I sober up."

"I knew it was bad," the voice said, coming closer, "but I had no idea you were this bad."

Darius rolled over until his face was pressed completely against the ground. "Do I know you?" he growled, voice muffled by the street.

"Is that comfortable?" the voice asked sympathetically.

"No," Darius replied.

"Well, I'm not surprised that you don't remember me." Darius wondered idly if he were already dead and this voice his conscience. "After all, the last time I saw you, you were kicking me through your window."

Darius picked his head up and finally met the eyes of the man standing over him. It slowly dawned on him that he was looking at another fugitive. A Vapros, he knew, but he couldn't think of the name. "What do you want, boy?"

The Vapros gave him a smile that was barely more than a grimace. "Neil," he said. "I'm Neil. And I need your help."

Darius moaned. "I don't help people, and especially not a Vapros."

"There's a revolution coming, Darius, and I want to know if you'll be a part of it. Someone has got to save your family."

Darius sat up angrily. "Listen," he growled, swaying a little, "my family can't be saved. I can't do it. I tried already. I'm the only hope for the Taurlum name now. I have to have as many children as I can. All the girls will be my wives!" He began to laugh. "And then I can have my own, new family. And drink until my steel heart stops beating!"

Neil sat on the ground next to him. "You're legacy phasing?"

"Call it what you want."

"That's unfortunate," he said. "My father went through a legacy phase once. He just wanted to protect his family line. He needed more kids, and it didn't matter where they came from. Your family and mine, they aren't so different."

Darius pulled a flask from the inner pocket of his cloak and took a large gulp. "You're talking to a wall, Vapros. I'm done. So is Michael."

Neil shrugged. "We could always use your help, and so could your family."

Darius growled, "Don't try to guilt me into this, you little bastard!"

Neil shook his head. "I'm not. But you have to make a decision soon. You can drink yourself to death, or you can help save your family and right the wrongs that have been done. The feud ends here, Darius. We can end it."

"My God," Darius said as he took another sip. "What the hell are you talking about? You sound like a preacher."

"I am preaching," Neil said confidently.

"Listen, kid," Darius mumbled, fumbling with his flask. It slipped between his clumsy fingers and hit the ground, but didn't break. "One day, you're gonna give up hope just like I have. And when you do, I invite you to grab a drink with me. Maybe I'll let you buy me a round." He looked excited by the prospect. "But until then, get out of my face with your damn hope. It's making me feel sorry for you. I don't give a damn about the feud. I was born hating your kind, but now I don't care."

Neil stood up and looked down at Darius's pitiful, hunched form. "In three nights," he said, "we will be at the First Church of Enlightenment deciding on a plan of action." He had decided on the meeting place based on their encounter with the preacher so many months ago. The Man with the Golden Light was the one who gave them the powers that started the feud; it was fitting that his shrine was the place for the feud to end. "I think we are going to find a way beyond the wall. You can either be a part of that or not. But we'd love to have you. At least think about it. We don't need to interact ever again after we get through. We could go our separate ways forever."

Darius scoffed and stowed his flask in his pocket. "Night, kid," he said and rolled over.

Neil sighed. "Goodbye, Darius."

Darius waited for Neil to exit the alley before pulling out his flask again. It was inscribed with his family crest's motto, "Iron Flesh and Iron Will." He stared at it wistfully, remembering when it had been the source of his greatest pride instead of his greatest failure. He remembered what it felt like to be so sure that he would be with his family again. He felt sorry for Neil. The Vapros boy had been right about one thing: the two of them, in spite of being from different families, weren't so different at all. Nobody stayed hopeful forever. Darius was sure Neil would soon give up and find a place in the gutter next to him.

Chapter Thirty-Six
The Slums
Bianca

Bianca stuck to the shadows and kept a firm grip on her knife. Her head was still spinning from her conversation with Neil. If they were actually going to follow her plan, she needed to raise as much money as possible. It was dangerous to walk through the slums alone, and she avoided it whenever she could, but tonight she had no choice. Every so often, she passed someone else walking alone and she held her knife a little more tightly and avoided eye contact. The faster she could get this over with the better.

Through the dimness, she barely made out someone coming toward her. She fixed her gaze on the ground, but from the corner of her eye she could see he wore a helmet shaped like a snake. She cursed under her breath and threw herself down a new alley, praying he hadn't seen her. The last thing she needed tonight was a confrontation with the Brotherhood of the Slums.

She saw him start down the alley after her and cursed a little louder.

"Sweetheart," he said, as she began to run, "where are you going in such a hurry?" Two more men in snake helmets were lounging at the other end of the alley. Bianca skidded to a halt.

"How are you tonight?" one of the new ones asked, getting to his feet.

"I'm fine," Bianca said. "And I'm in a hurry."

"Where are you off to?" he inquired. Bianca attempted to push past him, but he grabbed her arm and held her back.

Bianca's sigh seemed tired. "Please move," she said quietly.

The man who'd followed her down the alley finally caught up. "It speaks," he said, grinning. "And it has a beautiful voice." He unsheathed a dagger. "Why are you in such a rush?" he purred. "Carrying some money, maybe?"

Bianca wrenched free from the one holding her and brandished her own knife. "Do you really think I'm idiotic enough to waltz around the slums after dark carrying *money?*"

The three men exchanged confused glances. They were used to people screaming in terror at the mere sight of their helmets; this girl was unlike anyone they'd threatened before. "You must have something," one of them said finally. "Give us what you've got or you're in for an unpleasant evening."

Bianca reached for her purse. "Okay," she said, "you got me. Here it is. Just let me go." She held her money out to them. The first man reached for it, but just before he touched it she whipped her throwing knife into his chest. He stumbled and fell forward onto the grimy ground. Before the other two could react, Bianca was upon them. She drove her foot into one man's throat and kicked his legs out from under him, then grabbed the other man by his lapels and slammed him against a wall. She pulled another knife from her belt and held it against his throat. "Be very still," she hissed, "and I won't kill you." She heard the other man trying to sneak up behind her, and she lashed out with her foot and kicked him hard in the ribs.

"What do you want?" the man against the wall panted. She dug the knife a little deeper and he whimpered.

"I want to be able to walk through the streets without being assaulted," she said calmly. "Is that too much to ask?" The man looked at a loss for words. "Tell the rest of the Brotherhood to leave me alone," she ordered, letting go of him and stowing her knife.

"I …."

She brought her foot hard into his groin. As he fell, she brought it across his head, which quickly rendered him unconscious. "Thank you," she said, walking calmly back down the alley. She paused to yank her knife out of the chest of the first man. He screamed in pain. "Oh, calm down," she muttered. "I didn't hit any organs. You'll live."

Bianca passed four factories before she arrived at her destination. A large, shadowy figure in a huge, black coat stood on the corner waiting for her. "Anything?" she asked him.

He shook his head. "Not a lot of freelance work tonight. Maybe you should try out a factory job."

She shook her head. "You must have something."

"I have plenty of assassin jobs," he offered.

She shook her head again. "I don't kill people."

He sighed. "I know." He searched through the pockets of his coat. "What about this? The money is too good for it not to be dangerous. You'd have to be careful."

She took the crumpled piece of paper and scanned it. "This isn't what I usually do," she insisted. "I cause riots. I hunt down gang members. Doesn't anyone need that kind of work?"

He shook his head. "Not tonight, Bianca. I told you. It's an assassination or this. Don't act so high and mighty; I've heard you're no stranger to arson."

She looked at the paper for a minute. "Do you have any more details than this?"

"Our client wants this workshop gone. Burn it, demolish it, he doesn't care how."

"And he didn't say why?"

"You can guess why."

She handed the paper back and started to walk away into the night. "So are you in?" the man called after her.

She didn't stop. "The place will be gone by morning."

Chapter Thirty-Seven
Celerius Hideout
Lilly

Jonathan stumbled up the stairs with a box twice as large as he was. "Did we have to settle on the top floor of a building, Miss?" he asked from behind the box.

Lilly stood at the top of the staircase, examining the cargo her small army had accumulated. "This is discreet and out of the way. Don't complain. Just be happy we have a place at all."

"Yes, Miss," he said, finally reaching the top step and dropping the crate with a sigh of relief. "It's just . . . I fear each one of these steps is half as tall as I am. I just wish we didn't have to buy everything and move it in when it's the middle of the night."

She smiled for the first time in days. "You'll get used to it."

He sat on the crate and arched his back, trying to stretch out his aching muscles. "Are we still rich?" he asked hopefully.

Lilly gave him a distracted nod. She was inspecting cargo. "We're armed, too," she murmured a minute later. "We've been lucky." She turned to face her tiny army of Celerius guards. There were five of them left; they proudly wore their armor even though they were caked with mud to hide their original blue and gold colors. They all looked as exhausted as Lilly felt. Sleep had been scarce over the last six months. But things were finally turning around for the fugitives. With a heavy amount of bribery, Lilly had procured the attic above a bakery. It wasn't very big, but it had enough room for all of them to sleep comfortably on the floor. The owners of the place turned a blind eye to the fugitives' comings and goings.

"So," Lilly said to her guards, "here we are. We have a place to live, and we still have enough money from the treasury to afford weapons. I think the next step is obvious: recruiting. We have to make our army bigger, and I say we start in the slums."

The guards looked uneasy. "With all due respect, Miss," one of them said, "the slums and the Celerius aren't on good terms."

"They're poor," Lilly said. "We're rich. We can offer them money to help us. I don't see the problem."

The guard answered, "That is the problem. They won't be sympathetic to our cause. Your family turned a blind eye to their suffering. They'll be glad to return the favor."

"Anyone can be bribed," Lilly insisted, but the guards still looked troubled, so Lilly refined her plan. "The military, then. We'll see if anyone abandoned the army when the emperor attacked us. There could be allies there, right?"

The men nodded and Lilly smiled. "Fine," she said. "Tomorrow, we will start our recruitment. And in no time, the emperor will be dethroned!"

The men cheered half-heartedly and wandered toward the beds on the floor. Lilly went back to inspecting cargo. Weary as she was, she couldn't afford to sleep yet. There was planning to be done.

Bianca was good at blending in with the night, so it would be best to finish her mission before the sun was fully up. People noticed her more during the day. They stared at her ivory hair and whispered to each other about the girl dressed in armor. At night people didn't care so much about clothes. They were concerned with making it home or staying awake through their factory shifts. Nobody looked at her twice. Bianca stood in the middle of the street and stared up at the workshop she was supposed to bring down. It looked worn out and faded, and again she wondered why the client was offering so much money for this job.

She pulled a pin from her armor and jammed it into the lock on the front door. It clicked open easily. Bianca eased inside, closing the door gently.

"What the hell?" she heard a voice say behind her. She whirled around and found herself facing four Imperial guards. Three of them were holding playing cards, but one had thrown down his hand and groped beneath the table for a gun.

Bianca held up her hands defensively. "Don't shoot," she cautioned.

"You're trespassing," the guard with the gun said. "What are you doing here?"

One of her hands reached slowly for her knife. "Put the gun down," she warned. "I don't want to hurt you."

He pulled the trigger. Bianca saw his finger twitch and dove out of the way just in time. She sprang to her feet, took a running jump toward the guard, and jammed her knife between his ribs. "I told you not to shoot," she grumbled, kicking the two nearest guards across their faces as they tried to grab her. "You," she added, pointing her knife at the one unharmed man. "Don't move. Or you'll end up like them."

The guard tried to stand; Bianca leaped toward him and held her knife against his throat. "Don't move, please," she repeated, casually picking up one of the cards on the table and glancing at it. "I want some answers.

Why the hell are you here?"

"What do you mean?" the guard spat.

She set the card face down again. "This workshop makes guns, doesn't it?" she asked. He nodded. "It's tiny, though. It probably makes ten guns per day, if that. Why does the emperor have four men guarding a workshop that only makes ten guns per day?"

He didn't answer, and she pressed her knife a little harder against his skin. "Do you know who I am?" she growled in his ear.

He nodded. "Bianca Blackmore," he whispered. "You're the Taurlum killer."

She furrowed her brow. "I never killed any Taurlum. If you're talking about Darius, I just roughed him up a little. But I could have killed him. And I can kill you, too, if you don't give me some answers. What's so special about this place?"

He still didn't say anything, but his eyes flicked to a small trapdoor in the corner of the room. Bianca followed his gaze. "There's something through that hatch?" she asked. He didn't reply. "Stand up," she ordered, moving her knife so it was positioned between his shoulder blades. "You're going down there ahead of me. In case it's a trap."

He shot her a glare, but pulled open the hatch and started down a narrow staircase. Bianca followed closely. "How far down does this go?"

He looked miserable. "Real far," he said shortly. "I'd leave this alone if I were you, street girl."

"Not a chance," she said, prodding him with her knife.

They walked on in silence until they reached the bottom. Bianca looked around. The giant basement contained dozens of shiny factory machines. Looming in the distance was a pile of boxes. Peering through the dimness, Bianca made out dozens of unassembled rifle parts filling each box. "Those machines," she whispered. Her voice echoed. "They put the guns together, don't they? They're faster than the people who make them by hand." She glared into her hostage's eyes.

The guard didn't say anything.

She shook him roughly. "How many more places are there that do this?"

"None," he said. "So far."

Bianca clenched her jaw. "You have two choices. You can go up the stairs, out the door, and into the street. You can walk away from this place and never look back." He looked skeptical. "Or," Bianca said, flashing her knife, "I can kill you now."

The guard ran for the stairs and launched himself up to the ground floor with heavy footfalls. Above her head, Bianca heard the door creak open and slam shut. She knew he might tell the emperor who had destroyed the factory but she didn't care. This was one of her last nights in the city and soon they would know she was an enemy of the empire anyway. She overturned a large barrel of gunpowder and made a pile on the floor, then she pulled out some flint and dragged her knife across it. The sparks ignited the gunpowder and a trail of fire sprung up and enveloped the basement.

Bianca bolted up the stairs and out of the workshop as fast as she could. The ground shook as barrels of gunpowder exploded. In the distance, she could barely make out her former hostage running for his life. She walked calmly away from the factory, confident that nobody would look twice at her. She turned down an alley and started for the slums. Her job was done. It was time to collect.

Chapter Thirty-Eight
Vapros Hideout
Neil

Neil awoke with an idea. He groaned as he sat up and looked around for his brother. His new room consisted of a mat on the floor with a dusty pillow. Rhys was across the room, sleeping soundly on another mat. Their "house" consisted of an empty abandoned building they found in the working district. So far, it had sufficed as a suitable base. Neil walked over and lightly nudged Rhys with his foot. "Hey," he said. "Get up. I think I have a way to find Lilly Celerius."

Rhys didn't open his eyes or react to the nudge, but replied immediately, his voice clear of any hoarseness that usually accompanied waking up. "How do you know she'll come with us?"

Neil stared at his brother's motionless form. "Were you even sleeping?" he asked incredulously.

"Yes, until you kicked me." Rhys finally rolled over and looked up at his brother. "How do you know Lilly will come with us? Darius didn't want to. And I'm not even sure we should be looking at them for allies."

Neil turned to the closet and fished out his cloak. "Darius will come around if he sees other people joining us. After Lilly, we can look for his brother, Michael."

Rhys closed his eyes. "Michael's still in the markets," he said. "Someone told me he's all over the girls there. More than usual, he's trying to breed more Taurlum."

Neil raised an eyebrow. "How is he running around the markets and not being captured? That doesn't make any sense. Who told you that?"

"I don't remember," he said. "My brain needs a few moments to operate correctly. I was sleeping a few seconds ago, remember?"

Neil smirked. "Keep that brain operating; it might be the only thing keeping us alive."

Rhys smiled and opened his eyes again. "So, Lilly Celerius …." He got up and stretched. His hair stood out at funny angles, and Neil bit back a grin. "You think you can find her?"

Neil began fastening his cloak. "Rumor has it Lilly escaped with some guards."

"And?"

"Lately, someone has been buying weapons and armor from our arms dealer friend in the working district. Do you remember what was sold out the last time we went to buy knives?"

"Rapiers?" Rhys said with a smile.

"Rapiers."

Rhys grabbed his cloak from the closet. "I'll get Jennifer up," he said. "It's a good theory, Neil, a really good theory." He reached beneath his pillow and pulled out a knife. "Last time we saw her, Miss Celerius wasn't a big Vapros fan," he said, stowing the knife in his pocket. "I hope she won't hold a grudge."

Neil shrugged and mused, "Tragedy has a way of erasing past relationships."

Rhys gave him a half-smile. "I think that's a truth we can all appreciate."

Chapter Thirty-Nine
Celerius Hideout
Lilly

"Jonathan," Lilly said for the third time. "Do not touch the grenades."

Jonathan pulled his hand away from the weapon. "But Miss," he said dreamily, eyeing the grenade with fascination, "if I could learn to use one, I could help your army."

Lilly gave him a glare, and he snapped out of his trance. "I'm not a soldier, of course, Miss," he said sadly, "so I'll stop touching the grenades." He gazed at the crate longingly, but stopped when Lilly cleared her throat at him.

"Was it just me," she asked. "Or was the arms dealer who sold us these unbelievably creepy."

"Well, Miss, I don't wish to be vulgar, but that man is referred to as the Pig."

Lilly laughed. Jonathan looked confused and slightly hurt. "Jonathan, I don't think referring to a man as a pig is considered vulgar by any standard."

Jonathan loosened his collar. "But don't you want to know how he got that name?"

Lilly laughed again. "I think I can infer, Jonathan. Thank you very much."

"Just be careful of him," he said. "I don't want you getting hurt."

"Jonathan, that is truly adorable. I'm a Celerius. I have nothing to fear from perverted merchants."

Jonathan shook his head. "I've just heard stories, Lilly." Her eyebrows shot up. He had never used her first name before. "Miss Celerius," he amended quickly, reddening as he realized his mistake.

"I'll be careful," she promised. He nodded. His gaze strayed to the grenades again. "You know," she said hurriedly, and he looked at her again, "you've gotten quite protective of me lately."

He gave her a sad smile. "You tend to become protective of someone when you realize that they're the only thing you have left, Miss."

"Lilly," she said clearing her throat. "You can call me Lilly if you want to, Jonathan."

VICTORY LIES WITHIN
THE ASHES

Chapter Forty
The Markets
Neil

The Pig smiled, revealing a mouthful of rotting, yellow teeth. "Gee," he said smugly, "I'm not sure if I've sold anything to family members. That would be illegal."

Neil rolled his eyes. "Now, we both know that's a lie. Don't play games with me. Have you seen her or not?"

The Pig shrugged. "I mean, maybe I saw her. I just can't seem to remember. Maybe some coin would get me thinking."

Neil dropped a pouch on his counter. The Pig snatched it up, squealing greedily. "Have you seen her?" Neil asked through gritted teeth.

"She picked up twenty boxes of weapons last month. She had a few guards and a comically small servant come pick them up. They were on foot. Had to make a couple trips. The little one could barely carry one crate." The Pig chortled. Neil waited for him to finish. "And between you and me, Mr. Vapros ...." The Pig looked around dramatically and leaned in to share his secret, "she was quite enticing. You Vapros are gonna kill her, aren't you?"

Neil wrinkled his nose as the Pig's breath hit him. "What?"

"You're going to hunt her down and kill her, yeah?"

"No," Neil said thoughtfully. "Something else is going on. Hopefully she won't kill us. Thank you." He turned on his heel and marched across the street to where his siblings were waiting. "It was her," he informed them excitedly. "She sent her guards to get the weapons. And they came on foot. They're close."

Rhys furrowed his brow, thinking. "There was a room for rent above one of the bakeries around the corner," he said. "Remember? We checked it out before we found our house."

A thrill coursed through Neil's veins. "So we'll go ask the owners if it's still for rent," Neil said, his excitement building. "And if they say no, then we've got her!"

Jennifer sighed and examined her fingernails. "Or we've got some other guy who's renting the space and has nothing to do with the families."

Neil shrugged. "It's worth a try," he insisted and led the way down the road to the pub.

⚜

The Pig watched them go, grinning. "Idiots," he muttered, scratching at his giant belly. He ducked into the back room where a few of his shop workers were lying around. One of them belched. The Pig didn't bother to look disgusted. "The Celerius girl is hiding out near here," he said, with a belch of his own. "Those kids are going to find her. Follow 'em. Once the Vapros leave, bring her back here. If she's still alive, that is."

The men looked confused. One spoke. "You want us to kidnap a Celerius girl?"

The Pig nodded. "She's tiny. She won't be so hard. Knock her out while she's sleeping." He ran a hand over his bald scalp. "Just think," he said gleefully, "by the end of the night, I'll have a Celerius girl tied up in the back of my shop!"

The bell over the front door rang, signaling that a customer had arrived. The Pig glared at his men. "Go!" he mouthed, and they disappeared out the back door. He rushed around to the counter and put on a cheery grin. "Welcome!" he said.

The customer was a tall man in a mask. As he approached the counter, the Pig craned his neck back to meet his eyes. "Nice mask, guy," the Pig said. "What's that made of, steel?"

The man behind the mask stared deeply into the Pig's eyes. He had a bow over his shoulder. The Pig couldn't help but wonder what the bow was made of, and whether the man could be convinced to sell it. "I heard the conversation with your men," he said softly.

The Pig raised his eyebrows and looked at the door. "No way you could have heard that through the wall," he said stupidly. "No way you could have seen us in the back room."

The man shrugged and pulled the bow off his shoulder. "Nevertheless," he said quietly, fitting an arrow against the string.

The Pig looked around anxiously. "What the hell are you doing, guy?"

"Pig," he said. "You have posed as a danger to the one I am sworn to protect. For that, I am afraid you must die. I hope you find peace in the end."

Before the Pig could react, an arrow fired straight through his eye and he fell to the ground like a mason's sack of bricks. The masked man slung the bow back over his shoulder and exited the shop, leaving the arms dealer to rot. He mentally counted his arrows and then hurried off in pursuit of the Pig's men.

Lilly heard a noise on the stairs and immediately sprang into action. She grabbed a rapier from the nearest crate and pointed it at the door, ready to slice the intruder in half. The door creaked open and she came face to face with three Vapros. It wasn't exactly what she'd expected, but she swung her sword viciously at Neil's neck for good measure. "What are you doing here?" she growled as she repositioned it right beneath his chin.

Neil raised his hands to show that he was unarmed. Behind him, his sister and brother mimicked his surrender pose. "Listen," he said, "we heard you're starting a revolution. We'd like to invite you to the one already in progress."

"You've started one?" she asked, not lowering her sword.

"Yeah," Rhys piped up. "And we are gathering up all the others who want the emperor to die."

Lilly didn't take her eyes off Neil. "I'm in it to kill Carlin, mostly," she said.

Neil smiled the best he could with a sword at his neck. "That can be arranged, too."

Lilly lowered her sword and ushered Neil and his family into her makeshift house. She closed the door tightly behind them. "How did you find me?" she asked. "I was hoping to stay hidden."

"The Pig told us you bought weapons from his store," Jennifer said, examining her fingernails coolly. "We narrowed it down from there."

Lilly shuddered at the mention of the Pig. "How large is your rebellion?"

Neil shrugged. "We have no way of knowing actually. We are joining five villages outside the barrier that have been at war with the empire for years. We think that with their help we can win this thing."

She tried to keep her confusion concealed. "There are villages outside Altryon?" She hated that they knew more than she did.

"I know this is a lot to wrap your head around," Rhys said gently, "but if you're really considering the offer, come to the First Church of Enlightenment in two days. Once the sun sets, we will be there.

Hopefully so will the Taurlum."

"You're trying to unite the families?" Lilly shook her head and laughed. "It won't work."

"We think it could," Neil argued.

A small man in a blue coat came rushing out from around the corner. "Intruders!" he exclaimed, raising his arm. His hand clenched a small round object. "Shall I throw, Miss?"

Lilly looked down and gasped. "Jonathan. Put the grenade down." The servant, looking sheepish, gently replaced the weapon in a crate by the door. "They aren't intruders," she said. "I can't believe I'm saying this, but . . . they could be allies—maybe."

"Allies?" Rhys said hopefully. "Does that mean you're in?"

Lilly shook her head. "I don't know yet. I . . . we have to discuss it first. I'm not sure you can be trusted. You Vapros are known for tricking people in such a fashion."

Neil looked at his siblings. "We hope to see you at the church. I know we've fought before, but I think it's time to bury the hatchet. We don't really have another option. We need each other, if we're going to make it through this. Once we get outside this city, you can go wherever you want. We can all go our separate ways. But before any of that, we need to make it past the barrier."

She turned her sword over in her hands. "I'll keep that in mind," she said finally.

Jennifer reached around to open the door, and the Vapros materialized down the stairs and away. Lilly sighed and closed the door. "Get the guards in here," she said to Jonathan. "We need to talk."

Chapter Forty-One
The Oxblood Inn
Darius

Darius awoke in his rickety motel room bed feeling like he'd ingested acid. He stumbled to the window and groped for the latch before he realized it was already open. He pushed his head outside and took a gulp of air. The night wind against his skin was cool and refreshing. In only a few seconds, he felt alert enough to realize two things: first, that the window had been shut when he'd collapsed into bed, and secondly, there was someone else in the room with him. He whirled around just in time to see a long spike soar toward him. He ducked and the weapon embedded itself in the window frame.

Heart pounding, Darius stood up and yanked the spike out of the wall. It was attached to a long chain. He hadn't seen a weapon like this in months. The memories came rushing back instantly, and he closed his fist around the chain and turned away from the window. "It's been awhile," he said to the darkness.

A figure stepped out from the shadows and moved to stand in a pool of moonlight pouring in from the window. "It's been awhile since anyone wanted you dead," Anastasia said. She held out her hand. "I'd like my rope dart back, please."

He set her weapon down on the windowsill and stood in front of it. "Plenty of people want me dead."

She smiled confidently, her slanted eyes narrowing ever so slightly. "You won't trick me into revealing my employer," she said.

He took a step toward her. She held her ground. "I don't have to," he said. "I already know who it is. It's obvious."

She raised her eyebrows. "Is it?"

"You work for the emperor," he said, taking another step toward her. Anastasia smiled slightly, as if she knew the punch line to a joke he hadn't heard before.

"Not quite," she said, and before he could stop her, she dodged around him and lunged for the windowsill, catching the spike in her hands. He tried to grab her, but she slipped through his fingers. He lost his footing and staggered into the wall. She laughed. "You aren't so quick anymore, are you?" He swung his massive fist at her, but she dodged it effortlessly. He was breathing heavily. "What have you been doing?" she asked. Her tone almost sounded worried. "You're clumsier than last time—much clumsier."

"I'm a little out of practice," he panted.

She looked at him patronizingly. "Need a minute to catch your breath?"

He grabbed the bed and hurled it at her. She jumped back with a cry, but the bedpost struck her feet and sent her spiraling to the ground. Darius grinned. "No, thank you."

He approached and bent over to grab her, but she kicked him in the side of the neck. Her foot connected with a pressure point; Darius gasped and reeled backward.

"You're not as slow as I thought," Anastasia murmured, working her way to her feet.

Darius stood by the window, hand pressed against his neck. He prayed he wasn't bleeding. "I guess I'm not so out of practice after all," he said, hesitantly removing his hand and examining it in the moonlight. It was mercifully clean of blood.

Anastasia hurled her spike at him with a grunt, but this time he was ready. He caught it in midair and pulled hard. She went skidding across the floor, still gripping the chain. "I'm not going to die today, Taurlum," she hissed, jumping to her feet and throwing herself out the window. He saw her land on her feet like a cat on the street below.

In a rage, he threw the spike down after her. It landed almost two yards to the left of the target. Anastasia grinned up at him. "Until we meet again," she yelled, bending down to retrieve the rope spike and dashing down the street.

Darius shook his head in disbelief and turned to push his bed back into place. When it had been reset, he sat and buried his head in his hands. "I need to find Michael," he groaned, collapsing back into sleeping position and cursing himself for letting the assassin escape.

Chapter Forty-Two
Imperial Palace
Carlin

Carlin brushed past the guards and pushed through the doors into the throne room. The emperor didn't acknowledge his presence. He was lounging in his throne, gazing off into the distance. Saewulf sat by his side. Carlin cleared his throat. The emperor didn't move. "You wanted to see me?" Carlin said finally.

The emperor sighed and slowly turned his head toward the general. "I'm disappointed, Carlin," he said as he intertwined his fingers. Carlin couldn't help but notice Saewulf's stony face break into a tiny smile. "I am so very disappointed."

"About what?" Carlin demanded. "I've kept the savages under our boot. Our army is doing just as well as ever." Saewulf let out a small chuckle. Carlin glared at the servant and let his hand drift to the hilt of his sword. "Do you have something to say to me?" Saewulf didn't flinch.

The emperor stood and held up a hand for silence. "Six months ago," he said softly as he took a step down onto Carlin's level, "I sent you to murder the Celerius family. One of them escaped. Is she still at large?"

Carlin's jaw tightened. "Yes."

"And these Vapros, are they still at large?"

Carlin pointed desperately at Saewulf. "They were *his* responsibility!"

"And the Taurlum?" the emperor asked calmly, but there was a storm in his eyes.

Out of the corner of his eye, Carlin saw Saewulf laughing again. "Still at large," he admitted, bowing his head.

"Still at large," the emperor repeated. "As the general of my army, I expected you to be able to handle this in a matter of days. Not months."

Carlin gritted his teeth. "They're hard to find," he tried to explain. "It's hard to search through the whole city when I have other duties."

The emperor narrowed his eyes. "Oh, they're hard to find? My apologies, General; your total incompetence is forgiven in that case. I didn't realize *they'd be hard to find.*" Saewulf chuckled. Carlin wanted to plunge his sword into the servant's eye.

"Since they're *so hard to find,*" the emperor was saying, "I'll give you a little hint. Darius Taurlum is hiding in plain sight, drinking his pathetic life away. You just can't seem to find the right gutter to pick him out of. And Michael Taurlum, he's in the markets, seducing every young woman he can find. Not exactly subtle, and not exactly hard to find."

A bead of sweat traveled down Carlin's forehead.

"Lilly Celerius is prancing around the city flanked by an entire squad of armed men. And the Vapros spend their time either burning down the houses of my associates or recruiting prospective combatants in public places. And you can't catch a single one of them? Did you never think to send someone to a bar and wait for the Vapros to just drop in?" The emperor sighed heavily and began to pace in front of his throne. "Did I put the wrong man in charge? Virgil could have done this by now. Saewulf could have done this by now. Anthony Celerius could have done this in *one night,* if his own flesh and blood weren't involved."

Carlin couldn't look the emperor in the eye. "Father, I—"

The emperor whirled to face him. "Don't you *dare* address me that way." The smile was gone from Saewulf's face and an eerie silence filled the room. The guards in the room nervously shifted back and forth, unsure of where to go or how close to get to Carlin.

Carlin tightened his grip on the hilt of his sword. "Why not?" he asked. "Afraid your servants will find out you have a bastard for a child?"

The emperor stood completely still for a few seconds. The guards posted at the door sensed it was time to intervene and they approached Carlin. "Settle down, sir," one of them muttered in his ear. Carlin shook him off.

"Never say anything like that again, boy," the emperor hissed, "or I will have your subordinates cut you down. I don't care who your father is."

A guard put his hand on Carlin's shoulder (whether to comfort or restrain him, Carlin didn't know), and whispered, "General, maybe you should leave."

Carlin punched the guard so hard it sent him unconscious to the floor. The other guard attempted to subdue him, but Carlin's sword was through his chest before he even drew a weapon. Saewulf started to stand, but the emperor raised a hand, and he sat back down. "Calm down, Carlin," he boomed. Carlin froze, panting. "You have another chance. But I want to see progress. Start with the Taurlum."

Carlin sheathed his sword and glared at Saewulf, who returned the look with a lazy, little smile. "Yes, sir," he said, straightening his coat. The guard he had punched stirred and tried to stand; Carlin brought his foot down hard against the man's face. A sickening crack filled the throne room. "Keep your psychic on hand," Carlin said coldly as he walked toward the door. "I might need him later."

The room was silent as the giant double doors closed behind the general. "Your son is a bloodthirsty maniac," Saewulf observed casually.

The emperor nodded as he retook his seat. "I know," he said with the ghost of a smile forming across his lips. "That's what will make him so effective in our war."

Chapter Forty-Three
Vapros Hideout
Neil

"**W**e're nearly out of food already," Neil said to Jennifer as he rummaged through their cabinets. "I wish Lilly would have offered us some food. But then again, she wasn't exactly a gracious host." Neil smiled at Jennifer, but the joke was lost on her.

Jennifer sighed. "Maybe Rhys will bring some back?"

Neil shook his head. "Now that we might have the Celerius on board, Rhys is out trying to verify the legitimacy of Bianca's claims. He isn't looting tonight."

"Oh," Jennifer stared vacantly. "Maybe Rhys will bring some back."

Neil stopped rummaging. "You already said that."

"I did? Oh, forget it then."

"It's fine," he said nervously, moving to sit next to her. She had pressed herself into a corner of their tiny kitchen and hunched over to rest her chin on her knees. She didn't acknowledge her brother. "Are you okay?"

"Yes."

"Are you sure?"

She closed her eyes. "Yes."

"Are you lying to me?"

She finally looked at him. "Of course I'm not okay. I don't understand why you're okay."

Neil sighed and pushed his fingers through his hair. "I take it one day at a time."

"She was your sister, too," Jennifer said bluntly. "And you and Rhys just keep acting like we didn't lose her." There were tears in her eyes. "Didn't you care about her?"

"Of course!" Neil felt his eyes widen as Jennifer's tears spilled over onto her cheeks. "Of course we did. But if we're ever going to avenge her, we can't waste time missing her."

It was the wrong thing to say. Jennifer let out a sob. "Waste time missing her?"

He looked alarmed. "No, that's not what I meant. It came out wrong."

He expected her to pull out a knife and stab him then and there, but all she said was, "I've lost a lot of people, Neil."

He waited, but she didn't say anything else. "I've lost a lot of people, too, Jen." He wasn't used to comforting his sister. "I lost Victoria with you. And we both lost Mom."

She shook her head. "You didn't know Mom. You don't have memories of her tucking you into bed and reading stories to you, and teaching you how to walk." She stopped, interrupted by a hiccup, then continued, "And you didn't lose Victoria the same way I did. When you have a twin, you're born together, you spend your lives together and you have a connection. You can tell each other anything. Even all your deep dark secrets." Her nose was running and she scrubbed at it furiously with her sleeve. "But I did. And now I'm going through everything alone."

Neil didn't know what to say. "You have me," he tried lamely. "You can tell me your darkest secrets, if you want to." He pulled her into an awkward, one-armed hug. "I know I can't replace either one of them for you. But I can try, if you'll let me."

Jennifer sniffled. "Have you ever betrayed anyone?" she asked quietly.

Neil hadn't, and he told her so.

"When I was young, maybe Rhys's age, I had this friend," she said, wiping her eyes and sitting up. "Edward. I met him at the Opera House. He came out of his box, and Victoria and I went to talk to him. This was back when Victoria was too shy to go get gossip on her own." She remembered this with a giggle. It had been so long since Neil had heard her giggle. "He was sweet," she continued. "And he always said exactly what I was thinking. Nobody's ever thought like me before. Not even Victoria, really." She gave a shuddery sigh. A fresh wave of tears started down her face. "So we talked to him for awhile, I don't remember about what, and then the opera ended and we had to leave. Edward said he'd walk us out. Victoria went ahead of me, so I could hang back and have time with him alone. She could tell we had a connection." Jennifer unwrapped her arms from around her legs. "He walked me all the way home. I don't think he meant to. We just couldn't stop laughing, you know? And when I was about to go inside, he kissed me."

Neil tried not to look surprised. Jennifer had never seemed to be the romantic type.

"We made plans to meet again. We found each other at the Opera House, in the markets, in restaurants. We used to write letters in secret code and leave them at an abandoned stand in the market." She smiled faintly. "I think I loved him."

Neil couldn't help it. "What happened to him?"

Her smile faded. "I started my assassin training. I was busy all the time. And he was busy, too. He was going to join the military. He didn't want to, but it was his duty. Nearly all the Celerius join the military."

Neil nearly jumped to his feet. "Your boyfriend was Edward Celerius?"

Jennifer swallowed. "I never told anyone but Victoria. I knew people wouldn't understand."

"Jennifer!" Neil shoved his hand through his hair. "You can't just date a Celerius! Don't you see how wrong it is?"

Jennifer's eyes were shining with tears again, and Neil almost regretted his words. "The families aren't even technically related anymore. It's been nearly three hundred years," she said defensively.

"That's not why it's wrong. We were at war."

"Don't you see I didn't have a choice?"

"You could have chosen not to see him again."

She shook her head. "I couldn't have. He was so perfect for me, Neil." She took a deep, shuddery breath. "Dad sent me out on a few assignments, and I passed them all easily. He told me I was the best assassin candidate he'd seen in years. And then he gave me my first actual assassination. It was a more difficult test than the others, but Dad said he knew I could do it." She ran her hand over her ponytail. "It was Edward. I refused, of course. I told him I didn't want to be an assassin anymore. I couldn't tell him the real reason. He was enraged. He said he had information that, at that very moment, the Celerius family was plotting to kill me. My talents had not gone unnoticed. He told me they would be clever in choosing an assassin or a situation that I wouldn't suspect."

Neil's heart sank.

"I went to see Edward that night. I brought my knife. It was the first time I'd been to the Celerius estate. He let me in. He knew something was wrong. He saw me shaking." Jennifer was about to cry again. "He brought me up to his room and told me everything would be fine and that he loved me … but he reached for something in his pocket too quickly and I thought it was a weapon. I—"

"Stop!" Neil felt like he was being strangled. "You don't have to say the rest."

She closed her eyes and took deep breaths. "It was one of those secret letters we communicated with. I thought it was a weapon. I couldn't cremate him," she whispered. "I couldn't."

The room was uncomfortably silent as the gravity of Jennifer's story began to settle on Neil's shoulders.

"That's why I warned you. About Bianca, I mean. When she helped you in the markets, a long time ago. Assassins shouldn't have friends. It's too hard that way. I don't want ... I won't let you put yourself through everything I went through. It's not fair. None of it is fair."

"Jen ...." He didn't know what to say.

"And I know you want to be an assassin," Jennifer went on. "I know you want it more than anything. You think it will bring you glory and make you a Vapros hero and help you find your advanced abilities. None of it's worth it, Neil. *Not one second* is worth it because you have to live with yourself afterwards. And now I have to remember it forever. Now I have this." She pulled her shirt to the side to reveal a tattoo slightly above her heart. It was a skeletal hand clutching a heart. "I told Father I seduced Edward, so this was the tattoo he gave me."

They sat in silence for a few minutes. "I'm sorry," Neil said. "About everything you've gone through. But you can't blame yourself for Edward. You didn't know. You thought he would kill you first. You have to forgive yourself."

"I don't know how much longer I can keep this up," she said. "Any of it. The planning, the recruiting. This is all hopeless."

He shook his head. "This can't be hopeless. If we give up, they win. Saewulf wins."

"I know. But it's hard." She shook her head slowly. "What are you going to do when all this is over? Could you really just put all this behind you?"

"I'd try. I'd keep the family going. But not like it was before. I'm going to have a real family. A family that doesn't fight all the time."

"Every family fights, Neil. It's part of loving each other. Look at the two of us."

He couldn't quite believe his ears. "You love me?"

"Of course I do!" She punched his shoulder gently. "You're my baby brother."

"I know, it's just . . . you've never acted like it." He let out a breath. "What do you think you'll do when it's over?"

"I'm going to do something for Victoria," she decided. "It will be something big—maybe a memorial."

"I'll help you," Neil promised. "We'll build a statue of her and put it right in the nightlife district."

"You really think we'll make it out of this?"

"We will," he said. "I promise."

Jennifer laughed a little through her nose. "Don't make promises you can't keep, Neil."

"I can keep this one. I can try."

She stood up and dusted herself off. "I'm going to bed," she said. "It's been an emotional day. When Rhys gets home, tell him goodnight for me."

"I will." Neil stood up, too. "Jen?"

She was on her way to her bedroom, but paused. "Yeah?"

"I, um … I love you, too."

She nodded appreciatively and disappeared into her room. Neil cocked his head, listening carefully, but for the first time in months, he didn't hear quiet sobs coming from Jennifer's bedroom. He shook his head and tried to process everything she had just told him. Neil sighed and ran his fingers through his hair. He stared in the direction of Jennifer's door and smiled faintly. At last, all he heard was silence. Maybe there was hope for her, yet.

Chapter Forty-Four
The Markets
Michael

Michael wandered through the markets looking for a woman to occupy his time. He wasn't drunk yet, but planned to be by the time he hobbled home. He noticed a pretty young woman at one of the stands and he grinned. Target acquired. Before he could reach her, he was grabbed by the shoulder and yanked around.

"Darius?" Michael said, confused. "What are you doing here?"

"Someone just tried to kill me," he said bluntly.

Michael still looked confused. "But you're alive."

Darius seemed exasperated. "I'd realized that by myself, actually. I fended her off."

Michael wrinkled his giant nose. "That's curious. Who was it?"

"Remember that assassin who tried to kill me in the Imperial dungeon?"

"No."

"Oh, I see your mind's as sharp as ever. Look, I'm in trouble. I need a new place to stay. Where have you been sleeping?"

"Calm down, kiddo." Michael said, "Let's take this one step at a time. Who would want you dead?"

Darius shrugged. "The emperor does, but I don't think it was him."

"Maybe it was the other families," Michael suggested, sneaking a look over his shoulder. The woman was gone. A little dejected, he turned back to his brother. "They might want to take you out."

Darius shook his head wildly. "I talked to Neil Vapros the other day. He wanted to help me. He's trying to get the families together. Dammit! Michael, who wants me dead?"

Michael's ears perked up. "He wants to get the families together?"

"Yeah, they're meeting tomorrow night at the First Church of Enlightenment. They're trying to find a way over the wall. Focus, Michael! There's an assassin after me!"

There was panic in his voice, but Michael barely noticed. He rubbed his chin. "We should go," he said finally. "To the church, I mean."

Darius looked at him incredulously. "Are you serious? I thought we gave up on the revolution thing."

"We did," Michael answered. "But if people are going over the wall, you and I should be among them. Once we're outside Altryon, we're free men. No more being hunted." He leaned closer. "No more assassins."

"No more assassins." It sounded nice. "Fine, I'll be there. You too?"

"Absolutely, brother. I'll see you tomorrow night."

Darius turned on his heel and walked back the way he had come, leaving Michael to scan the streets, looking for another girl to occupy his time.

Chapter Forty-Five
Imperial Dungeon
Carlin

Carlin stared through the bars at his captive with a wistful smile on his face. Ever since he had achieved a position with the empire, he had loved spending time in the dungeons. A new wing had been added and nothing supplied him with more joy than wandering around the dark halls. A raspy voice called from the top of the stairs. "Oh, Carlin," Saewulf hissed. "You've picked such an odd place to pout."

Carlin scowled in Saewulf's general direction. "Leave me alone, servant."

Saewulf effortlessly used his powers to glide down the staircase to Carlin's side. "Such an interesting revelation that was," Saewulf mused with a dark smile. "I can't believe the emperor never thought to tell me about his connection with you."

Carlin glared forward, not bothering to face the psychic who was practically dancing around him. "I don't understand why he would. He's not particularly proud."

Saewulf thoughtfully pulled his long, orange hair away from his eyes and tied it into a ponytail. "If you would, I'd love a little clarification. How did you come to be?"

"Well," Carlin said bitterly, "when a man and woman like each other very much …."

Saewulf chuckled, his voice trickling out like cold water. "Was that a joke? From you?"

Carlin nodded. "The emperor once had a mistress before he was actually the emperor. I was born. I shouldn't have been."

"Interesting," Saewulf said. "It seems even he had a legacy phase. It's not just family members."

"You don't need to be trying to spread your legacy to have children," Carlin responded. "He wasn't, anyway."

Saewulf shrugged and peered into the cell at a prisoner for a moment. "Well, this explains your latest promotion."

Carlin finally turned to face Saewulf and his hand moved to the handle of his sword. "Pardon me, Saewulf. Care to repeat that?"

Saewulf wasn't intimidated; instead, he looked rather amused. "Carlin, are you honestly trying to tell me you were promoted purely because of your skills as a tactician or a strategist? Grow up."

Carlin looked ready to pull his sword. "I was given no advantage," he replied. "Ever! I grew up poor and joined the empire the second I could. And then I worked for it. I worked every damn day until my fingers bled and I couldn't continue."

Saewulf shrugged. "It's just odd. I heard that you blew through the ranks to your current position. It takes most generals nearly their entire lives to reach such a status. Well, all generals except Anthony Celerius. But with his strategic mind and swordsmanship, how could he not reach general quickly? How old are you Carlin? Forty? Forty-five? Celerius was only thirty when he became general."

"And look where he is now." Carlin spat as he drew his sword. "I put my blade through his chest and then I had his body burned. And he deserved it."

Saewulf sneered. "Because he was better than you? Because he was in your way of becoming a man your father would notice?"

Carlin clenched his sword and hissed, desperately trying to avoid playing Saewulf's game. "No," he managed, "he deserved it. I trained with him and rose through the ranks with him, but he was always praised because of skills he was born with."

Saewulf back-pedalled a few steps as Carlin advanced. "Oh, I see," he cooed. "It wasn't fair?"

"You're damn right it wasn't fair!" Carlin roared. "I spend every second training and bettering myself and some kid speeds through the ranks because he was born with certain skills? People who take advantage of their birthright and hold it over the rest of us are not to be admired as gods. They're to be exterminated as abominations."

Saewulf nodded thoughtfully and his smile began to fade. "That's a popular theory," he said. "But not everyone who's born into privilege is an abomination, Carlin."

"The families are," Carlin said. "Them especially—the Vapros, the Taurlum and the Celerius. They don't belong out there with the innocent people. That's why I come down here. To remind myself where they really belong." Saewulf pivoted on his foot to look into the cell where Carlin had been staring. Inside was a body with arms outstretched, straining against chains that suspended him from either wall like a demented scarecrow. An iron mask had been fitted over his face and small air holes were visible. "They belong in one of two places: here in these cells or in the ground."

"That's Sir Vapros, eh?" Saewulf asked. "What's with the mask?"

"It limits his air," Carlin said. "He needs air to materialize. They all do.

With the limited supply, he's left helpless."

Saewulf paused for a moment and then turned to leave. "It's been good to speak with you, Carlin. It's always interesting to see what makes psychopaths like you tick."

"Go to hell," Carlin murmured as he was left to examine the helpless prisoners.

Chapter Forty-Six
First Church of Enlightenment
Neil

"No one is going to show up," Jennifer said glumly. She was lying flat on her back behind the alter, throwing her knife into the air and catching it by the handle before it hit her face. The trick made Neil nervous, but Jennifer never missed.

The First Church of Enlightenment wasn't a place Neil had ever spent a lot of time. He didn't believe in The Man with the Golden Light as deeply as his father did. He'd never really stopped to consider religion at all. He didn't know why the "Man" had chosen his family to gift or why he'd picked them to protect the city or why he'd never intervened when the feuding became heated.

Maybe he thought the feud couldn't be fixed.

"I say we head home now and pretend we never had this terrible idea to rely on our greatest enemies," Neil said.

"Yeah," a booming voice said from the door. "Enemies can be a bunch of flaky bastards, can't they?"

Neil jumped up from his sitting position on the stage and materialized down into the pews to get a better look. "Darius?" he said, squinting. The Taurlum swaggered down the aisle. "You look sober. And bathed."

Darius rolled his eyes. "That's because I am. You're a deductive genius." He leaned against the pulpit. "I'm not used to being in the same room as a Vapros without trying to kill it," he admitted, looking down at Jennifer.

She snorted. "Welcome to desperation," she said, tossing her knife up again. Darius plucked it out of the air, catching it by the blade, unaffected by its sharpness. She glared at him, but didn't get up. "Did you bring your brother?"

"Michael's supposed to meet me."

Rhys poked his head out from the back room where he'd been combing the cabinets for bottles of wine. "There's nothing back here," he reported. "Which is a shame because I doubt Darius Taurlum will be able to see straight without a little—" He cut himself off quickly when he saw Darius standing on the stage wielding a knife. "Hello," he said nervously. "I don't believe we've met. I'm Rhys."

Darius handed the knife back to Jennifer and lumbered over to Rhys. "Darius," he said, catching Rhys's palm in a crushing handshake. Rhys winced.

"Don't hurt him, Darius," Neil said. "We need him in top shape. He's the brains behind this operation."

"Oh, you're a brain?" the Taurlum asked, dropping Rhys's hand. Rhys nodded. "What good is a brain in a fight?"

"I do battle strategy," Rhys said calmly.

"Battle strategy?" Darius looked thoughtful. "Okay. Let's say I'm going up against four Imperial Guards armed with bows and arrows and I'm not wearing any armor. What weapon do I use?"

Rhys's calm expression didn't falter. "Easy. You're a Taurlum, you would use a hammer." Darius opened his mouth, but Rhys wasn't finished. "But if you want to know which weapon you should choose, I would suggest a shield. You could use it to block arrows since you don't have armor and then, when they're out of ammunition, you could swing it like a club. Most people don't carry them because they're large and impractical, but that wouldn't matter to you."

Darius almost looked impressed. "That's not too bad, Rhys."

Rhys shrugged. "I just know a lot about battle strategy."

"Don't be modest," Jennifer called from her place on the floor. "Rhys knows a lot about everything."

"Everything?" Darius repeated.

"Almost everything," Rhys amended quietly.

"So, you know what the most sold item was in the market last year?"

"Apples," Rhys said without missing a beat. "Followed by salt, bread, and rice."

Darius wracked his brain for a harder trivia question. "Richest merchant in the market?"

"Well, it was Sir Taurlum, until the attack," Rhys said, brow furrowed. "But once he was gone, the man who runs food distribution was the richest. But then the Pig started branching out and selling more products. He used to sell exclusively weapons, but then he added masks and armor to his inventory and profits shot up. So the richest man in the markets is the Pig."

"He was the richest man in the markets," said a feminine voice from the very back of the church, "until two days ago, when he was murdered along with all his employees." Lilly Celerius glided down the aisle, head held high. Jonathan followed close behind.

Darius looked slightly let down. "Don't let it get to your head, kid," he told Rhys. Rhys shrugged. "Celerius, I reckon?" he said, turning to the newcomer.

She barely nodded at him before ascending the steps onto the stage and turning to Neil. "When you told me you talked to the Pig, you neglected to mention that you killed him."

"We didn't kill him," Neil said defensively.

"Oh, please. They found arrows in his body. The Vapros are well known for using crossbows."

"That's true, but not anymore," Rhys said. "Until recently, we couldn't afford them or their ammunition. We didn't have any reason to kill the Pig. He was alive and well when we left him."

"I'd believe him," Darius muttered to Lilly sarcastically. "This kid knows everything."

"Well, I would be lying if I said I was distraught. Given the state of the city, it comes as no surprise. Poverty drives people to extremes." Lilly walked by the group and planted her feet next to Jennifer. "Are we all here? Can the planning begin?"

"The Nose isn't here yet," Neil pointed out, glancing at Darius. The Taurlum didn't look offended by the use of his brother's nickname.

"We'll catch him up," Darius said. "Let's get down to it. I say we start by finalizing the plan to make it past the wall."

Jennifer scoffed. "Subtlety be damned, I suppose."

Darius eyed her indignantly. "We Taurlum aren't known for subtlety."

Jennifer raised her eyebrows. "So I've gathered."

"I have a friend who knows a way out," Neil said hurriedly before a fight could break out. "I didn't bring her to this meeting because I was under the impression it was a family member only sort of gathering." He glanced pointedly at Jonathan.

The small servant reddened. Lilly looked mildly annoyed. "He goes where I go."

"Just like a Celerius to make a power play on our first peaceful meeting," Darius grumbled.

"Actually that seems like a Vapros kind of move," Rhys whispered.

"Anyway," Neil pushed on, "there is only one main door in the wall. It's used by soldiers and is heavily protected. I don't like our chances of sneaking through that way. But there is also a lesser-known back door."

"Explain," Lilly said.

Neil wanted to snap at her. He smothered the instinct and continued. "There is a special gate protected by a small guard house. It's near the Taurlum mansion. Guards use it to bring supplies out to the army, without attracting enemy attention. Sometimes they bring things in from the outside, too, like prisoners of war or negotiators. It opens once a month."

"I think I've seen that building," Darius muttered.

"The next opening is tomorrow night," Neil said.

Lilly looked skeptical. "So soon?"

Darius looked at Rhys and grinned. "I'm sure there's a battle plan, right, buddy?"

Rhys didn't return the smile, but he nodded calmly. "We go as fast as we can," he said. "We bring everything we have. We attack with our powers and we don't give them any time to regroup or call for reinforcements. Once we make it out, we scatter into the wilderness."

It wasn't exactly what Darius expected. "Sounds a little risky."

"I know," Rhys said, "but it's the best we can do."

"Why can't I just punch my way through the wall?" Darius asked. "Then we could go whenever we want."

"The wall is near thirty feet thick, two hundred feet high, and made completely of solid rock. It was built by dozens of family members. It is truly the greatest architectural marvel to date," Rhys said. "The wall is also constantly manned and guarded. Tunneling would be loud and by the time we were halfway through we would have the entire army on our backs."

"One question," Darius said. "Will there be booze outside the barrier?"

Rhys shrugged. "Maybe. If not I could teach you how to make it before we all split up."

Darius gasped. "You can do that?"

"Yes. It's simple fermentation."

Darius threw his hands into the air happily. Lilly rolled her eyes and cut off his cry of jubilation. "My group is five soldiers and four dozen crates of weapons. How do you propose we transport that?"

Rhys thought for a moment. "You might have to leave it behind."

Lilly looked offended. "I don't have impenetrable skin or materializing powers! I need armor. I need weapons!"

"You can bring some of it," Rhys said, "just not all. Darius could help you carry a crate or two."

"Anything for you," Darius said mockingly.

"You'll have to leave the guards, too. We can't sneak that many people through the wall. They need to stockpile weapons and prepare for the revolution," Rhys said.

Lilly looked like she wanted to argue more, but Neil cut in. "Listen, Miss Celerius. I understand you have different needs than we do. And you're used to being in control. Not now though. Everyone needs to check their ego at the door. That includes you, Darius and us."

She opened her mouth to respond but suddenly tensed up and raised one hand in the air. Her eyes closed. "Miss?" Jonathan said urgently, speaking up for the first time all night. "Is it happening again?"

Lilly snapped out of her trance and gasped. "Don't panic," she said, "but there are twenty men gathering outside."

Jennifer jumped to her feet. "What makes you say that?"

Lilly trembled. "Over the last month, I developed advanced abilities," she whispered. "I can feel sound waves and vibrations in the ground. I sense a large gathering of people walking outside. They're making a formation around the front doors. They know we're here. They're coming for us." She closed her eyes and stretched her arms out, reaching through the empty space in front of her. "There's a back door, yes? I can feel it."

"There's a door, yes," Neil said, a pang of jealousy coursing through him. Was he the only one without a heightened ability? "What brought upon your new powers?" he asked.

"I heard my father had been murdered," she said, and it wasn't in her usual icy tone. It sounded sad, and Neil remembered that he wasn't the only person who had lost someone in this war.

"We should split up," Darius suggested. "Meet in the orchards before sunrise. It's easy to hide in there. I've done it before."

"Okay," Neil said. "Lilly, you and Jonathan take the back door." They sprinted away, Jonathan falling behind almost immediately. She paused for a moment to let him catch up. "Darius, you—"

Darius grinned like a madman and charged straight through the wall and into the street, effectively forming his own way out. "Damn Taurlum fool," Jennifer grumbled.

"A fool who's on our side," Neil reminded her. "We can take the rooftop exit." He materialized to the uppermost balcony and then over to a ceiling beam. He grinned as he rematerialized, remembering the days when using his powers like this winded him for days. Now it was as natural as breathing. Jennifer and Rhys joined him on the beam and together they materialized toward the small door that opened up onto the roof.

Rhys led the way onto the rooftop and was immediately greeted by a volley of arrows. He gasped and materialized across the street on a new rooftop; the arrows continued toward his siblings. Neil felt a sharp pain across his arm and let out a cry. Jennifer sliced an arrow out of the air with her knife. "Neil, go!" she screamed as she began to panic. She had taken care of the first arrow, but seemed too disoriented to materialize. Neil gathered his concentration and materialized across the street next to Rhys.

Rhys was putting archers to sleep right and left. Neil ducked behind a chimney and pressed hard against the wound on his arm. It wasn't much more than a cut but it was bleeding a fair bit. "Where's Jennifer?" he yelled.

"She just disappeared!"

Right on cue, Jennifer appeared next to them. She looked more disoriented than Neil had ever seen her. Neil grabbed her wrist. "Come on!" He materialized to the street. The arrows followed him, shooting in perfect arcs over the roof of the building. He and Rhys took off running. Jennifer lagged behind, gasping sharply with every step. Neil dove around a corner, out of range of the archers, and slid to the ground. When Jennifer collapsed next to him, he wrapped her in a hug. "We almost lost you."

Jennifer shook her head. A few tears fell down her face. "I ...." She took a few shallow breaths. "I can't ... do this."

"You can do this," he assured her. "Remember what I said? We can't give up. Or they'll win."

Jennifer shook her head wildly. "I can't, Neil."

Rhys knelt beside them solemnly. "Neil," he said, "her back." He looked like he was going to be sick. Neil ran his hand down his sister's back. His stomach turned as his palm slid over a jagged fragment of an arrow. The end had broken off, making it harder to see, but the tip wedged tightly into what could only be her lung. "Jennifer?" he said cautiously. "Do you feel okay?"

She smirked. Her ponytail had come undone, but she didn't care, or maybe just didn't notice. "Don't patronize me," she said faintly, "I'll be fine."

Neil rolled her onto her side and examined the wound. He and Rhys exchanged a glance. Rhys shrugged and shook his head. "Neil," he whispered. "I don't know."

"It's bad, isn't it," Jennifer said. "You don't have to pretend."

Neil let her lie down. "It'll be okay, Jen," he said. "I promise."

Jennifer laughed. "Don't make promises you can't keep, Neil."

Neil felt his eyes welling up. "No, Jen, I can keep this one. We just need to find someone who can heal you—a doctor."

Jennifer shook her head. "Don't. I'd honestly rather just let it end now."

Neil pounded his fist into the ground. "Don't say that!"

"It's okay," she breathed. "You know better than anyone that I can't keep going through this without Victoria—"

Neil cut her off. "This wound is not that bad," he told her fiercely.

"I couldn't do it without her," she managed. Her eyes fluttered closed. "Couldn't do it alone."

Rhys lost his composure and began to sob.

Neil grabbed Jennifer's hands to comfort her and realized with a sinking heart that for the first time in her life they were cold. She sputtered for a moment and managed to keep speaking. "Don't be an assassin," she begged Neil. "It's not how you think it is. I spend so much time being angry ... and alone."

"I won't," he promised, gripping her hands tightly. "I won't."

A smile ghosted across her face. She whispered something hoarsely and then with one last sigh of relief went limp in his arms. Neil buried his face in her body and wept as he felt the crushing weight of another loss.

It could have been hours later, or maybe only seconds, but the next thing Neil knew was Rhys's hand on his shoulder. "I don't think we can take her to the other side of the barrier," he said, voice cracking with tears. "We have to ... you know."

Neil looked up at Rhys with red-rimmed eyes. "I don't think I can do that."

Rhys nodded. "I know. But she deserves to be ... she doesn't deserve to be left here all alone." He put his hand against her neck. "I'll do it, if you don't want to."

Neil wiped his eyes and put a hand on her neck next to Rhys's. "I can do it," he said. Together, they watched Jennifer's body slowly dissolve into ash and float away, carried up over the rooftops by the wind.

Chapter Forty-Seven
The Orchards
Darius

Darius made it to the orchards before anyone else. He had been sitting in a tree for over an hour, holding as still as he could in case any soldiers had followed him. In spite of the danger he'd narrowly escaped, a thrill built in his stomach. He'd forgotten how much he loved going into battle.

Dawn was just breaking when he heard voices coming from below his perch. He swung himself down, grinning as he prepared to pummel the enemies. He stopped his fist just in time as he recognized his new unlikely allies. "You made it!" he said to the Vapros boys, smiling at Rhys. He didn't smile back. "What's wrong?" Darius asked casually. "And where's the girl?"

Neil looked at the ground. Rhys shook his head silently.

"Oh," Darius said. He tried starting a sentence but the words wouldn't form correctly. He tried again. "Well, if it means anything, I fought her a few times. She was brave and strong as hell."

Neil looked up. "Yes," he said. "She was." Darius pretended not to notice the tears in his eyes.

A rustling in the trees made Darius's ears perk up. "Careful," he whispered, crouching over like a predator about to pounce. "There's someone here."

Neil and Rhys materialized into the branches of the tree, but Darius stayed on the ground. The thrill in his stomach was back. The rustling came closer, and he knew he should hide. He couldn't take on an ambush without his hammer, but he couldn't help it: he wanted to fight again.

A figure burst through the bushes and before Darius could make out a face, four hands came down from the tree and grabbed the unwanted guest. In a flash, Neil and Rhys materialized to the ground, holding a struggling girl between them.

"What the hell was that?" the girl gasped.

Neil threw her to the ground. "You just materialized," he said, panting a little. Materializing with another person was a lot harder than going alone. "Why did you follow us?"

The girl struggled to her feet and pushed her hair out of her face. Darius finally recognized her. "Anastasia," he growled. He planted his foot against her shoulder and kicked her hard. She toppled over. "You might be the most persistent person I've ever met. That doesn't seem to have worked out for you too well." He leaned over her. "Who sent you?" His voice came out in a roar that was so loud the Vapros boys flinched.

She didn't flinch, just turned her head and spat on his boot. "Go to hell."

Two sets of footsteps rustled into earshot. Darius groaned. "Who is it now?"

The footsteps stopped. "What happened here?" Lilly's voice asked.

Darius glanced up. "This girl has tried to kill me three times. It's time to find out why."

Lilly cocked her head and looked at Anastasia. "She won't talk?"

"No," Darius said. "And I think I'm going to pull off her fingers."

Anastasia gasped.

Lilly shook her head quickly. "No, allow me," she said. "I'll make her talk."

Jonathan *(of course Jonathan was here,* Darius thought) spoke up. "Miss, I don't know if you should do this."

"Jonathan," she said calmly, "I can handle it." She bent down to place her hand on Anastasia's forehead. "You see, this power I've developed started out as a weapon of sorts."

Anastasia began to shake spastically.

"What's happening to her?" Rhys asked curiously.

Lilly kept her eyes closed. "I can send energy through things. When I do it to the ground and the air, nothing really happens. But when I do it to people they react poorly."

Anastasia screamed.

"Just tell us why you're trying to kill the Taurlum," Lilly said soothingly, "and I'll make it all go away."

"The Nose!" the assassin screamed. "Michael Taurlum hired me!"

Lilly took her hand away. "There's your answer."

Darius shook his head. "She's lying," he growled. "Michael is my brother."

Lilly moved to put her hands back on Anastasia's forehead, but the hostage shrieked, "I swear it was him! He wouldn't tell me why! Please, don't touch me!"

"If Michael hired you, then you must know where he is," Darius said. "If you don't tell me now, I will crush you in my hand like a stick."

Anastasia trembled. "He's in the old Taurlum mansion. The Imperial Guards know he's there, but they haven't captured him. I don't know why."

Darius looked confused. "He's living in my house?"

Anastasia nodded, but he wasn't paying attention to her anymore. "I have to find Michael," he said to his group of allies. "I have to get to the bottom of this."

Neil shook his head and felt rage begin to well up in his chest. "This was you."

"What?" Darius asked turning his attention away from Anastasia. Neil was upon him in a second, swinging his knife rabidly. It bounced off Darius's stomach and he stumbled backwards. "Whoa kid! What the hell do you think you're doing?"

"Someone ratted us out. Someone told the empire where we were going to be and now Jennifer is dead. This is because of you and your damn family!" Neil advanced slowly. He could feel heat coming off every part of his body. Rhys stepped in front of him and raised his hands calmly. Neil said, "Don't defend him."

"I'm not." Rhys had tears in his eyes too. "But think, Neil, settle down and think. Darius was there, too. So was Lilly. If Michael knew we were going to be at the church, then it must have been *him*. If this was anyone's fault, it's purely Michael's. And Darius is just as confused as we are. He was betrayed."

Neil glared at Darius over Rhys's shoulder. "This was such a mistake—trying to get the families back together. This feud is in our blood. Trusting you is just going to get us all killed."

"Listen kid," Darius said slowly, "I'm just trying to figure this out. I had nothing to gain from your sister getting killed. All I want is to know what's happening. I'm going to find Michael right away."

Neil sheathed his knife and stumbled backwards. He ran his fingers through his hair and tried to think. "I'm sorry, but you can't," he said. "Every day we stay here is another day we risk our lives. The gate won't be open for another month. We're leaving tonight, with or without you."

Anastasia took this opportunity to jump to her feet and sprint away through the brush. Lilly started to chase after her, but Darius grabbed her arm to stop her. "Don't bother," he growled. "We have to find Michael."

"What if she goes to the emperor?" Lilly said.

"She's not working for the emperor," Darius growled. "She's working for someone else."

"And that someone else appears to be Michael," Rhys said.

"Look," Darius said growing annoyed, "I'm confused about all of this. I don't know why Michael would do this, but I've got to go see him. I've got to know what's going on."

"If you go after your brother, you'll have to go alone," Neil said. "The rest of us are getting out of here."

"I'll meet up with you before we leave, then."

Rhys's brow was furrowed. "Michael never showed up to the church …"

"He's the one who told me I should go," Darius said. "He said he'd meet me."

"But he never did," Rhys confirmed. "And instead, we were ambushed by the Imperial Army. The same Imperial Army that's letting Michael live in your old house."

"What are you implying?" Darius said as he noticeably clenched his fists.

"Michael could be feeding the emperor information in exchange for his own freedom," Rhys said.

Darius punched a tree trunk so hard it toppled over. "My brother is not a traitor. This is something we just need to clear up."

"Maybe not, but it all adds up, don't you think?"

Darius started walking. "I'm getting to the bottom of this," he said. "If you want to come with me, you can. If not, I understand."

Rhys scrambled after him. "I'll go," he said. Darius looked down at him and smiled. It wasn't the usual ferocious Taurlum grin, but an unidentifiable smile, maybe one of gratitude. At first, Neil felt hope, maybe they could learn to overcome the feud. But those feelings were quickly replaced with skepticism. He definitely didn't want Rhys to be alone with two Taurlum, especially if one was working for the emperor. "Rhys—" he started, but his brother interrupted.

"If Michael ordered this attack, then it's his fault Jennifer is gone. I want revenge too, Neil."

Neil was still unsure. His head was swimming. "Fine," he said as he rubbed his temples. "You can go kill Michael, but not yet. None of us has slept all night. You need a few hours rest before you go killing anyone."

"We aren't going to kill him," Darius protested, but he did look exhausted. "We're going to get an explanation. My brother would never betray our family."

Neil didn't believe that, but he nodded. "Just rest first. Rhys and I have had a hard day."

"Well then follow me," Lilly said. "My home can accommodate us all."

Chapter Forty-Eight
Robert's Shack
Robert

Robert took off the coat Victoria had given him and hung it carefully in the closet. He sighed and rubbed his hands against his forehead. It had been another long night.

He had been working for months, ever since Jennifer Vapros hunted him down, told him that his love was dead, and begged for his help in the revolution against the emperor. He spread his propaganda throughout the slums, begging people to join the cause. A good number of people had joined at first. Lately, though, it was becoming harder and harder to recruit new members, especially with the Brotherhood's growing numbers. People just wanted to feel safe, and leading a war against their leader didn't accomplish that goal. He and Neil had considered working with the Brotherhood, but they quickly began to realize that they were far too unpredictable.

Robert grabbed a bit of stale bread from the counter. It tasted terrible. He didn't mind. Stale bread was as good as a feast in comparison to starvation.

Suddenly, he heard a slight creak behind him. He paused mid-chew and narrowed his eyes. Without warning, he whirled around and threw his chair into the figure behind him and then rolled to his desk where his musket was waiting. Before he could reach it, a throwing knife pinned his sleeve to the wall. "Relax," said a calm female voice. "I'm not here to kill you. I just want the rest of my money."

Robert pulled the knife out of his sleeve and stood. He examined the female for a moment. "It wasn't enough?"

She shook her head. "It was enough for a workshop. You didn't mention I'd have to take down an entire factory."

Robert groped under his desk for his pouch and tossed it to her. "I didn't know it was an entire factory," he admitted as she caught it. "It makes sense though. I was wondering how they produced so many guns."

The girl opened the pouch and scanned the contents. "Not enough."

"Not enough?" Robert started to panic. "It's all I have! Look around. This isn't exactly a palace."

"It's not enough."

"You aren't even supposed to be here," he said. "That's why I hired a middleman. How did you find me?"

"It wasn't hard. I asked around and did some persuading. You aren't as anonymous as you think, Mr. Rebellion Leader." She shook the pouch at him. "And it's still not enough."

He held up his hands. "I don't have anymore. If you want further payment, you'll have to talk to one of my benefactors—Neil Vapros."

"Neil Vapros is giving you money?"

"He's helping me get the revolution started."

"You're Robert Tanner, then," she said. "You're the one stockpiling weapons for the revolution."

He nodded. "Who are you?"

"Bianca Blackmore."

"Right. I've heard of you. I'll get you the money, I promise, I just don't know …."

"Forget it," she said shoving the pouch back into his hands. "No charge."

He looked at his money in disbelief. "Seriously?"

"Yes." She started for the door. "And for the record, I'm sorry about Victoria."

He tried to smile. "I'm coping with it the best way I know how."

She paused, one hand on the doorknob. "Starting a revolution?"

"That's one way to do it."

"Those Vapros," she said. "They sure do know a thing or two about forbidden love."

He laughed once. "Tell me about it."

"Well, Mr. Tanner," Bianca said, still facing the door, "it was a pleasure doing business with you. Keep stockpiling weapons."

"Wait." Robert set the pouch on his desk and moved toward her. "Maybe we can help each other out some more. There are more gun factories being started …."

"I'm going on a trip," she said. "Outside the city. But I'll be back. And when I am, I'll need your weapons."

He took a bite of bread. "Safe travels, then."

She gave him a wistful smile. "Easier said than done."

Chapter Forty-Nine
Lilly's Hideout
Neil

illy led them to her safe house, and the group followed her up to her rented attic. "This is definitely nicer than where I live," Darius said as he took a seat at Lilly's kitchen table.

"We took a lot of money from my home before it burned," Lilly explained. "We can afford the rent here. And we paid off the owners to keep their mouths shut about us living here."

Jonathan went to the cabinet, pulled out a loaf of bread and a bottle of wine, and placed it in the center of the table. No one took a drink and Darius noticed. "Nothing to drink, tiny shadow man?" he taunted.

Jonathan seemed more confused than offended by the insult. "It is improper for servants to drink with their superiors," he said. "And ... tiny shadow man?"

Darius tore off a piece of the bread. "You're never far behind ... Lilly." It was a struggle to use her given name. "Kind of like a shadow."

"I am like her shadow," Jonathan said emotionlessly. "I won't let harm come to Miss Celerius."

No one else reached out for the bottle. Not even Darius. "You don't drink?" Darius asked the table.

Lilly shook her head. "Not anymore. Not after it almost cost me my life."

The Vapros boys murmured in agreement. Darius sighed and handed the bottle back to Jonathan. "I guess there's no time like the present," he grumbled.

Jonathan replaced the bottle in the cabinet and returned to the silent table awkwardly.

"So, we already know you're always at her heels," Darius said to the tiny servant. "Say a horde of troops came after 'Miss Celerius.' What would you do?"

Jonathan looked determined. "I would not have to do anything," he said confidently. "Miss Celerius is fully capable of handling attackers herself. But if I needed to step in, I would kill them."

Darius chuckled. "You?"

"Yes," his eyes narrowed fiercely. "All of them."

Darius grinned. "Well, I'm glad to have you on our side, tiny savage," he said, patting Jonathan on the back. He pitched forward, unprepared for the Taurlum's strong hand against his shoulder. Darius pulled back immediately, muttering an apology.

"What do you guys think you're going to do when you get outside the wall?" Rhys asked, chewing thoughtfully on a piece of bread.

Lilly drummed her fingers on the table a few times. "Well, I had an uncle who was banished," she said finally. "I'll try to find him."

"What about joining the war against Altryon?" Neil asked.

"I'd get to that eventually. I want to find my uncle first." She ripped off a chunk of bread as properly as she could. "I haven't had a family in a long time. I've lost a lot of people to wars. I'm not so eager to jump right into another one."

"I understand," Neil sighed. "I'm not sure if I'd join the war, either," he admitted quietly.

Rhys nearly dropped his bread. "What?"

Neil covered his face with his hands. "Do you ever think about how things could actually be better if we didn't have to be a part of the Vapros family? Or the way it used to be, anyway."

"We have to save our family," Rhys said.

"I know that," Neil muttered. "But do you really miss it? Do you miss the pressure? Do you miss being beaten? Do you really miss everything Father did to us?"

"Stop." Rhys said. "I know you got the worst of it, but Father was good to Jen and me."

"Really? Because to me, it looked like he wouldn't let you be a human being. Do you ever wonder what it would be like to be able to be a normal person or even wear spectacles for that matter?"

Rhys sighed. "Okay, so he wouldn't let me wear spectacles, but that doesn't mean I want to abandon him. And he never did anything to Jen. She was fine—"

"You're a smart kid, Rhys," Neil interrupted. "You're smarter than I am. So don't sit there and pretend that at the end of the day Jennifer was okay. Don't pretend that you didn't notice anything."

Rhys was silent, but his jade eyes teared up. Neil's eyes flicked over to Lilly and he sighed. "Look, we can talk about all of this later but I think we both know that there were a lot of things we didn't know about Jennifer. Let's not insult her by saying she was 'fine' when we both know she wasn't."

Neil stared at him for a moment and then ran his hands through his hair. "I love our Father," he continued, "and I want to see him and the rest of the family free, but I've lost a lot of people, too. I only have two really important people left. I would rather take them and run far away. Just keep them safe with me."

"Two important people?" Darius echoed. "Who's the second?"

"She's a girl from the streets. You wouldn't know her." Neil thought for a second. "Actually, you would. Do you remember the girl who knocked you out in the markets once? The day before you attacked the Opera House?"

Darius laughed a little. "How could I forget?"

"Well, that's Bianca, my best friend. She's the one who told me about the back gate in the barrier."

Darius laughed again. "I can't believe I'm relying on a street girl who made me a laughingstock."

"She's not part of your family, though," Lilly mused. "This isn't her war. Would she still want to leave with you?"

"Would Jonathan want to leave with you?" Neil countered.

All eyes turned to the servant. "Miss Celerius is my duty," he said formally. "I have no choice but to leave with her."

"Right," Neil said. "But do you want to? Are you happy about going?"

He didn't miss a beat. "Of course I am."

"And what about the fighting?" Darius jumped in. "This isn't your war, Shadow Man."

Jonathan reddened. "My family has served the Celerius for generations. I may be a servant, but I still wear a Celerius military coat." To prove it, he carefully adjusted one of the buttons on his oversized jacket.

Darius wasn't satisfied. "If Lilly died, would you continue on?"

Jonathan looked at his hands. "I serve the Celerius family, in life and in death." He didn't sound completely sure. He wouldn't meet anyone's eyes.

Darius, sensing it was time to let the subject drop before Jonathan cried, moved on. "What about you, Lilly?"

"What about me?"

"You have a military coat. Why? Most Celerius girls don't choose to be soldiers or wear the coat everywhere."

She smiled. "I am not most girls."

Darius opened his mouth to continue his interrogation, but Neil jumped in before he could offend anyone else. "Why are you asking so many questions, Darius?"

Darius said, "I've spent my life hearing stories about how horrible your families are, and now I'm about to go into battle with you. It's probably about time I learn some truths, don't you think?" He looked at Rhys. "I already know you're a brain. But what about your brother?" His eyes settled on Neil. "What about you, kid? Got any stories to tell? You seemed like a more enthusiastic guy when we first met. I miss the preaching."

"I don't feel like preaching anymore," Neil replied. "I've lost both of my sisters, I'm not sure how I feel."

"I'm used to losing people," Darius tried to be comforting. "It's been happening since I was born. Taurlum would go on raids, and a few wouldn't come back. You learn to live with it."

This didn't make Neil feel better. "Well, I'm running out of people to lose." A silence settled over the table as each person remembered the loved ones lost.

"I have a question for you," Jonathan said boldly to Darius. The Taurlum looked mildly surprised. "Sir Anthony used to talk about his adventures in the Taurlum Coliseum. Is that a real place?"

Darius laughed, "Of course it's real!" The Coliseum was in the basement of the Taurlum mansion. It was a giant battle arena where prisoners were pitted against animals, soldiers, and sometimes members of the Taurlum family. He'd grown up watching fights to the death.

"And is it as horrible as they say?" Jonathan asked.

"I used to play in it with Michael when there were no battles going on. It was like a playground as a kid. I even fought in it for real once. I won— clearly."

"Did you fight my brother?" Lilly asked.

Darius shook his head. "I don't remember Anthony Celerius, but if he lived to tell the tale, then whoever he was fighting is long gone. Coliseum battles are to the death."

Lilly shuddered. "That is absolutely gruesome."

"What about Nicolai Taurlum?" Rhys asked. Neil felt a thrill course through his veins. Nicolai Taurlum, the Sewer Man, was one of his favorite myths. "Is he real?"

"Yeah, Uncle Nicolai was real. People talk about him, but I don't really remember him too well. People say he was the biggest Taurlum."

Neil's jaw dropped. "He's real?" he said incredulously. "Did he really escape the Imperial Guards and live in the sewers?"

Darius shrugged. "I have no idea. He probably ditched the sewers years ago, if he did survive."

"Oh." Neil was disappointed.

Rhys yawned. "I'm going to sleep," he announced, rising from the table. Darius followed suit. "We have a big day ahead of us."

Neil agreed. "A gate to get through, a Taurlum to kill—"

"We aren't going to kill him," Darius interrupted. "He's innocent."

"A Taurlum to talk to," Neil amended. "Either way, we should all get to bed."

They began to strip off their armor. "So, the Vapros eating children: true or false?" he heard Darius ask Rhys as they settled into their positions on the floor. Neil closed his eyes. The last thought that entered his mind, before he drifted off to sleep, was one of confusion. For once in his life, he had shared an amicable moment with his lifelong enemies. But where did the feud end? Was it something that could be overcome or was it something destined to continue forever? Could he ever really trust Darius and Lilly or were they just using him to escape? Would they then try and kill him and his brother?

⁂

Neil awoke to the sounds of Jonathan sweeping the room. He sat up and rubbed a hand through his hair. "You do this every morning?" he asked, eyes squinted against the light pouring in through the window. It had to be about midday.

Jonathan didn't look up. "Anything Lilly needs," he said, not pausing in his diligent cleaning.

Neil whistled. "Why didn't we ever have servants as loyal as you? When we were attacked, all our servants ran for the hills."

Jonathan shrugged, still not looking up. "I don't have anyone else. Carlin's men killed my parents that night. Lilly is the only family I have left. I took a vow to care for her a long time ago."

Neil groaned as he stood up. "Have you seen my armor?"

"It's being cleaned by one of the guards," Jonathan replied, sweeping his small dust pile into a dustpan. "I'll have it to you soon."

"Wow. Thanks." Neil flopped back down onto the floor. "Any ideas about what you're going to do once we're outside the wall?"

"Lilly's going to join the rebellion, eventually, of course," Jonathan said, tucking the broom away in the corner. "But I'm not cut out for that life. I'll wait until she joins up and then I'd like to settle down. Find a nice girl, start a family. Lilly pulled me aside last night to talk to me and told me that once we're outside the wall she wants to free me. Let me live some other kind of life."

"Any wife of yours would be lucky," Neil said.

"Well, one thing is for certain. She'd never have to lift a finger."

"It's funny," Neil said, folding his hands behind his head and looking up at the slanted roof, "I've spent all this time wanting to start a revolution, but now that it's happening I think I want the same thing you want."

"A family?"

"Yeah." He rolled over to look at Jonathan. "Do you think that's weak?"

Jonathan shook his head. "I think it's admirable. War is fueled by hatred. A family is something to love."

Neil smiled slightly. "How many hours until sunset?"

"About four. You all slept very late. But I suppose you deserved to."

"Well, now I'm up," he declared. "Time to train."

❈

"So, tonight's the night," Darius said, dropping into push-up position in the middle of the room. "How do you Vapros prepare for a battle?"

Rhys watched Darius do a few push-ups. "We practice our balance. It helps with materialization." He looked toward the door as Neil entered. "You're awake," he noted. "Finally. Where's Lilly?"

"No idea," Neil said.

"Miss Celerius is preparing for the day," Jonathan supplied.

Darius paused mid-push-up. "So she's training?"

"She's doing her hair."

"What?" Darius almost dropped himself. "That's how she prepares? She combs her hair?"

Jonathan seemed confused by the question. "Um . . . yes?"

Darius rolled his eyes and muttered something that sounded distinctly like, "Women."

Neil materialized up to the rafters of the attic and let himself fall. A few inches before he hit the ground, he materialized back up to the ceiling and caught a rafter in his hand. Meanwhile, Darius dusted himself off and moved to sit on a dusty couch. "That's all you do to warm up?" Neil asked between materializations. "A handful of push-ups?"

Darius followed the bouncing Vapros with his eyes. "I weigh four

266

hundred pounds," he said casually. "It's a good amount of lifting. And anyway, I'm already stronger than the Imperial Guards. I was just working out because Rhys says it's 'necessary' if I'm going to go into battle."

"You weigh four hundred pounds?" Rhys asked with interest. "I never would have guessed that. Your footsteps aren't as loud as I would have expected."

Darius flexed his bicep. "Skin of steel comes with the weight of steel."

The door to another room opened and Lilly stepped in. Her hair and makeup were done to perfection. Neil let himself land on the ground and pushed a hand through his hair a little self-consciously. He'd hardly even looked in a mirror the better part of six months. "Good morning, gentlemen," Lilly said, taking a seat beside Darius on the couch. "Training for this evening?"

Darius nodded and fell back into push-up position, this time using only one arm. Rhys looked impressed. "Four hundred pounds," he said under his breath. "Unbelievable."

"Does anyone want to spar with me?" Lilly asked. "You know, to practice for tonight?"

Darius laughed. "You don't want me," he assured her. "I'm nowhere near as fast as you."

"I'll do it," Neil said.

Lilly pulled two wooden swords out of the crate on the floor and tossed one to him. "Be careful, Vapros," she warned as she whipped her sword around in a circle. "I've been training." Neil brandished his sword confidently and lunged at her. She was expecting it, blocked him effortlessly, and parried. Before she could finish him off, he materialized behind her. She ducked beneath his weapon and blocked his sword. But just barely. "You've been training too," she exclaimed, preparing to strike again.

"Living as a fugitive gave me a little practice," Neil said, swinging his sword toward her neck.

She dodged the blow and quickly swiped her sword against his back. "Gotcha!"

He stumbled forward, wincing a little at the pain. "Best two out of three?"

She smiled triumphantly and patted daintily at her hair. Inexplicably, it had all stayed perfectly in place. "You're on, Vapros."

For the first time in six months, Darius slipped on his strategically placed armor, covering his pressure points. It took a few minutes to get used to the weight, but he felt powerful with it on his shoulders. "Everyone ready?" he asked, turning to his fellow warriors. Everyone had bathed and looked considerably better. The Vapros boys were still strapping on their leather armor, but Lilly looked prepared for battle in her blue and gold military coat. "Tonight's the night we leave Altryon behind." Darius grinned as he flexed his muscles experimentally in his armor.

"It's weird," Neil said, flipping up his hood. "This is where I was born, took my first steps, said my first words."

Lilly weighed different swords in her hands. "Hopefully we'll take our last breaths here, too," she murmured. "Once this war is won, we'll be back."

Rhys nodded. "We leave as fugitives, but we will return someday as free men. And women," he added quickly at a glance from Lilly.

"The sun is setting, Miss," Jonathan said excitedly. "It's time!"

Lilly smiled and sheathed her sword. "My guards have elected to remain in the city so that we can move more inconspicuously. It means fewer weapons, but it's also a greater chance of survival."

"Is Bianca coming with us?" Rhys asked Neil.

"I don't know. Honestly, I think she was planning on leaving anyway, with or without us. She might already be there. I sent a letter with a messenger, so hopefully that'll reach her."

"No more stalling," Darius ordered. "Let's go!" He led the way down the steep staircase and out the back door, heaving a large cloak over his shoulders to hide his shining armor. He needn't have bothered; the city was empty tonight.

The group walked together down the quiet streets to the market, sticking to the shadows in case a stray civilian happened to walk by. The Taurlum mansion loomed in the distance. Darius kept his eyes fixed on his old home. Michael was in there. *Could Michael have told the emperor about the meeting in the church? Was it Michael who had hired an assassin to kill him? No,* Darius thought furiously. *Michael would never do that. Michael would have an explanation.*

They reached a road that split in two directions. One was paved with marble. It led to the front hall of the Taurlum mansion. The other was a small dirt road that curved around behind the mansion, ultimately to the secret barrier gate. "Well," Darius said. "I guess this is it." He took a step onto the marble path. Rhys followed.

"Be careful," Neil said softly. After a second of hesitation, he pulled Rhys into a hug. "Don't trust either of them," he whispered. "I don't feel good about this whole thing."

Rhys smiled calmly. "We're just going to talk," he reminded his brother. "There's no danger."

"I still don't feel good about you in a room with two Taurlum," Neil murmured.

"Good luck, sir," Jonathan said to Darius.

"See you on the other side, Shadow Man."

Rhys and Darius walked side by side down the road. "Darius," Rhys said. "You do know there's a chance we'll have to fight him."

Darius shook his head. "Michael and I are brothers. He would never try to hurt me."

"Right." Rhys let silence fall over them for a few minutes. "Darius?"

"Yeah?"

"You trust me, right?"

Darius snorted. "You're a Vapros. I trust you as much as I would trust a Vapros, I suppose."

"Ok, do you at least agree that my knowledge about things is usually pretty accurate?"

Darius didn't like where this was going. "I suppose."

"I'm just saying that there are a lot of things that just aren't adding up. You have to prepare yourself for that."

Darius nodded reluctantly. "I will. But he's not behind this. Trust me. I know my brother."

"I hope you're right," Rhys said softly. "I truly hope you're right."

Chapter Fifty
The Altryon Gate
Neil

Neil saw Bianca before she saw him. His pulse quickened. She was leaning against the nearest building, still wearing her armor trimmed with fur. He quickly materialized next to her. "Hello," he whispered in her ear. "What's up?"

"Neil!" She wrapped her arms around him almost sympathetically. His letter had detailed the situation with Jennifer.

He returned the hug. "What's the situation?"

"Five guards," she replied. "I could have taken them out on my own, but I'd like someone to get rid of the bodies. Also, it doesn't seem fair that I get to have all the fun."

He grinned. "What about outside the wall?"

"No idea." Lilly and Jonathan approached. "Ah," Bianca said, "it's the rich girl. How've you been, rich girl?"

Lilly offered a little smile. "I've been working hard," she said. "You still couldn't beat me, street girl."

"I remember you being pretty quick," Bianca said. "Ready to take out some guards?"

Lilly whipped out her sword. "Born ready."

Bianca led them around the corner and pointed up. Two soldiers patrolled the top of the wall. "Watch this," she mouthed. She pulled out two knives, one in each hand, and threw them at the same time. Both met their marks; the guards fell off the wall, shouting. Neil materialized right below and caught them by the necks, cremating them before they even hit the ground.

One of the guards on the ground heard the commotion and came running toward the Vapros boy, but Lilly jumped out of the shadows and sank her sword through his heart. Neil sprinted over to disintegrate him while Lilly and Bianca each took out another guard.

It was over in less than ten seconds. Neil kicked through piles of ash. "That's the most people I've ever dematerialized in a row," he panted.

"My God," Jonathan breathed. "That was incredible. They just dissolved!"

Neil nodded, trying desperately to catch his breath. "It takes a lot out of you."

Jonathan didn't seem to notice Neil's exhaustion. "Those first two didn't even land!" he said, awestruck.

Neil laughed a little at Jonathan's incredulity. "It's a handy little talent."

"How do you do it?"

"It takes concentration. We take the same energy we use to teleport, but we channel it into another person instead of ourselves. They aren't capable of reforming, like we are, so they just turn into ash." Jonathan's jaw was hanging open. Neil smiled. "It's a lot easier to do it to people who are already dead. When you try to cremate living people, their bodies fight back. They have their own energy that keeps them glued together. My father can manage it, but I'm nowhere near strong enough yet."

Lilly and Bianca caught up to them. "Ready?" Lilly asked, "We have a city to escape."

Neil walked up to the giant gate and pulled it open. Instead of spitting them out into freedom, it opened into a long corridor with another gate at the end. It was so close, he could have materialized right up to it.

Unfortunately, there were about thirty guards standing in his way.

"Well, well, well," said a voice from behind the many guards. "That was almost too easy."

The soldiers parted and General Carlin walked between them, brandishing a broadsword. Lilly snarled and raised her own weapon.

"Oh, please." Carlin said, rolling his eyes at Lilly. "Did you really think we wouldn't find out about your escape attempt? The Vapros brats have been advertising it all over town."

Neil reddened. Carlin noticed.

"We have our spies," he said, smiling. "Michael Taurlum was very helpful."

Lilly gasped. "I knew it," she muttered. "Stand down, Carlin," she commanded. "In the name of my brother, Anthony Celerius, I order you to call off your soldiers!"

Carlin laughed. "In the name of Anthony Celerius? Anthony is dead. I killed him myself. Sent you the ashes in a box, remember?"

Lilly narrowed her eyes. "Stand down or I will—"

Before she could finish the threat, she and the rest of her group were thrown against the wall and suspended in midair by an invisible force. "I'll take it from here, General," a cold voice said. Neil's heart sank as he recognized Saewulf. "Ah, one of you is a Vapros," he said delightedly, making his way through the ranks of soldiers. "Do you remember me? It's been too long!" His hands began to glow. "Let's see if you die as easily as your family members."

Chapter Fifty-One
Taurlum Mansion
Darius

The Taurlum mansion didn't have a lock. The front door was designed to be so heavy that only a Taurlum could heave it open. With a grunt, Darius forced through the door and beckoned Rhys inside behind him.

Their footsteps echoed against the marble floor. Rhys let out a low whistle. "Nice place," he said, admiring the high ceilings. "Much different from our house."

Darius didn't say anything. He couldn't quite believe he was home. He had long ago accepted that he would never set foot in this entryway again, yet here it was, looking as splendid and regal as the last time he saw it. He pressed his palm against one of the columns and closed his eyes. It was like he'd never left. If he concentrated hard, he could almost hear his family's voices echoing down the hallways.

"Where's Michael's room?" Rhys asked.

Darius opened his eyes and exhaled. "Upstairs," he said quietly. "I'll show you." He led the way through a maze of staircases and hallways, pausing at each one to touch a portrait or gently straighten a tapestry. It didn't feel like his house was deserted. Any second now, someone would come around the corner and ask him if he wanted to go out and get a drink. It would be like nothing had ever happened, the past six months were just a dream.

"This is his room," Darius said, rapping his knuckles against the door. It fell open. Michael's room was empty. His bed was stripped of its sheets, his dresser overturned, his clothes spilled out over the floor. A fine layer of dust covered it all.

"It doesn't look like anyone's been here for a long time," Rhys whispered.

"Why are you whispering?" Darius asked, lumbering into his brother's bedroom and pulling the dresser into its upright position. "You're acting like somebody died in here."

"Somebody did die here. A lot of people died here." Rhys still wouldn't set foot in the room. "Did you not realize that?"

Darius shook his head. "Taurlum don't die," he explained. "They're all imprisoned."

Rhys shook his head slowly. "Taurlum have weaknesses, same as everybody else. You and your family aren't gods. You're mortal men. And some of you died in the attack that night."

"You may know a lot," Darius said, steadying himself against Michael's dresser, "but you're wrong about this."

Rhys sighed. "I'm sorry," he whispered, "but I don't think I am."

Darius held perfectly still for a moment, then stormed past Rhys and down the hallway. "Michael's not here," he growled. "We're leaving."

"Wait!" Rhys had to materialize every few steps to keep up. "Is there anywhere else he could be? Any places he used to spend a lot of time?"

"The roof," Darius said, not slowing down. "That way." He gestured vaguely. "Find it yourself."

"Darius!" Rhys grabbed his arm and held on tightly. The Taurlum didn't even slow down. "We need to find your brother!"

"Maybe my brother is dead," Darius growled. "Just like the rest of my family apparently is! I don't need to listen to your condescending Vapros attitude."

"He's not dead," Rhys said calmly. "You saw him two days ago. He has the answers you need. Remember why we came here?"

Darius finally stopped. "Right." He put his face in his hands and took a few deep breaths. "The roof—this way." He started up a long staircase and threw himself against the door at the top. It burst open with a noise so loud that, for a moment, Darius thought he'd ripped it completely off its hinges. "Michael?"

Michael turned around and gazed with droopy eyes at his intruders. "Darius," he said lazily as he raised his jeweled arms. "Glad to see you made it home."

"What do you . . . you never showed up at the church. You said you'd meet me and then you didn't come."

Michael gave him a slow smile. "No, I didn't. I had more important things to do."

"That assassin came back," Darius said. "She tried to kill me again."

"Did she?" Michael shook his head and took a step toward them. The jewelry on his wrists clinked softly, like cruel, quiet laughter. "But she failed, I see."

"I'm still alive, aren't I?" Darius didn't like the look in Michael's eye.

"Indeed." Michael stopped. "What a pity," he said harshly.

Darius stared. "What a . . . a pity? Michael, what are you talking about?"

"Anastasia," he said loudly, and the assassin stepped out of the shadows. "He's still alive."

Anastasia looked furious. "Not for long," she growled, reaching for her spike. Michael held out a hand to stop her.

"You have tried to kill him three times," he said softly, and Darius felt his jaw drop. "Give up. You clearly aren't capable. I'll do it myself."

"Michael?" Darius's throat was dry. "What are you talking about?"

Michael turned and gazed over the city. "Several months ago, when that Vapros boy attacked our house, I realized how easy it would have been for him to kill one of us," he said vaguely. "We were stronger, of course, but he had the element of surprise. We barely saw him coming. And I started to wonder. What would have happened if he'd reached his target? What if he had killed our grandfather. Or even our father?"

"Neil's not so bad," Darius said quickly. "The Vapros aren't so different. I actually think the feud can end. Stop what you're doing Michael."

Michael didn't appear to hear him. "So I took a look at Father's will, just to see how things could have ended up. You can imagine my surprise when I discovered that he left everything to you."

"So what? I'm his son!"

Michael turned back and glared at Darius. "His *youngest* son," Michael hissed. "He didn't leave anything to me. The elder. The rightful heir. You would be the new 'Sir Taurlum.' He preferred you. He's always preferred you."

Darius could barely breathe. "So you tried to have me killed over some money? I would have shared it with you. You know that."

"It's not about money!" Michael was starting to lose his composure. "It's about the fact that our father loved you more than he loved me! Our entire family did! And for what? I decided to leave for a girl and despite our 'break-up,' I am still considered a deserter. A failure. As long as you're alive, Darius, I will always be second best. And it's not in a Taurlum's nature to settle for second." Michael gestured toward Rhys. "I see you brought a friend. Now you're fraternizing with a Vapros. This is exactly why you have always been completely incapable of leading this family.

You are consorting with our greatest enemies."

Out of the corner of his eye, Darius saw Rhys start to reach for his knife. "So you hired an assassin to kill me once I was in prison?" he asked.

Michael laughed hollowly. "I'm the one who put you there."

"I don't understand."

"How do you think the Imperial Guards found you so quickly? Who do you think alerted them that someone would be attacking the Opera House that night?"

Against his will, Darius whispered, "It was you?"

A few raindrops fell from the sky. Michael shrugged his shoulders. "Of course it was me. I was hoping you'd die resisting but there was no such luck. So I took other precautions. I didn't plan on the army ousting us, though. I was forced to hide for a while. One night, Carlin caught me in the markets. He was going to kill me, until I offered him something better: every other family member. I told him I could find all of you, and he told me he'd give me my weight in gold for each one. I sent my assassin again, but then you found me and gave me everything—five fugitives under one roof. I'm a free man, thanks to you. I can walk down the streets with my head held high. Now I'm free to build my legacy: a legacy where I can be free of the things that haunt me. Free of my mistakes." He straightened a few of his bracelets and continued to stare into the distance. "And tonight, I'm going to kill you."

"Are you that stupid? You really think the emperor is going to live up to his end of that bargain? Once he captures us, you will be at the top of the most wanted list."

Michael shook his head. "You're wrong. The emperor needs me. He attacked our family without knowing enough about our businesses. He can't run them without my help. He realizes my value in restoring economic order." Michael continued, his voice dangerously calm. "So tonight it ends, brother. Part of me always knew I'd have to be the one to do the deed. Part of me knew I couldn't have someone else do it for me. It'll be over quick. You've lost a lot of weight."

"This is crazy," Darius said. "You're crazy."

"Shut up!" Michael roared deafeningly loud. "I will not have my motives questioned by the likes of you. What were you doing with your life, anyway? Drinking it away? Your death won't even matter." Anastasia began to spin her spike-chain. "This is where it ends, Darius."

Darius clenched his jaw. He trembled. "Then let's end it—bare hands, man to man."

Michael curled his hands into fists and leaped at Darius, who met him halfway with a force just as mighty. They collided with a sound as loud as thunder. Michael recovered first. He swung his full might into Darius's jaw; the blow sent a shockwave through the air. Anastasia tried to hurl her spike at Darius, but Rhys materialized in front of it and deflected the blow with his knife. Anastasia growled and slammed her foot across his face in a roundhouse kick. He tried to materialize behind her to put her to sleep, but she anticipated it and whipped the spike at him, forcing him to dodge and duck.

Across the roof, Michael was quickly getting the better of Darius. He swung faster and harder than his brother and Darius was having trouble getting his arms up to block. "You never understood!" Michael roared as he swung with all his might. "I have the strength of a god! Why should I be treated like a mortal man?"

Darius delivered a punch to Michael's stomach that would have killed a normal man. "You're not a god," he yelled back angrily. "Taurlum have weaknesses, same as everybody else. You are treated like a mortal man because you can die like a mortal man!"

The rain fell hard now. Michael lashed out with a strike Darius wasn't strong enough to block. He hit the ground so hard it left a Taurlum-sized crater. "All evidence to the contrary," Michael retorted, grabbing

Darius by the front of his armor and slamming him back into the floor. Darius struggled to get up, but Michael pinned him down with one hand and began to beat him with the other. "Am I not a god?" he shouted. "I don't bleed. Mortals bleed!"

Darius's breastplate crumpled. Michael ripped it away and delivered more blows to his now-unguarded upper body. "I have never felt tired. Mortals tire!"

He punched Darius's face. "I've never been hungry. I've never felt weakness. I have never been in pain. Am I not a god?" he roared.

Darius kicked his feet up into Michael's chest, sending him staggering backwards. He rose, panting, and raised his fists.

Rhys materialized behind Anastasia and grabbed her neck, but before he could put her to sleep she pulled her elbow back into his gut. He stumbled and materialized out of range of her spike. He was growing tired. The energy it took to teleport was taking its toll.

Darius leapt at Michael like a feral animal. He ripped off his brother's breastplate and delivered a crushing blow to his chest. Michael staggered but didn't fall. He charged his brother with enough force to crush a boulder. Darius yelled and began to fire punches at Michael, who grabbed Darius around the waist and hurled him across the roof. With his brother out of the way, Michael dropped to his knees and planted his palms on top of the mansion. A dark grin crossed his face.

Darius realized what was going to happen a mere second before it occurred. "Rhys!" he screamed. "He's going to …."

Large cracks in the marble radiated from around Michael's ringed fingers and spread across the roof. Darius ran to Michael and kicked him hard enough to break his concentration, but the damage was done. The roof began to crumble under the weight of the Taurlum boys. Michael didn't seem to notice, or maybe he just didn't care. He leapt with reckless abandon at Darius. He landed on his brother's back. The rain made the marble slippery. Darius dug his heels in to avoid going over the edge. "As I recall," Michael hissed as he caught Darius around the neck, "creating earthquakes is quite godly."

"You sound tired," Darius said, bucking Michael off his back. "That's strange. Do gods tire, Michael?"

Michael fell into a crouch, smiling evilly. "You fought well, brother," he said. "But those words will be your last." And he pounced with all his might at Darius.

Chapter Fifty-Two
The Altryon Gate
Neil

Carlin paced the ground in front of the immobilized and suspended intruders. "Your little servant is still trailing after you?" he asked Lilly with a slow smile. "I killed your parents, you know," he added, looking at Jonathan with cold eyes. "They were tiny, stupid looking slaves, too."

Jonathan tried to reply, but Saewulf's powers made it impossible to open his mouth. Carlin laughed. "So," he said conversationally, "who shall we dismember first, Saewulf?"

Saewulf shrugged.

"I say we start with the weakest and work our way up," Carlin continued without waiting for a response. "We can start with the girl with the knife."

Saewulf squinted, and Bianca began to shudder.

"Stop!" Neil breathed even though no one could hear him. "Don't hurt her!"

Bianca screamed. Neil desperately tried to focus his energy to materialize out of Saewulf's hold, but he couldn't muster enough energy. Bianca's cries distracted him. He struggled, concentrating harder than he ever had before, and felt the energy run through him in an unfamiliar way. It coursed through his fingers instead of settling in his stomach. Something was happening, something different, something he'd never felt before.

Suddenly, a bolt of smoky fire exploded from his fingertips and landed straight in Saewulf's eyes. He howled and clapped his hands over his face, dropping his prey. The soldiers stared at him in shock. A few of them clumsily assembled their weapons, but Neil threw another bolt of smoke and fire that tore through their formation. He looked down at his hands incredulously. This must have been his advanced power, finally coming into play!

Neil ran past Saewulf's screaming form and knelt down next to Bianca. Carlin started to swing his sword down on the Vapros, but he was blocked by Lilly. "Carlin," she said calmly. "You and I have unfinished business."

"Get out of my way," he snarled.

Lilly lashed out so quickly her blade was invisible and nicked his shoulder. He howled and jumped backwards, then narrowed his eyes. "All right," he said, "you first, then your fire-throwing friend."

Lilly raised her rapier. "You're going to die here, Carlin. For everything you've done to my family, death is a mercy."

He grinned. "Then allow me to be merciful," he said with a mock bow, and he lunged at her.

Neil pulled Bianca out of range of the sword fight and helped her sit up. "Are you okay? What hurts?"

She groaned and stood up. "I'm fine. Take care of the psychic. Jonathan and I will take care of the guards."

Jonathan, who had been trying his best to stay out of the way of any fighting, looked up at her with wide eyes. "Really?"

She reached into a pocket in her armor and handed him a flintlock pistol. "Really."

He closed his fingers around the gun and smiled. "Let's do this!"

"Be safe," Neil pleaded, and then he turned to face Saewulf. The psychic had regained standing position. A red scorch mark covered his neck and crept onto the right side of his face. A few strands of his orange hair were singed. Neil's thoughts flashed instantly to Jennifer.

"That was a nice trick, Vapros," Saewulf spat. "But you're still going to die. I will rip your bones out of your flesh."

Neil smiled sweetly. "Are you sure you're okay to fight, Saewulf? You've looked better." He let his energy flow down to his fingertips. His hands glowed white with heat, and just as Saewulf raised his arm to immobilize Neil, he let fire explode from his body. Saewulf dodged around the ball of fire, but his concentration was broken.

"It seems we're evenly matched," Neil said, heating up his hands again.

"Don't insult me," Saewulf growled. "I am superior."

"Prove it." Neil felt his hands getting hot.

Saewulf scowled as he raised his arm. "I'm about to."

Chapter Fifty-Three
Taurlum Mansion
Darius

"How many more times can you vanish, kid?" Anastasia taunted as she whirled her chain. "You look sleepy."

Rhys panted heavily. "I could do this forever," he gasped, "but I don't think I'll have to."

She laughed. "You're right." She wasn't even out of breath. "You'll die before you get the chance to do it again." She whipped the chain at him fiercely. He dodged it without materializing. The roof beneath him was crumbling thanks to Michael's earthquake. He could barely keep his footing. On the other side of the roof, Michael pounded on Darius, who had retreated to the edge of the roof and was trying desperately to protect the pressure points in his neck. "I thought you were a warrior," Michael grunted. "Sorry—my mistake." He shoved Darius hard. "I wonder if a fall from this height would kill you?"

Anastasia threw her chain at Rhys one more time. The Vapros let himself collapse, and the spike sailed harmlessly over his head and instead nicked Michael Taurlum's neck. Anastasia gasped and dropped the chain. Rhys grabbed the weapon before she could get it back and threw it expertly into her stomach. She fell to her knees.

Michael pressed his palm against his neck, eyes wide. "No," he whispered, pulling his hand back and holding it at eye level. It was covered in blood. "No!"

Darius lunged and wrapped both hands around his brother's vulnerable throat. "You made a horrible mistake, Michael. It didn't have to end like this."

Michael cried out and frantically tried to pry Darius's hands off his neck, but when he spoke, his voice was almost calm. "Are you going to do it, Darius? Are you going to kill me?" he asked, while tears of anger raced down his cheeks. "You're my brother. Do you think you can do it? Can you send me to the place where I've sent so many: countless men, warriors or not? Not to mention the woman I loved." He saw Darius's eyes soften. "Let me go, brother. Think about the future of the Taurlum family."

Darius loosened his grip, and Michael wrenched himself free. He pulled a small knife from the back of his armor and tried to jab it into Darius's stomach. Snarling, Darius yanked the blade away from him and caught him by the throat again. "I have thought about the future of the family," Darius growled. "And you don't deserve to be part of it."

Michael screamed wordlessly as Darius kicked out and sent his brother over the edge of the roof. They heard him hit the ground, his armor clanging against the marble road. Darius peered over the edge. His brother's limbs were twisted into a broken mess. He was covered in blood. There was no chance he'd survived, not when he was already vulnerable. Darius closed his eyes and sank to the ground. He'd done it. Michael was dead. He'd killed his own brother. He didn't feel accomplished. He didn't feel relief. He felt like a monster.

"Is he dead?" a small voice asked. Darius opened his eyes to see Rhys, his hair plastered to his head by rain.

"Yeah," Darius croaked.

Rhys patted Darius's shoulder. "You did the right thing."

Darius shook his head. "Doesn't feel like it." They shared a moment of silence as they reflected on the conflict that had just occurred, "What about her?"

Rhys looked over his shoulder at Anastasia, who was lying on the ground with her eyes closed. "I just put her to sleep," he said. "She'll be okay, if she finds a doctor when she wakes up."

Darius sighed. "We should go. I don't want to ever come back here."

Rhys nodded sympathetically. "Okay. Let's go. We have to meet the others outside the wall." He and the Taurlum walked side by side back into the house. "And be careful," Rhys added as they started down the stairs. "This house could collapse at any second."

Chapter Fifty-Four
The Altryon Gate
Neil

"**S**hut the damn gate!" Carlin roared as he swung at (and was blocked by) Lilly. "Don't let them slip past you!"

The guards made for the exit, but Bianca and Jonathan got there first. Bianca began to cut down any guard who came her way while Jonathan held out his pistol threateningly. Carlin scowled. "This won't last," he said as he brought his sword around hard enough to disarm a normal man.

Lilly's blade flashed like lightening. "I'm faster than I used to be."

She twirled and whipped the sword past his knees. He jumped backward silently, then lunged so quickly she didn't see it coming. His blade only grazed her thumb, and it healed over quickly. Lilly couldn't help but cry out in surprise. Carlin gave a maniacal laugh and swung the sword within an inch of her neck. "Still faster," he hissed, eyes shining.

A few feet away, Neil threw a fireball right at Saewulf's chest; Saewulf caught it with his psychic powers and hurled it back at him. Neil materialized out of the way just in time.

"Come on, cousin!" Saewulf snarled. "Can't you do any better than that?"

Neil sent another fireball at his adversary. "Cousin?"

Saewulf grinned and raised his arm, catching the fire with his powers again and this time letting it burn out in midair. "Don't tell me you actually haven't figured it out yet," he said idly. "Look at me. I have otherworldly powers. Sound like anyone else you know?"

Neil nodded. "You're from the fourth family," he noted. "I think I've known for a while. There used to be four brothers, but one of them was killed in the first great battle."

Saewulf laughed. "And they all said he was killed by savages, didn't they? They forgot to mention that they're the ones who killed him." He cackled at Neil's confused expression. "Oh, yes, Vapros. My ancestor was the strongest of the brothers. Of course he survived that battle! He should have gone on to rule Altryon. He wanted to lead the Imperial Army, eradicate the savages, and make Altryon safe forever. Perhaps even eliminate the need for a wall. His brothers weren't quite so ambitious. So they killed him."

Neil shook his head. "I have a feeling there's more to the story, Saewolf. If they killed him, he was probably a power hungry, maniacal bastard like you."

Saewulf wrinkled his nose in disgust and continued. "No! They were threatened by his power. Fortunately, they didn't know he had already sired a child. The legacy phase is a beautiful thing, don't you agree? My ancestors escaped the city and began their life out there." He raised his arm and trapped Neil with his powers. "I spent my entire life enduring hell you couldn't even imagine. But now my family has returned for one reason—to end your miserable little lives." Neil made two fireballs in his hands and blasted Saewulf's force field apart. Neil landed on his knees, panting. "You're getting weaker," Saewulf said confidently. "You just gained your new abilities. You can't hope to control them so early."

Neil struggled to his feet. "I wasn't planning on controlling it," Neil said as another blast of fire sent Saewulf stumbling backwards.

Saewulf raised his hands just in time to ward off the flame. Neil could see him buckling under the pressure, but his own vision became blurry, too. He took deep breaths and forced himself to keep going. "That's a lot of fire," Saewulf called from behind his defenses. "Must take a lot of energy."

Neil felt the heat in his hands begin to fade. His lungs weren't working anymore. Saewulf laughed and cleared away the smoke with his powers, then lifted Neil and slammed him against a wall. "It's over," he hissed, and in that moment, Neil realized what scared him so much about Saewulf. He had darkness in his eyes, with the desperation of a survivor; someone who was starving for something. Neil could do nothing but close his eyes and wait for the end.

✦

Lilly knew she'd been getting stronger, but apparently Carlin had been training hard, too. "Give up?" he asked, repeatedly swinging his broadsword against her rapier.

She slashed so close to his head that she sliced off a few strands of his hair. "Never."

He swung down so hard that he let out a grunt. It was enough. She dropped her sword. Grinning, he swung again and gave her a shallow cut on her shoulder. It healed over before she had time to bleed. She dove for her sword, and he sliced into her side. This cut took longer to heal. "You're afraid," Carlin said, an evil grin splitting his face. "I can feel you losing hope."

Out of the corner of her eye, Lilly saw Saewulf lift a struggling Neil against a wall. She looked into Carlin's cold eyes. "Give me a second," she said as she made eye contact with the suffocating Neil. Moving as fast as she could, Lilly grabbed her fallen sword and ducked under Carlin's next swing. She bolted over to the psychic and tore into his back with her sword. Saewolf screamed and dropped Neil. Staggering to his feet Neil sent a jet of fire just over Lilly's shoulder to where Carlin was standing with his sword above her head poised to strike. The general was knocked off his feet and to the floor with a loud thud. "Thank you," Lilly said. Neil leaned heavily against the wall, gasping, and gave her a nod.

Suddenly, a loud clang echoed through the entire room. Lilly turned to see that the gate that led to everything beyond Altryon was sliding closed. "We're almost out of time!" Lilly yelled. "Come on, Neil!"

Evidently, a guard had managed to cut its supports before he was killed. Bianca and Jonathan came running toward them. "The gate!" Bianca screamed. "We have to go now!"

Neil was shaking his head. "Rhys," he breathed. "Darius."

"We might not get another chance!" Bianca begged. "They'll find their own way out!"

The gate had fewer than forty feet left. Suddenly, the room began to shake as loud footsteps came running down the hallway. "Reinforcements have arrived!" bellowed Darius, tearing through the hallway. Rhys followed at his heels.

Darius leapt in front of the closing gate and shoved against it. It shuddered, but he was strong enough to keep it from closing any farther. "Go!" he yelled. Rhys ducked through first, followed closely by Bianca and Lilly. Neil, still drained of energy, threw himself through next and collapsed to the ground. Jonathan brought up the rear. Just before he made it to the gate, he tripped over the blue military coat that had always been too big for him. Before he could scramble to his feet, he froze and began to rise into the air. Behind him, Saewulf had his arm raised, fury in his eyes. "Lilly," he taunted angrily. "Come back inside and lay down your weapon. Or watch your little friend die an agonizing death."

Lilly gasped and started back through the gate. Darius, who was starting to lose his grip, wouldn't let her through. "Don't do it," he groaned in pain. "He'll kill you."

"I don't care!" She tried to push past him, but at that moment, for the first time in his life, Darius's strength failed. He let go of the gate and collapsed to the ground outside the wall.

Lilly threw herself against the bars, screaming, "Jonathan!" She reached through the gate, trying to grab him, but he was out of reach.

Saewulf shrugged. "No matter," he said. "Your friend will die, and then we will make it through the gate after you. I'll have you in my grasp by morning."

"He's not a Celerius!" Lilly screamed. "He's not in a family! You have no reason to kill him!"

"There is always a reason!" Saewulf roared as his eyes began to blacken again. A dark grin crossed his face and he lowered his arm. Jonathan dropped to the ground. "Lilly!" he cried, rushing to the gate.

Tears streamed down Lilly's face. "Your coat," she lamented quietly. The jacket had a huge tear ripped in the side where he'd fallen.

"It's okay," he assured her. "It's fine. The thing never fit me anyway."

"Any last words, Celerius slave?" Saewulf asked lightly.

Jonathan didn't take his eyes off Lilly. "Miss," he said. "I only disobeyed one order you ever gave me."

"It's okay, it's okay, I forgive you."

Saewulf clucked his tongue. "Those are terrible last words," he said, reaching out to crush Jonathan's neck. Lilly screamed.

"And for that disobeyed order," Jonathan choked, as he reached into his pocket and pulled out the grenade, "I am sorry."

Lilly knew what was going to happen and had time to throw herself out of the way. Saewulf saw it a second too late, and all he could do was raise his arms to protect himself. "Goodbye, Miss," Jonathan said, closing his eyes.

Lilly screamed as the grenade went off, consuming Saewulf and Jonathan and all the guards behind the gate. The deafening sound rang through the air and, in an instant, silence fell. The only audible noise was the crackling of the remaining embers and Neil's wheezing. "Jonathan!" Lilly staggered to her feet and tried to run back. Darius got up and dragged her away from the gate. When he set her down next to Neil, she collapsed into a heap and sobbed.

Neil didn't know how to comfort her. He should have been used to this by now. He wanted to say something, to tell Lilly her servant was a hero, or assure her that the pain of her loss would fade with time, but he couldn't quite form the words. Instead he turned his head away from her and looked out over the horizon for the first time.

The vast rolling hills of green grass were illuminated by the full moon. This was the same full moon Neil had seen a thousand times inside the city, but somehow out here it seemed brighter. Its light was strong enough to reflect off the lush blades of grass, so the whole landscape glittered as if the ground was adorned with the finest jewels. Layer upon layer of sparkling hills laid out at their feet, each one a little taller than the one before. And yet, the most unsettling, wonderful thing of all was that no wall interrupted nature's flow. This also took his breath away, but the feeling was different.

Neil didn't know how long he looked at the hills. Lilly's voice broke him out of his trance. "His ridiculous coat," she said hoarsely as Neil remembered Jonathan. "He would never take it off."

"We have to keep going," Rhys said as gently as he could. "It's only a matter of time before they open the gate and come after us. We need to be far away by then."

Lilly wiped tears out of her eyes. "Yes," she said. "We have to press on. I believe that was what he would have wanted."

Bianca started to put a hand on Lilly's shoulder, but thought better of it. She turned to Neil instead. "Where do we go from here?" she asked. The landscape was vaster than anything they had ever known.

Neil pulled his hood over his head and pointed out into the distance. "We move forward," he decided. "Wherever that may be."

"Time to run," Darius said, flexing a bicep experimentally.

"Yes," Lilly said, rubbing more tears out of her eyes. "Hopefully for the last time."

Chapter Fifty-Five
The Markets
Carlin

Carlin spat some blood into the street and shook his head in fury. He'd avoided the blast from the grenade, but it had caused damage to his army. Not to mention his gate. The heat had fused the door into the wall. There was no way to open it now. The brats were lucky this time, he fumed, but he'd get them in the end. As he walked, he thought about what was to come—telling his father of his failure. He would be scolded and possibly even demoted. His hatred and anger grew until he couldn't stand it any more. He reached the nearest stone building, removed his glove and began to strike his fist against the wall. He felt his face grow hot as blood dripped down his hands and he screamed in fury. After a minute or two, he began to tire and slipped his glove over the bloodied hand.

He continued down the street, calmer this time. Just when he was exiting the markets and nearing the nightlife district, an arrow flew and embedded itself into his shoulder. It had been perfectly aimed so that it went straight through the chink in his armor. Carlin howled and ripped the arrow out of his skin. He whirled around, looking for the source, but the streets were deserted. "Who's there?" he yelled, drawing his broadsword and whirling it threateningly.

A calm voice came out of an alley. "Seek out the families," it said, "and the next arrow will be in your neck."

Carlin stepped closer to the alley. "I'll kill you for this."

A man in an iron mask and a blue coat emerged from the shadows. He pulled out a thin sword of his own and leapt through the air. Carlin raised his sword to block but his hurt shoulder and damaged hand slowed him enough for the masked figure to gain an advantage. Carlin's sword fell to the ground with a clang. He gasped and backtracked hurriedly, examining his surroundings for another useable weapon. "Who are you?"

The masked man lowered his sword. "You have been a danger to the one I am sworn to protect," he said in a hard voice. "I advise you not to remain a threat any longer." Carlin leapt for his sword but the masked figure was too fast. He brought his foot across Carlin's head so hard that he saw stars. He tried to stand but the figure stomped his head against the cobblestone street. Carlin felt his nose crack. He remembered that he had a pistol in the back of his armor. He pulled it out and fired blindly at his assailant.

He lifted his head and, with relief, realized that his attacker had vanished. He was able to pull his damaged body off the ground and spat a mouthful of blood into the street. He exited the alley, limping and bleeding heavily from his nose. As he walked down the street in the opposite direction of the gate, he fumed to himself about how badly things had gone. If the Vapros boy hadn't suddenly developed his advanced powers, the Empire would be sleeping soundly. He heard footsteps running down the street after him and drew his sword viciously. A small soldier raised his arms in fear. "What do you want?" Carlin roared furiously.

"We ... we're still digging through the wreckage, sir," the soldier said quietly. "The emperor needs to be alerted of our progress. What should we tell him?"

Carlin sheathed his sword and exhaled deeply as he began to remove the armor covering his shoulder wound. "First, get me a doctor and prepare my convoy. Tell him we lost his psychic but we're on our way outside the wall. The fugitives will die. I'll make sure of it."

Chapter Fifty-Six
Outside the Wall
Neil

"How's Lilly?" Bianca asked, staring at the rising sun in the distance. She was fascinated with this new world; Neil could see it in her eyes. After traveling for hours, they'd made camp on top of a distant mountain. They had taken turns staying awake to watch for any soldiers who might be following them.

"She'll survive," he said, sitting down next to her. "Darius and Rhys were both with her all night."

Neil glanced covertly at his comrades. Darius was telling some loud, ridiculous story about his drunken, teenage grandfather unknowingly taking home some cross-dressed man. Rhys was smiling and writing in a small notebook, only half-listening. It was obvious that Darius was trying to cheer up Lilly and, surprisingly, it actually seemed to be working. *That's brave of him*, Neil thought. Darius was covering it well, but Neil knew he had been seriously traumatized by killing his brother. Darius put on a courageous smile and told a story about his grandfather's drunken exploits.

"It's easier to hate people you don't know," Neil muttered to Bianca.

"What?" she asked.

"Nothing," he said. "It's just an odd feeling. Being here with them …"

Bianca nodded in understanding. Darius appeared to be nearing the end of the story because he was getting louder and Lilly and Rhys laughed out loud. Neil was curious about the ending, but something weighed on his mind: a Taurlum had killed Rhys's mother, Jennifer had killed Lilly's brother, and Neil, if he had completed that first mission, would have killed Darius' grandfather, the very same grandfather who had mistakenly brought home a rather questionable date. That nameless, faceless target that Neil had been coldly assigned to assassinate was someone's grandfather. Neil thought about the countless others who had been murdered: the centuries of hatred and senseless violence, with each family convinced their side possessed righteousness and justice. And yet, there they were, sitting and laughing in each other's company. It wasn't the end of the feud, and such hatred and meaningless death could never be erased in a day. Neil knew that. But it was a step in the right direction.

"And how do you feel?" she asked quietly. "About being out of Altryon, I mean."

He thought about it for a minute. "Free." He raised a hand to shield his eyes from the brightness of the rising sun. "And I'm glad you're here with me."

She smiled, eyes still trained on the sunrise. "I'm glad to be here. I'll be with you until the very end."

He looked down at her, and she finally lifted her eyes to meet his. "I'm very glad you're with me," he repeated quietly, and before he could think, before he could talk himself out of it, he leaned down to press his lips against hers.

"You're up early," Rhys said from behind them.

"Just watching the sun come up," Bianca said briskly, but she was grinning. "Excuse me." She walked away toward the others and began to gather her gear.

The ground shook as Darius rolled up into push-up position and began to pump his arms vigorously. He let out an exhilarated yell. "First day outside the city!" he grinned. "Let's go!"

"So are we splitting up now, or are we going to keep this partnership going?" asked Rhys.

Neil looked at the group and noticed that they appeared to be silently asking the same question. "Why don't we stick together until we find someplace to settle—some civilization."

Lilly cracked her knuckles and sighed loudly as she prepared to stand. Her eyes had a fading redness that had been caused by all her crying. She picked up her sword and stroked the blade thoughtfully. "So, Captain Vapros," she said, looking at Neil as she stood up, "what are we looking for?"

"A new place to call home," Neil said, giving her a half-smile. She returned it.

"Then let the search begin," Darius said. He trotted down the mountain and into the unfamiliar expanses.

For the first time in his life, Neil felt truly free—free from the city that expelled him and his family, free from the emperor that wanted him dead, and free from the feud that had consumed his life. An unfamiliar feeling settled in his heart as he led the group down the mountain. For the first time in so many months, he felt hope.

Acknowledgements

❧

I would like to acknowledge and thank the following people for their special contribution to *The Sparks*.

First and foremost, I want to thank my parents, Kelly and Steve Prue, for their incredible support and endless man-hours as early readers and editors.

Secondly, I wouldn't have been able to accomplish this without the help of the editors who pushed me into endless revisions over the past year. Elizabeth Feins, who was spectacular at trimming the fat and bouncing ideas back and forth; Kelly McNees, for fourteen pages of single-spaced feedback that forced me to dig deep and mold the book into something I could be proud of; and Julie Mosow, who helped as a fresh pair of eyes and was able to give instrumental plot advice.

I would also like to thank those who were willing to give me advice and guidance in my initial venture into publishing. That includes Michael Neff and everyone at the New York Writers Pitch Conference who initially taught me about what it means to be original and assured me that I was on the right track with this novel; Claire Anderson-Wheeler at Regal Literary for her wonderful advice about the industry; my acting manager, Cinda Snow, who has always stood by me and who I hope to repay when I'm a big movie star; and Howard Schott for teaching me to put in every last bit of work and for inspiring me to love reading and writing.

I am also incredibly grateful for everyone at Barringer Publishing who decided to take a chance on me and put endless amounts of work into the final product. Jeff Schlesinger was the driving force behind this team and was always available when I needed advice or help. Special thanks to Lisa Camp for her wonderful graphic design of the cover and the map of

Altryon. Also, thanks to Jessica L. Delashmit, whose eagle eyes caught those punctuation and plot holes that touched up and finalized the book.

I'd also like to thank Roland Scarpa, for his unparalleled photography and for the starving artist discount; and everyone at PR by the Book for their excellent work in making sure the book could get into the hands of as many readers as possible.

David and Courtney are, of course, to be included for being the original inspiration for the book and my writing. I couldn't have asked for better siblings. Also, to the rest of my wonderful extended family for being incredibly supportive of everything I do.

A special thanks to Seacrest Country Day School in Naples, Florida, for their endless support, love and time. Erin Duffy and the entire faculty have been absolutely fantastic in encouraging me to follow my dreams and make Seacrest my second home, not to mention my wonderful classmates who have inspired me daily to pursue what I love. I will be giving a portion of the proceeds of this book to the school because I have seen firsthand the difference they make in children's lives.

Last, but certainly not least, Drew Harrison. He was my first best friend, and I've yet to meet another person with his unique intelligence and creativity. Without him, I never would have had the courage to disregard the naysayers and follow my dreams.

About the Author

A night of insomnia inspired teen author Kyle Prue's new trilogy, *Feud*. His interest in reading declining, he endeavored to write a three volume series that he and his peers wouldn't be able to put down. The trilogy will be completed with *The Flames* and *The Ashes*.

Currently a high school senior, Kyle is passionate about writing, acting, and stand-up comedy. He trains at Second City Comedy Club in Chicago, where a number of SNL actors have started, and performs improv at LA Connection in Los Angeles. Kyle lives with his family in Naples, Florida.